## Nighthawk hadn't meant to kiss the pretty White Eyes photographer.

But when he touched her soft skin, inhaled her sweet scent, saw her eyes widen in awareness, his need to taste her mouth took over.

From the moment he'd met her, he'd lost the ability to think rationally—a dangerous thing for an Apache warrior who prided himself on always being clearheaded. But as soon as Mariah Corbett entered his life, everything had changed.

Though aware of the danger, Nighthawk couldn't make himself stop. He wanted to kiss Mariah, and so he did, with little forethought given to the consequences.

And when she recovered from her initial shock and pressed against him with an urgency that took him by surprise, concern about his loss of clear thinking faded.

His thoughts centered solely on the woman in his arms and the desire spreading through him like wildfire. . . .

# APACHE LOVER

# HOLLY HARTE

LEISURE BOOKS  NEW YORK CITY

A LEISURE BOOK®

October 2000

Published by

Dorchester Publishing Co., Inc.
276 Fifth Avenue
New York, NY 10001

ISBN 0-8439-4779-9

Printed in the United States of America.

# APACHE LOVER

# AUTHOR'S NOTE

*Apache Lover* begins a series of books featuring the proud and courageous people called Apache, in particular the Chiricahua Apache whose home territory was southeastern Arizona. Through these books I hope you will come to appreciate and respect the Apache life-way as much as I have.

The culture of the nineteenth-century Apache was both complex and fascinating. They were extremely generous to others in their band and absolutely fearless when fighting the enemy. Their religion was a mystical combination of beliefs and ceremonies. Obtaining supernatural power, receiving visions from the Spirits, and fear of ghosts and witches all played a significant role in how they lived their lives.

Join me now for the story of former Chiricahua Apache warrior Ethan Nighthawk and Wild West photographer Mariah Corbett, then watch for my next book in the series, *Apache Destiny*, in October of 2001.

—Holly Harte

# Chapter One

*The mountains of southeast Arizona Territory, 1864*

Tu Sika flinched, the storm intensifying with his every stride. The Thunder People must be extremely angry. He had never seen their arrows create such a fiery display across the sky, never heard them shout so loudly from their homes in the clouds. He spared a quick glance over one shoulder, hoping to see his friends Chino and Nacori. They hadn't been far apart, trying to pick up the trail of a deer they'd been tracking, when the sudden thunderstorm blew across the mountains. The brightness of a sunny midday had abruptly changed to the deepest of nighttime shadows, and somehow he and his friends had become separated. Tu Sika could only hope the Great Spirit would keep them safe.

Another shout from the Thunder People boomed

off the rocks, making the earth shudder beneath Tu Sika's feet. As the first splats of rain hit the rocks around him, the wind picked up, whipping strands of his hair across his face and pelting his bare back with stinging grains of sand.

He had nearly reached the protection of a small cave when the hair on his arms and nape stood up. In the next moment, the area around him suddenly lit up with the blinding flash of another lightning-arrow, this one striking a nearby tree. His ears rang with another resounding shout of thunder. His nostrils filled with the scent of charred wood. The earth shook violently, jerking his feet out from under him and tossing him through the air as if he weighed no more than a feather. He landed on his back with a grunt. Dazed, he lay still, barely aware that the storm's fury had already begun to recede.

A few minutes later, Tu Sika stirred. Blinking at the glare of sunshine, he tested his limbs for injury, then slowly got to his feet. A short distance away, he found Chino and Nacori, who agreed to his suggestion to end their hunting trip and return to camp.

His friends walked in silence beside him for a long time, apparently as deep in thought as he.

Finally Tu Sika said, "One of the Thunder People's arrows was so powerful, it threw me to the ground. While I lay there, I had a dream. But it was not like any dream I have ever had. I think it was a vision, because the Spirits talked to me."

Chino and Nacori exchanged a look, then Chino said, "The Spirits also spoke to us in a dream-vision."

Tu Sika stopped in midstride and turned to face his

friends. "You speak the truth? The Spirits talked to both of you?"

The two nodded in unison; then Chino spoke. "Like you, we were knocked to the ground by one of the Thunder People's arrows. That is when the Spirits sent us the dream-visions."

Tu Sika remained silent a moment, looking at the two young men he considered his closest friends— friends he'd had for nearly all his sixteen seasons of life. "Did you understand their meaning?"

"I have been thinking about what I saw in the dream the Spirits sent me," Nacori replied, "and what they said to me." He gave his head a shake. "But I do not know the meaning."

"It is the same with me," Chino said. "I do not know what the Spirits were trying to tell me." He looked at Tu Sika. "Did you understand what the Spirits said to you?"

"No. The images and words were clear. Clearer than any dream I have had. But the meaning is not."

"A lightning-arrow striking so close to us," Nacori said in a low voice, "is said to be a warning that something bad will happen." He glanced first at Tu Sika, then at Chino. "Do you think that is so?"

"I do not know," Chino replied, then drew a deep breath. "When we return to camp, we should go to Spotted Wolf. He will tell us if we are in danger."

"*Au*—yes," Tu Sika replied, then started walking again. "He will answer our questions." Spotted Wolf, a shaman in their band with much power, could tell them if the lighting strike was really a dire warning, as they'd been taught. Spotted Wolf would also know the meanings of their dream-visions.

# Holly Harte

*Tucson, twelve years later*

"Well, would ya look at that. The town marshal's got himself a prisoner. Looks like an Injun. And he's naked."

Mariah Corbett nodded. "That's nice, Uncle—" Her head snapped up, the collection of photographs on the table in front of her forgotten. "Did you say naked?"

Ned Corbett grinned. "Figured that would get yer attention. Okay, so I exaggerated a mite. He's just half naked."

Mariah rose from her chair and crossed the parlor of the hotel suite she shared with her uncle to where he sat by the window. "And don't call him an Injun. That's horribly insulting." She stopped beside his chair, taking care not to bump the stool supporting his splinted right leg, then leaned forward to look out the second-story window.

Indeed, the marshal was escorting a handcuffed man down the street, a man whose copper-colored skin revealed him to be an Indian. She couldn't see much of his face, only his high cheekbones and slightly hooked nose. And just as her uncle said, the man was half dressed. Bare-chested and barefoot, he wore only a pair of skintight trousers. She stared at the man's muscular thighs, buttocks, and back for a long moment, wondering what had caused the scar on the right side of his lower back. Shifting her gaze higher, she watched the early-morning sun make the long strands of his ink-black hair sparkle with a hundred pinpoints of light.

For some reason, looking at the man left her breathless, her fingers itching to skim over skin she knew would be smooth and warm to the touch, her hands eager to run through hair she knew would be as soft as silk. Absently rubbing her palms on her skirt to ease the strange tingling, she wondered what crime he'd committed.

After the marshal and his prisoner disappeared around the corner, she exhaled a deep breath before straightening and turning away from the open window. "I'm going out for a while," she said in an oddly husky voice. She bent to adjust the pillow beneath Ned's leg. "Can I get you anything before I go?"

He shook his head, the movement making a lock of silver-streaked light-brown hair fall onto his wide forehead. "If yer thinking of looking for someone to take my place, don't waste yer time. If ya haven't found anyone by now, I doubt yer going to."

Mariah smoothed the hair off his forehead, then pressed a kiss to his tanned cheek. "I can't give up. Not yet. I keep hoping someone new will arrive in town." As she headed toward her bedroom to fetch her hat and handbag, she said, "Someone who won't pay attention to all the talk about the possibility of Apache raids."

She returned to the parlor and saw the troubled look in Ned's blue-green eyes, the frown pulling down the corners of his full lips. She knew that expression. Once again, he was blaming himself for breaking his leg soon after their arrival in Tucson three weeks earlier, an unfortunate accident that left her without a photographic assistant. Adjusting her hat pin to hold her hat more securely atop her upswept hair, she moved closer to her only living relative.

Swallowing the sudden lump in her throat, she said, "Don't fret, Uncle Ned. I'll find someone." She laid a hand on his shoulder. "I'm sure of it."

"Ya know, girlie, maybe ya should scrap yer plans to take photographs of the scenery around here." He lifted a hand to grasp hers. "Maybe the folks in Tucson are right about the Apache taking up raiding again. If the rumors we've been hearing are true, it won't be safe for ya to go traipsing around the countryside."

"You know I can't give up. I always finish the projects I undertake, no matter how strong the potential for danger, and I have no intention of changing now. And you know as well as I do that in order for me to take photographs, I have to have an assistant."

"And what if ya find someone who'll work for ya? Do we have the money to pay wages?"

She gave him an indulgent smile. "We'll get by, so stop your fretting, okay?"

Ned nodded, gave her fingers a squeeze, then dropped his hand back to the arm of his chair. There was no point in pushing the issue. He knew all too well how determined his niece could be once she set her mind to something. Closing his eyes, he released a long sigh. Maybe he'd been wrong to instill such independence in Mariah. Maybe he shouldn't have taken her in after the deaths of her parents, his only brother and his sister-in-law, fourteen years ago. What had he been thinking, a thirty-year-old bachelor, trying to raise a twelve-year-old girl? He should've found a good family to take her in, a family that would have known the proper way to raise a young girl.

"Uncle Ned?" Mariah's voice pulled him from his painful musings. "Are you all right?"

"Fine. Fine." He made a shooing motion toward the door. "You run along. I'll just sit here for a while. There's a nice breeze comin' in the window."

"I won't be gone long."

"No rush, girlie. Take yer time."

Nighthawk stared at the bars of the jail cell, anger churning in his gut. He should have known better than to get involved. But when he heard the cries from the room of one of the bordello prostitutes, he couldn't stop himself from going to her aid. Though Carmen tried to stop him, he ignored her objections, pulled on his trousers, and headed down the hall.

He found the source of the cries struggling to get dressed while trying to defend herself against a customer who had apparently awoken in a foul mood and turned his rage on her.

Though men from his own band of Chokonen Apache occasionally beat their wives after drinking too much of the White Eyes' liquor, Nighthawk didn't condone such behavior. His distaste for the mistreatment of women began when he was a child, known then by his boyhood name Tu Sika. He'd witnessed the punishment leveled on a woman by her drunken husband for some minor offense and swore he'd never lift a hand to a woman. After having a vision experience, he had been given a new name, in keeping with the Chokonen life-way; from then on he had been called Nighthawk and became a fierce Apache warrior, yet he never broke the promise he'd made as a boy. A promise he had expanded to include stopping

13

others from mistreating women—even women who sold their bodies for a man's pleasure.

His mouth twisted into a scowl. Carmen was right. This time, he should've stayed out of it. But he had to get involved, had to defend the helpless. And look where trying to be a Good Samaritan—as Father Julian called those who helped the less fortunate—got him. He snorted with disgust. Two other bordello customers, who'd also paid to spend the entire night in a prostitute's bed, had heard the frightened woman's screams and had charged down the hallway in their underdrawers to join the fray. Yet when the marshal arrived, he acted as if the other men weren't there.

Nighthawk had tried to explain that he hadn't started the fight, was only trying to come to the aid of an abused woman, but the marshal turned a deaf ear. Instead, he announced that Nighthawk was under arrest for disturbing the peace, refused a request to let him retrieve the rest of his clothes, and hauled him off to jail.

Nighthawk snorted again. Just when his hatred and distrust of all White Eyes had begun to subside, tempered by the relative peace between their peoples the past four years and Father Julian's kindness, he discovered that the anger he'd nurtured for nearly half of his twenty-eight years hadn't abated entirely.

The morning's events had taught him a valuable lesson. When three white men and one Indian were involved in a fight, the Indian was always the one at fault—no questions asked. Until such biased attitudes died, there would never be lasting peace between the White Eyes and the Apache.

Though Nighthawk knew he'd saved the prostitute

from a severe beating, and in the process given the abusive drunk a well-deserved black eye and maybe a cracked rib, bitterness and anger at the inequity of his treatment by the marshal continued to smolder in his belly.

Since he hadn't slept much the night before, he stretched out on the lumpy jail-cell mattress and crossed his arms over his chest, one hand wrapping around the small buckskin pouch suspended from a narrow leather necklace. He closed his eyes, then cleared his mind of everything but the need for sleep. Soon he slipped into the peaceful darkness of slumber.

*Nighthawk continued walking down the road, his moccasins sending up little puffs of dust with each step. When he came to a fork in the road, he stopped. Closing his eyes, he waited, listening. Soon he heard it, the call of his namesake, the piishii. When he opened his eyes, he saw the small speckled bird sitting on the ground a few feet in front of him.*

*"Show me which path to take," Nighthawk said to the bird.*

*"Follow me," the nighthawk replied, then spread its wings and flew down the road to the right. Nighthawk did not question the decision but immediately started down that same road. As the bird increased its speed, Nighthawk walked faster and faster, eager to see what lay ahead. Just as the nighthawk had shown him the town of Tucson on one previous occasion and Father Julian on another, he knew the bird had something new to show him.*

*Soon the bird disappeared, but Nighthawk could*

*make out something, a shadowed shape, farther down
the road. He squinted, trying to bring the object into
focus. He couldn't be certain, but it looked like a
human form—a woman with hair as pale as morning
sunlight. As he drew closer, the image began to fade,
finally disappearing altogether in a misty swirl.*

*When Nighthawk reached the place where the mys-
terious image had appeared, he noticed something on
the ground. He dropped onto one knee, then reached
toward what lay in the dirt. Just as his fingers were
about to make contact, he recognized what he was
about to touch. Sucking in a sharp breath, he jerked
his hand away.*

*Two feathers from the* niishjaa—*owl—lay on the
ground, and he would not risk touching them.*

Nighthawk opened his eyes, awakening as he always
did immediately after having a vision, each detail still
vivid in his mind. Ever since his visit to Spotted Wolf
twelve years earlier to tell the shaman about nearly
being struck by lightning and to have his first dream-
vision explained, he'd learned to draw a distinction
between simple dreams of no consequence and those
sent to him by the Spirits. The one he'd just experienced fell into the latter group. The fact that he'd
awakened as soon as the vision ended, as if someone
had spoken to him, confirmed the importance of what
the Spirits were trying to tell him.

He stared at the ceiling of the jail cell, letting the
vision replay in his mind. It was similar to the others.
He always saw himself walking down a road that
eventually divided. When he reached the fork, he
never knew which path to take. Then the nighthawk

came and showed him the way. This time the bird led him to a woman—at least, the wavering shape seemed to be that of a woman. In his previous visions, such as when he saw the town of Tucson, he'd been able to make out more details. After he went to Tucson, another vision revealed a bearded man wearing the long black robe of the White Eyes' religious leader. Several days later, he met Father Julian and immediately recognized him from the image the Spirits had shown him.

But in the vision he'd just experienced, the only things clearly visible were what appeared to be a woman with long, light-colored hair and—he shuddered at the memory—owl feathers.

As a child he'd been taught, as had all generations of Apache before him, to fear owls. He still remembered his parents telling him that owls were ghosts of the evil dead. When people died, they had explained, those who had led good lives went to the Spirit World, but the wicked turned into owls. When he was nine or ten years old, a member of his band saw an owl while out walking one evening. The next day, the man's horse suddenly went berserk, throwing him to the ground and trampling him to death. The horse was the gentlest in the man's herd and had never thrown a rider or displayed aggressive behavior. Everyone said that the man's encounter with the owl had spooked the horse.

From then on, Nighthawk understood that contact with an owl—whether actually seeing one or simply hearing the bird's call—was a bad omen. Though he couldn't be certain if seeing owl feathers in a dream-vision fell into the same category, he didn't want to take any chances, and he offered a quick prayer to ask the Spirits for protection.

Again he slept, and this time no vision awakened him.

Midmorning of the following day, Nighthawk heard a commotion coming from the marshal's office. He'd already learned he would be set free before noon and hoped that whatever was causing the disturbance wouldn't interfere with his scheduled release. When the door separating the office and the back room containing two small cells finally opened, he glanced up, expecting to see the marshal. What he saw halted the breath in his chest.

A woman whose pale-yellow hair matched the color of morning's first sunlight stepped into the room. When her gaze found his, she approached the door to his cell. "Marshal, would you be so kind as to leave us alone?" she said, though her gaze never left Nighthawk.

"Here now, Miss Corbett, that ain't a good idea. I think—"

"*Isn't* a good idea, marshal. And frankly I don't care a fig what you think. Just leave us, please."

The marshal opened his mouth, snapped it shut, then sputtered something unintelligible before backing out of the room and closing the door.

Nighthawk's shock gave way to amusement. He had to bite the inside of his cheek to halt a smile, the look on the marshal's face well worth having his release delayed a few minutes. Shifting his attention to the woman standing just outside his cell, he rose from where he sat on the bunk. As he slowly moved closer to the bars, he studied her face.

Her eyes were a deep green, her face oval-shaped with a slightly pointed chin and a straight, narrow nose. He inhaled, drawing her sweet scent into his lungs. His body's instant reaction stunned him. Shifting his stance to ease the sudden tightness in his groin, he dropped his gaze to her full bosom, small waist, and the flare of feminine hips.

"If you're finished giving me a once-over," she said in a clipped voice, "I have some business I'd like to discuss with you."

His gaze snapped back to her face, one eyebrow lifted in question. "What business could you have with me?"

Mariah's eyes widened. "Your English is far better than I expected." The flash of irritation in his black eyes made her add, "I didn't mean any disrespect. Some of the townsfolk said the local priest had taught you English, but I had no idea . . . Well, that's not important."

Nighthawk folded his arms over his chest. "I knew some English before I met Father Julian. And I could speak Spanish long before that. But you are right. How well I speak any language is not important. So, I ask you again. What business do you want to discuss with me?"

Mariah cleared her throat, shifting her gaze from the bulging muscles of his bare chest and the small buckskin pouch dangling from a strip of leather tied around his neck. "My name is Mariah Corbett, Mr. Nighthawk, and I need your assistance." Noticing the flattening of his lips, the narrowing of his dark eyes, she paused, expecting him to speak. When he didn't, she continued. "I'm looking for someone to help with my equipment. My uncle normally works as my assistant, but he broke his leg right after we arrived in town several weeks ago, and I can't wait for his leg to heal."

Nighthawk stared at the woman for a moment. Though he'd been in Tucson two years, the open way White Eyes called each other by name still surprised him. To his people, names were very valuable, and calling a person by name to his face was considered impolite. Pushing those thoughts aside, he said, "You want me to take your uncle's place?"

She nodded.

"And what is your equipment?"

"I'm a photographer, Mr. Nighthawk. Going on photographic field trips requires a lot of equipment in addition to the usual supplies. Food. Bedding. Clothes."

"You plan to take one of those field trips?"

"Yes. More than one, in fact. I was invited to display my work in the Colorado Pavilion at the Centennial Exposition in Philadelphia. My exhibit is called A Photographic Documentation of the American Southwest, but it won't be complete until I add photographs of this part of Arizona Territory. The Exposition opened last month, but there's still time to display my work, provided I find a replacement for Uncle Ned quickly."

"You are not afraid to leave town?"

She tipped her head to one side. "Should I be?"

"If you have been in town for several weeks, then you must have heard the rumors."

"Oh, that," she replied, making a dismissive gesture with one hand. "I can't worry about rumors. I believe in taking chances, living life to its fullest, so a little danger makes it that much more exacting. And if I should meet my end while I'm taking photographs, then at least I will have died doing what I love."

When he didn't respond, she said, "So what do you say, Mr. Nighthawk? Will you be my assistant?"

Nighthawk stared at her for a few moments. His gaze moved slowly over her face, then came to rest on her pale hair. Though he wanted to say he couldn't help her, the memory of his vision from the night before halted his refusal. Exhaling heavily, he knew what he must do.

"Yes, I will work as your assistant, but only if you give me your word that you will obey my instructions if we encounter danger."

Her chin came up, her lips thinned, and two splotches of bright color appeared on her cheeks. A full minute passed before the tightness left her features. "Okay, Mr. Nighthawk. In case of danger, I agree to obey your instructions."

"That is not good enough. I want your word."

She huffed out a breath. "All right. All right. I give you my word."

"That was not so painful, was it?" he said, a smile quirking the corners of his mouth. "And do not call me mister. I am Nighthawk. Or Ethan, if you prefer." His smile quickly fading, he wondered why he'd mentioned what names she could call him, especially given his earlier thoughts on the subject. Father Julian called him Ethan, which he finally had accepted, so perhaps that was the reason for his statement to her.

Mariah nodded. Summoning a smile, she said, "And please call me Mariah." She stuck her right hand through the bars of his cell. "Do we have a deal?"

Nighthawk eyed her small hand for several seconds. How would he react to touching the woman the Spirits had predicted he would meet? Mentally preparing himself, he slowly lifted his hand to clasp hers. As soon as his skin made contact with hers, he realized he never could have prepared himself adequately for the reality of touching her. A stab of desire sliced through his body—a stab so intense, his knees nearly buckled. Through sheer determination he stayed on his feet and managed a choked, "Yes."

She gave him a quizzical look, then withdrew her hand from his. "Good. The marshal said you're about to be released, so I'll . . . uh . . . wait for you outside. Then we can discuss the details of the first trip I want to make."

Nighthawk watched her leave the room, still aching from her touch and wondering again what purpose the Spirits had for bringing the intriguing Mariah Corbett into his life.

# *Chapter Two*

"Why were you arrested?" Mariah bit her bottom lip and stifled a groan. *Drat, I leaped before I looked again. Uncle Ned will be furious if he finds out I didn't ask that question before leaving the jail.* Hoping her initial impression of Ethan Nighthawk hadn't been wrong, she waited for him to respond.

Nighthawk cast a sidelong glance at her, then shifted his gaze back to the dirt street in front of them. "Is this a test to see if I give you the same answer the marshal gave you?"

"I . . . um . . . didn't ask the marshal."

Nighthawk's eyebrows lifted. "Then why are you asking now?"

"As your employer, I have a right to know why you were arrested."

"You have already hired me, so what does it matter?"

"It matters because if you've murdered someone, then I'd . . . I'd promptly retract my offer of employment."

"Do you think the marshal would have released me this morning if I had been arrested for murder?"

Mariah frowned. "Well, no."

His only response was a grunt.

Her frown deepened. "You still haven't answered my question."

Nighthawk came to an abrupt halt and turned to face her. "I stopped a man from beating a woman, but he did not like my interfering and came after me. Other men joined the fight, but when the marshal arrived, he arrested only one man. Me. For disturbing the peace." He drew a deep breath, then added, "Does that satisfy your curiosity?"

The anger burning in his dark eyes should have stilled her tongue, but she ignored the warning. "But that's not fair! Gallantry should be rewarded, not punished with an arrest. And besides, you weren't the only one fighting. The marshal should've—"

"There is little fairness when it comes to the way my people are treated. Something you"—he pointed a finger at her—"a spoiled White Eyes, would know nothing about."

"Spoiled!" She glared at him, her eyes narrowed to slits. "How dare you call me spoiled?" She thumped his chest with two fingers, making the buckskin pouch bounce. "Everything I have, I've worked hard to get. Nothing was given to me, do you understand?" She gave his chest another thump. "Nothing."

Nighthawk's own irritation faded. He found her display of temper amusing and at the same time arousing, though he took care to hide both reactions. Absently rubbing his chest to ease the burn of her touch, he watched the rapid rise and fall of her breasts. He wondered if she'd be just as wild in his bed, then quickly squelched such a tantalizing thought. Dropping his arm to his side, he shrugged. "Whatever you say, Miss Corbett." He turned and resumed walking.

His sudden capitulation left Mariah momentarily startled. Hurrying to catch up, she said, "I told you to call me Mariah, remember?"

She couldn't be certain what another of his grunted responses meant, but sensing he would say no more on the subject, she let the matter drop.

After they'd walked in silence for a few minutes, Mariah came out of her ruminations to realize she didn't recognize their surroundings. "Where are we?"

"Maiden Lane."

Mariah's eyes widened. "Really? So this is what the tenderloin looks like."

Nighthawk flashed her an annoyed glance. "What do you know about tenderloin districts?"

"Just that men go there to drink, gamble, and seek pleasure."

"Seek pleasure." His lips curved in a mocking smile. "An interesting way of describing what goes on here."

"Would you rather I say, 'fornicate with some harlot till he's too weak to stand'?"

He couldn't stop his smile from breaking into a grin. "If Father Julian heard those words come out of your mouth, he would be shocked speechless. You do

25

not speak the way he says proper ladies are supposed to."

Mariah's cheeks heated with a blush. "No, I'm sure I don't. Though Uncle Ned is forever warning me against letting my mouth leap ahead of my brain, I still have a tendency to say whatever's on the tip of my tongue and damn the consequences."

Nighthawk chuckled. "To my people, there are few offenses greater than being accused of lying. Speaking the truth is a good quality."

"I agreed, but Uncle Ned doesn't always see it that way."

"You are family. He is only trying to protect you."

"I know," Mariah replied with a sigh. Deciding to shift the topic of their conversation, she said, "Why are we on Maiden Lane?"

"To get the rest of my clothes. After the marshal arrested me, he refused to let me go to Carmen's room to finish getting dressed."

"Carmen's room?" As his meaning sank in, Mariah nearly stumbled. "Oh, the fight the marshal broke up was in a bordello," she said in a low voice. Her head suddenly spinning, she heard his affirmative reply over the buzzing in her ears. Why the thought of Nighthawk's spending the night in the bed of a prostitute named Carmen caused her such distress, she couldn't imagine. Pushing the disturbing thought to the back of her mind, she drew a steadying breath and forced herself to concentrate on her reason for coming to southeastern Arizona Territory.

When Nighthawk stopped in front of a large adobe building, she hoped she sounded businesslike when she said, "After we fetch your clothes, I'd like to discuss—"

"We?"

"Of course. We'll go inside, fetch your clothes, then when we come out, I want to—"

"No, *I* will get my clothes. Women cannot go inside unless they work there."

"Fine," she replied, lifting her chin. "I'll wait here."

Nighthawk wished he hadn't allowed her to accompany him to Tucson's tenderloin district, but ever since meeting her he'd been thrown off balance, his thoughts in a jumble. He rubbed a hand over his jaw, then said, "Okay, but stay right here, and speak to no one. Do you understand?"

"Why wouldn't I?" Mariah said a little more sharply than she intended. "We both know your English is damn near perfect."

He scowled in response.

"Go on," she said, nodding toward the door. "Go get your clothes. When you get back, I want to discuss our first photographic field trip."

He stared at her for several seconds, then nodded. As he turned, he said, "Remember what I said."

She gave him a forced smile, though she had the sudden urge to stick out her tongue. As soon as he disappeared through the bordello door, her smile faded. His bossing her around rankled. After all, she was used to giving the orders, not receiving them. Though she'd agreed to follow his instructions in case of danger, she made a mental note to remind him she was the boss the rest of the time.

Nighthawk returned a few minutes later to find Mariah standing exactly where he'd left her. Thankful she'd done as he asked and come to no harm, he felt the inexplicable knot of apprehension in his belly begin to ease.

Mariah turned at his approach, her gaze dropping to his dusty boots, then moving upward to linger on the shirt covering the wide expanse of his muscular chest. Though now fully clothed, he still set her heart to pounding against her ribs and spawned an insistent throbbing between her thighs. She wanted to ask about the small buckskin pouch he wore around his neck, the leather thong visible through the open collar of his shirt, but she didn't dare trust her voice.

As they started back toward the main section of town, Mariah finally managed to pull herself together enough to speak. "Now, about our first field trip. We should—"

"Would you mind delaying this discussion long enough for me to clean up?"

She hauled back on her impatience. "Certainly. Why don't you come to the hotel in an hour? I know my uncle will want to meet you." Her uncle! She bit back a groan. Dear Lord, she hadn't even considered what Uncle Ned would say about her hiring an Indian to be her assistant. Well, it was too late. The deed was done.

"Fine. Where are you staying?"

"The Palace. The suite on the second floor."

After Mariah left him at a barbershop with a sign advertising hot baths, she headed for her hotel, contemplating both her decision to hire Ethan Nighthawk and her uncle's reaction. She'd spent the better part of the day before trying to find someone to hire as her assistant. And as on her previous attempts, her

28

offers were met with the same reaction: curt refusals. Then one man facetiously suggested she hire a "tame Apache" to be her errand boy. Though he and his friends laughed uproariously at the suggestion, she immediately saw merit in the idea.

When she asked for a name, the men laughed even harder. At her insistence, they finally gave her Ethan Nighthawk's name, adding that she'd find him lodged in the town jail. Mariah figured they probably thought that last bit of information would dissuade her from following through on their suggestion; they had no way of knowing it had the opposite effect. Certain Ethan Nighthawk was the man she'd seen the marshal escorting through town earlier that day, she became more determined than ever to speak with him.

Now that she'd met Ethan Nighthawk, she realized the people of Tucson were dead wrong if they really believed he was no longer, to use their words, a savage red devil. If he gave a "tame" impression, Mariah felt certain it was only because that's what he wanted people to see, but beneath his facade he was anything but tame. In fact, he was probably the most dangerous man she would ever meet. Yet for reasons she didn't completely understand, she didn't fear him. Rather, she found him fascinating and exciting, his blatant masculinity attracting her in ways she'd never imagined.

And soon they would be spending days, even weeks, together in the Arizona wilderness while she continued her photographic work. The thought made her shoulders ripple with a shiver of anticipation. She refused to analyze whether her reaction stemmed from getting back to the work she loved or being alone with Ethan Nighthawk.

An hour later, Nighthawk made his way down Meyer Street to the Palace Hotel. He crossed the lobby to the staircase, pointedly ignoring the glare of the man behind the desk.

As he climbed the stairs to the second floor, he wished he could tell Mariah he'd changed his mind, but he knew he wouldn't. If he were to offend the Spirits by ignoring the messages they sent him in his visions, he could face punishment of illness, bad luck, or even death. The Spirits had predicted he would meet a woman with pale hair the day before Mariah Corbett walked into the jail, so there was no mistaking the reality of the matter. She had been brought into his life for a purpose—a purpose the Spirits had yet to reveal. And until they did, he'd have to deal with the outspoken, all-too-tempting Mariah as best he could.

He exhaled a deep breath, then raised a hand and knocked. The door swung inward almost immediately to reveal Mariah. Something about her expression set off an alarm in his head.

"Is there a problem?" He glanced past her and saw the man sitting by the window. "Has your uncle changed your mind about hiring me?"

"He tried," she said, a smile easing the tightness around her mouth. She stepped back from the door. "Come in and let me introduce you."

After the introduction, the two men spent several seconds silently sizing up each other; then Ned said, "I'll be honest with ya, Nighthawk. I'm against this.

No offense to ya, but the situation with the Injuns . . . er . . . Apaches sounds too unstable for me to allow my niece to go traipsing off with one of 'em. I can't risk her getting raped or worse."

Nighthawk's jaw tightened. "Apache do not rape women."

"That ain't the way I heard it," Ned replied.

"What you heard is wrong. The warriors of other nations may rape the women they capture, but my people do not. It is against our way of life."

Ned stared long and hard at the proud man standing a few feet away, then finally nodded. "Okay, I believe ya. I still don't cotton to this idea of hers. But as she constantly reminds me, she's no longer a girl who needs my permission. Especially when it comes to her photographic work." He heaved a long sigh. "So, if yer still interested in taking over my responsibilities while I'm laid up"—he flicked a glance at Mariah—"and are willing to put up with her stubbornness, then I reckon ya got the job."

Nighthawk looked at Mariah. The glare she directed at her uncle told him she longed to make a comment, but her lips remained pressed together in a firm line. Stifling his amusement, he looked back at Ned. "I am definitely interested."

Ned shifted his gaze back and forth between his niece and the man he and Mariah had argued about for nearly an hour. Something in the man's reply made him wonder if there could be a double meaning to his words.

Ned cleared his throat, then said, "Well, then, have a seat, and let's talk about the work you'll be doing for my niece."

Nighthawk eased down onto an upholstered chair opposite Ned's. When he first arrived in Tucson two years earlier, he thought he'd never become accustomed to the White Eyes' world. Living in buildings rather than brush wickiups or tepees made of buffalo hides. Sitting on fancy furniture. Sleeping in beds rather than on blankets or animal-skin robes on the ground. To his own surprise, he'd soon learned to appreciate the conveniences of the White Eyes, though there were times he longed for the simpler Apache life-way. The rustle of Mariah's skirt pulled him from his musings.

He watched her move past his chair and take a seat on the settee. Once she was settled, Ned said, "I assume yer familiar with the countryside in this part of the territory."

Nighthawk looked at the older man and nodded. "This land has been home to my people for many generations. I was born and raised here. I know every mountain peak, every valley east to beyond the Rio Grande and south far into Mexico."

Ned nodded. "Good. Good. Though Mariah won't be needing to go as far as New Mexico Territory or down into Mexico." He turned to look at his niece. "She's looking to photograph just this part of Arizona Territory, right, girlie?" When she nodded, he said, "Why don't you tell Nighthawk yer plans for yer photographs so he'll know what yer looking for?"

Mariah turned her gaze on Nighthawk. As she outlined her plans for the series of landscape photographs she wanted to take to complete her exhibit for the Exposition, she tried not to stare at the way his hair, still damp from his bath, clung to the sides of his face

32

or the way his muscles flexed beneath his white cotton shirt. Somehow she managed to get through her explanation, then finished by saying, "Do you have a suggestion on where we should begin?"

Nighthawk had lots of suggestions, but he doubted Mariah would appreciate knowing that the first one on his list was stripping off her clothes, layer by layer, then slowly exploring her naked body with his hands and mouth. Forcing his attention away from such tantalizing thoughts, he said, "I know of several places."

She flashed him a brilliant smile, bringing back his previous line of thinking and sending a surge of desire pulsing through his body.

"Wonderful," she said, leaning forward in anticipation. "Can we leave right away? All I have to do is finish packing a few personal items. My photographic equipment is already packed in boxes. I've already spoken to the man at Smith's Corral about renting a wagon, so if you'll—"

"Wagon?" Nighthawk frowned. "We cannot use a wagon."

"But how will we haul my photographic equipment?"

"Pack animals."

"The corral has mules," Ned said. "Reckon Smith wouldn't care if we rented them instead of a wagon."

"Mules?" Mariah's brow wrinkled while she considered the change in her plans. "You're sure there's no other way?"

"There are few roads where we will go. Mules and horses are the only way to get into the mountains."

"Yes, of course. I should have realized that. Well, then, it's settled." She rose from the settee. "Let's go to Smith's Corral. I'd like your opinion on which mules to rent."

Nighthawk's eyes widened. "Now?"

"Yes, now," she replied. "I want to leave tomorrow, so we need to take care of this right away." When he didn't move, she said, "Please."

He glanced at Ned. The older man grinned, then said, "At least she said 'please.' "

At the corral, Nighthawk made quick work of selecting four pack mules. Deciding on a saddle horse for Mariah took a little more time. She claimed to be a competent rider, but he finally convinced her the skittish mare she'd picked wouldn't be a good choice in the rugged terrain where they were headed. She reluctantly agreed to let him select her mount. Ignoring the poorly concealed disgust on the corral owner's face, he inspected each horse carefully, finally choosing a chestnut gelding with a more docile nature.

After Nighthawk indicated his choice, Mariah said, "I'll be right back. I need to speak to Mr. Smith in private."

She followed the corral owner into his small office, then said, "Do you want my business, Mr. Smith?"

Smith turned, a look of surprise on his sun-weathered face. " 'Course I do."

"Then I suggest you stop looking at Mr. Nighthawk as if he were a fresh pile of horse dung."

The man's mouth dropped open, then snapped shut, his blue eyes blazing with ire. "Now, look here. I'm entitled to my opinion, and I don't like Apaches one iota, tame or not."

"Yes, you are entitled to your private opinions," she said, leaning closer. "But I won't do business with anyone who displays open and callous disregard for the feelings of others."

When he started to speak, her glare silenced him. "Has Mr. Nighthawk ever done anything to you?"

"Well, no, not personally. But that don't—"

"He's a human being, Mr. Smith, just like you and me, and for that reason alone he's entitled to be treated with respect. If you can't see fit to do that, I'll take my business elsewhere." She straightened, paused for a moment to let her words sink in, then said, "Have I made my position clear?"

He rubbed his bristled jaw with the back of one hand. "Yeah, I got yer point."

"Good, then let's discuss your rental fees."

When Mariah stepped out of the office a few minutes later, Nighthawk pushed away from the corral fence. Her stiff posture catching his attention, he kept his gaze trained on her face. As she drew closer, he could see her flushed cheeks and the remnants of anger swirling in her green eyes. Cupping her elbows with his hands, he said, "Is something wrong?"

"Not anymore. Mr. Smith and I reached an understanding."

"Understanding?" His gaze narrowed. "Did he do something to you? Are you all right?"

"I'm fine, and, no, he didn't do anything to me. I had a talk with him about the way he treated you, and now that he—"

"You what?" He dropped his hands from her arms and took a step back.

"I told him I wouldn't tolerate the way he treated you, and if he wanted my business he'd better change his attitude."

A muscle in Nighthawk's jaw jumped. "I do not need you or anyone else defending me."

"I know that. But I couldn't bear the way he looked at you, and when you didn't say anything, I had to."

"If you plan to scold everyone who gives me a look you do not like, you will be giving many lectures."

Mariah didn't respond for a moment but just stared up at his harsh expression, her mouth pursed in a thoughtful frown. Finally, she said, "How do you stand it?"

He shrugged. "I have learned to ignore the looks people give me and the things they say."

She put a hand on his arm. "You don't deserve to be treated that way."

The sympathy he heard in her voice touched a nerve he thought had lost its sensitivity and ignited his temper. Shaking off her hand, he said, "No, I do not deserve to be treated like I am filth. Just as the Apache did not deserve to be killed for wanting to stay on land that was the home of our ancestors. Or to be forced onto reservations, where we are treated like cattle in a corral. Or to have the White Eyes break every promise they ever gave us." He squeezed his eyes closed, struggling to control his temper. He took a deep breath, exhaled slowly, then opened his eyes. In a softer voice, he said, "All Apache deserve to be treated better. Not just me."

Mariah's throat tightened at his obvious pain and anger. She longed to reach out to him, to offer comfort, but she didn't dare touch him again. When she could speak, she said, "After being treated so badly, why did the Apache agree to a peace treaty?"

At first she thought he wasn't going to answer. He

36

just stared off at some unknown point in the distance, his arms crossed over his chest. After a moment, he released a deep breath, then began speaking. "The Apache are a people from many bands. Each band has its own name. Mine is the Chokonen, but the White Eyes call us Chiricahua.

"After many years of battling the White Eyes, our leader realized we had to end the fighting. He said resuming a war with the White Eyes would mean the death of not just the Chokonen but of all Apache. He said the only way to survive was to live in peace. When the government of the White Eyes sent a soldier to our camp with an offer of peace, our leader talked with him for many days. Our leader agreed to a treaty only when he was promised that a reservation would be created on our homeland and that he would be allowed to select the Indian agent for the new Chiricahua Reservation.

"Some Chokonen saw the White Eyes' agreement to those terms as another trick, but our leader would not change his mind. He did not completely trust the White Eyes, especially the soldiers, but he was weary of fighting and of so many deaths. He told us he had finally accepted the fact that we were outnumbered and that the ways of the Chokonen had to change. He believed the only way for us to survive was for him to agree to the treaty and make peace with the White Eyes."

"Were you one of those who thought the treaty was another trick of the American government? Is that when you came to Tucson?"

Nighthawk shook his head. "I stayed on the reservation after the peace treaty was signed. But the first

years were a time of much discontent. Many Chokonen did not want to abandon the old ways and were
not comfortable with the new ones. I, too, was unhappy with the changes, but I respected our leader too
much to openly defy his wishes. So I tried to do as
he wanted by better understanding the White Eyes. I
learned English from our agent and the men he hired
to work on our reservation. I watched and listened to
the White Eyes who delivered supplies. Then, two
years ago, our leader passed on to the Spirit World.
He was much loved and respected among our people.
We grieved a long time."

He drew a deep breath, the memories of those days
still painful. After releasing his breath, he continued.
"Before our leader died, he named his oldest son,
Taza, to replace him. But Taza did not have his father's strength of leadership. Soon there was a split
among our people. Some even left the reservation."

"And you were one of those who left?"

Nighthawk stared down into Mariah's upturned
face, contemplating how he should respond. Since the
Spirits had foretold his meeting this woman, did they
expect him to tell her the truth? Though he decided
the answer had to be yes, he still chose his words
carefully. "I left, yes, but not for the same reason as
the others. I left the reservation and came to Tucson
because the Spirits told me to. In a vision."

# Chapter Three

Mariah blinked up at him, then her lips parted in a smile. "A vision. That's pretty funny." She chuckled. "For a minute there, I thought you were serious."

"I am serious."

She sobered. "Are you telling me you actually had a vision that told you to come to Tucson?"

"I was not told. I saw the town in my vision and knew the Spirits wanted me to come here."

"And you expect me to believe that?"

When he nodded, she put her hands on her hips and gave him a withering glare. "Look, if you don't want to tell me the real reason you came to Tucson, just say so and stop making up ridiculous stories."

Nighthawk stared down at her, momentarily stunned by her reaction to his claim. Realizing she hadn't known him long enough to trust what he told her, he decided not to pursue the issue. "We should drop the subject."

"Fine with me."

He finally pulled his gaze from her flushed face. Once again he found himself wondering if this woman's fiery temper carried over to her passion. He scowled at the direction of his thoughts, then forced the notion of Mariah as a sexual partner from his mind. He cleared his throat, then said, "I have some things to take care of before we leave town. What time should we meet in the morning?"

"An hour past daybreak."

He nodded, then turned and walked away.

Mariah watched him disappear from view, suddenly struck by the notion that one of the "things he had to take care of" might be another visit to Maiden Lane, another night spent in Carmen's bed. Chastising herself for thinking of him with the prostitute and, worse, for the sharp sting of irrational jealousy the idea spawned, she lifted her chin and straightened her shoulders. She didn't have time to stand around mooning over a man; she had final preparations of her own to make before beginning her field trip.

Her priorities back in order, she headed for the Palace Hotel, determined not to think about Ethan Nighthawk for the rest of the day.

Mariah arrived at Smith's Corral long before dawn the following morning. She hadn't slept well and decided, rather than doing any more tossing and turning, to put the time to better use. While the sleepy stablehand she'd rousted from his bed held a lantern, she double-checked all the various crates, satchels, and bags containing her photographic equipment, personal belongings, and provisions, which she'd had delivered to the corral late the previous afternoon. Once she was satisfied everything had been packed properly, she oversaw the loading of the pack mules. She held her breath while the strongboxes containing her precious cameras were hefted onto a mule. Exhaling a sigh of relief, she carefully secured the boxes, not trusting the chore to anyone else. After everything had been loaded, she went back to the hotel to tell her uncle good-bye and to retrieve one last piece of baggage.

By the time she returned to the corral, the sun's first rays had begun piercing holes in the blue-black night sky, creating enough light that she no longer needed a lantern. She quickly secured the final item to one of the mules, then went into the stable to fetch the chestnut gelding. A few minutes later, she led the horse outside to await Ethan Nighthawk.

She tried not to worry that he might not show up, that he'd changed his mind about being her assistant. Just because she'd arrived so early, she couldn't expect him to do the same, not when the time they'd agreed to leave was nearly an hour away. But as the minutes ticked by, her fear grew. Surely he would arrive a little before their appointed hour of departure.

As if she'd conjured him with her thoughts, she saw him coming toward the corral, leading a brown-and-white pinto. Easing out a relieved breath, she let her gaze rake over him before he spotted her. His shoulder-length hair remained loose, though he'd tied a strip of red cloth across his forehead to keep the thick black strands off his face. He wore another cotton shirt and the same skintight buckskin trousers but had exchanged his boots for knee-high moccasins with turned-up toes. The tops of the moccasins had been folded down several times, then tied in place with strips of rawhide. The headband and moccasins emphasized his Apache heritage, a visible reminder that she had hired a potentially dangerous man to be her assistant. Yet his rugged good looks and blatant masculinity didn't stir fear but a far more dangerous reaction. Desire.

Mariah licked her suddenly dry lips. Her pulse pounded against her temples, and a dull throb swirled low in her belly, then settled between her thighs. She gave her head a shake to clear her senses, chastising herself for reacting like a wanton trollop to Ethan Nighthawk. Wrapping her fingers around the cheek strap of the gelding's bridle, she led the horse toward the street.

Nighthawk's gaze snapped to the movement in the shadows just outside the stable's double doors. Recognizing the chestnut gelding as the one he'd selected for Mariah, he shifted his gaze to the person walking beside the horse. His eyes narrowed for a moment, then went wide with surprise. He hadn't expected Mariah to arrive at the corral ahead of him.

As he drew closer, he noted the long plait of yellow hair hanging over her right shoulder, the slightly curly tail of the braid brushing her breast. Struck with the sudden urge to finger that tuft of hair, to cup his hand over the rounded flesh beneath, he tightened his grip on his horse's reins and forced his gaze elsewhere.

Her style of dress came as another surprise. Gone were her fancy high-necked dress, full petticoats, high-heeled shoes, and foolish little hat. Instead, she wore a plain, open-necked blouse tucked into a knee-length split skirt, and a pair of high-top, low-heeled, laced boots. Behind her, he could see a sensible, large-brimmed hat hanging by its chin strap from the saddle horn.

Mariah Corbett was not like any woman he'd ever known. She spoke her mind with a frankness he found refreshing, possessed a boldness of spirit he found admirable. And she set his blood on fire with no effort whatsoever. He scowled at the direction of his thoughts. He didn't want to like this white woman's frankness, didn't want to admire her spirit, and he didn't want to desire her. Yet, being honest with himself, he realized he had already started liking and admiring Mariah, and he definitely desired her.

Once again, he wished the Spirits would tell him their purpose for bringing this white woman into his life. In the past, he'd always waited patiently for the Spirits to reveal their plans. But this time he chafed at the wait, constantly hoping the Spirits would speak to him soon. If they didn't, he feared routing Mariah from his memory once they went their separate ways would prove to be a difficult, if not impossible, task.

Nighthawk met Mariah halfway across the stable yard, her smile of greeting instantly easing his frustration. Still angry at himself for allowing this woman to affect him so easily, he took a sharp tone when he said, "If you wanted to leave earlier than we decided yesterday, you should have said so."

Mariah's smile faltered at his terse words. She lifted her chin and sent him a chilling glare. Though she longed to make a scathing remark, she didn't want to risk having him back out of their arrangement at

43

the last minute. Instead, she said, "The time we agreed on is fine. I got here early because I couldn't sleep." She lifted a shoulder in a shrug. "The excitement of our field trip, I suppose."

His momentary anger vanishing, he nodded, taking care to hide his amusement at her efforts to control her temper. He cast a quick glance at where the four heavily burdened pack mules stood dozing inside the corral fence. "Are you sure you did not forget something? An overstuffed chair or a feather mattress? Or maybe you would like to take an entire bed."

"A bed? What are you—" Clamping her mouth shut, she studied his face in the soft gold of the dawn's light. At first his stoic expression revealed nothing, but then the slight twitching of his lips, the sparkle in his eyes, gave him away. Irritated at herself for allowing him to rattle her composure so easily, she flashed him an annoyed look. "That's not funny. Being a photographer requires lots of equipment, and I assure you I haven't packed anything that isn't necessary for this trip."

He shrugged, the movement stirring his long hair and drawing her attention to something she'd missed earlier.

"What in the world?" She leaned closer, narrowing her gaze to stare at one ear, then the other. "You're wearing earrings!"

He stiffened. "Most Apache wear *jaatul*—ear strings."

"Really?" she replied, studying them. Each had some sort of blue bead dangling on a heavy circle of thread that had been inserted through the hole in his earlobe and tied. "Did it hurt having your ears pierced?"

"I do not remember. Like those of all Apache, my ears were pierced when I was a few weeks old. It is done so Apache children will hear things sooner and obey more quickly."

She stared at him, amazed at this new lesson in the Apache lifestyle. Then she turned and grabbed her hat from the saddle horn. Settling the hat on her head, she said, "Guess we'd better mount up."

He took a step toward her. "Let me help you."

Though Mariah was capable of mounting the horse on her own, she couldn't find the words to refuse his offer. He moved closer, laced his fingers together, then bent his knees. With his face just inches from hers, his musky male scent filled her lungs, making her head swim and her breathing labored. She squeezed her eyes closed for a second, swallowed hard, then lifted her left foot and placed her boot in his laced fingers. Though she longed to put her hands on his shoulders, she forced herself to wrap her fingers around the saddle horn, then swing her right leg over the horse's rump. As she lowered herself onto the saddle, she murmured her thanks.

Nighthawk moved one hand to her ankle and guided her foot into the stirrup. "You are welcome," he replied in a raspy voice, fighting the urge to slide his hand up her leg to explore her calf, her thigh, her—He jerked his hand away before he gave in to temptation.

As he took a step back, he glanced up at her. The heat of desire simmering in her green eyes caught him by surprise. His body responded instantly, heart pounding against his eardrums, his manhood swelling and throbbing with need. Drawing a shaky breath, he broke eye contact. His gaze landed on the leather scabbard hanging from the right side of her saddle.

"Do you know how to use that?" he said, nodding toward the gun in the scabbard.

Mariah followed his gaze to her Winchester carbine. "Of course. Uncle Ned said it was important for me to know how to use both pistols and rifles." She pulled the brim of her hat lower, then tightened the chin strap. "I'm good with a pistol, but I'm better with a rifle, especially this carbine."

Nighthawk gave her a thoughtful stare, then turned toward his horse. Though amazed by Mariah's latest revelation, he didn't doubt her claim.

A few minutes later, they left Smith's Corral. Nighthawk rode out first, leading two of the pack mules. Mariah followed with the other pair of mules trotting behind her gelding.

The first several hours of their trip were accomplished in silence, for which Mariah was grateful. The lingering effects of Ethan's nearness when he'd helped her mount hadn't abated. She'd never experienced anything like her body's response to the man riding ahead of her. She'd come to Arizona Territory for a purpose. She had to remember that. Her photographic work always took precedence over everything else in her life. She still had a list of goals she wanted to accomplish—places to go, photographs to take—goals that left no room for a man. Even a man as appealing and exciting as Ethan Nighthawk.

She glanced over at him, admiring his easy grace in the saddle, his body moving as one with the pinto.

Once again, she felt the powerful pull of this attractive yet mysterious man. Needing to find a distraction from her line of thinking, she jerked her gaze from his broad back and concentrated on the dusty road ahead of them.

She searched her mind for a topic of conversation, then finally said, "I was just thinking about what you told me yesterday. About the leader of your people. The one who died."

"What about him?"

"You never said his name. You mentioned his son's name but not his."

"Why are you asking?"

Mariah frowned. Unwilling to admit the truth, that she wanted to know everything about him, including the name of his former leader, she shrugged. "Just curious."

Nighthawk stared at her for several seconds, his lips flattened into a thin line. At last, he said, "Our leader was called Cochise by both Mexicans and White Eyes."

"Cochise." She pursed her lips. "I read something about him, but I can't remember when. Maybe it was when he agreed to the peace treaty." After a moment, she said, "What was his Apache name?"

"I cannot speak his Apache name."

"Why not?"

"You are a White Eyes. You would not understand."

"Try me."

He jerked back on the reins and swung his horse around so he faced Mariah. When she halted the gelding a few feet from his pinto, he said, "Apache do not say the name of those who have passed to the Spirit World unless it is absolutely necessary. Usually we say, 'he who is gone.' Or, if we must speak the name, first we say, 'the one who used to be called.' " Seeing the confusion on her face, he added, "To speak the name of the dead in any other way might summon their ghost."

"Ghost?" Her eyes went wide. "You believe in ghosts?"

He nodded. "The Apache life-way has always believed in ghosts. We are taught to fear them because they are dangerous, capable of luring the living into the world of the dead. So we are careful not to do anything that might summon a ghost."

"And speaking the name of a dead person can do that?"

He nodded again.

She thought about that for a moment, then said, "What happens if someone accidently summons one of these ghosts?"

"Sometimes nothing. But usually the person will get ghost sickness."

Mariah silently repeated his words, then gave him a pointed stare. "Are you making this up?"

He glared at her. "No. Ghost sickness is real. I have seen it myself. A powerful medicine man is needed to chase away the ghost."

She continued staring at him for several seconds, trying to decide if he was pulling her leg. Nothing in his expression confirmed her suspicions; he genuinely appeared to believe what he'd told her. At last she said, "Do you have any idea how bizarre all of this sounds?"

The corners of his mouth lifted in a faint smile. "It is true the Apache life-way is much different than the ways of the White Eyes. But so are the ways of the Chinese."

"You know about the Chinese culture?"

"Yes. When I first met Father Julian, I knew some English, but I could not read," he replied. "He taught me how, then encouraged me to borrow books from his library to improve my English. He has books on many subjects, including China." He didn't wait for her reply, ending their conversation by swinging his horse around and touching his heels to the pinto's sides.

Mariah watched him ride away, dumbfounded by what he'd just said. Urging her horse forward, she wondered about the puzzle of the man known as Ethan Nighthawk and what other interesting pieces of information he had yet to reveal about himself and his Apache heritage.

As Nighthawk rode ahead of Mariah, he could feel her staring at him, the intensity of her gaze searing his back through the fabric of his shirt. Trying to ignore the burning of his skin, he turned his thoughts to a subject that had plagued him for many months: finding a place where he belonged.

The Spirits had instructed him to go to Tucson. Told him he would meet Father Julian, who'd improved his English and taught him to read and write, yet he still didn't feel he belonged with the White Eyes. He'd spent his early years training to be a warrior and many of his adult years putting those skills to use. And he had yet to find a reason for an English-speaking Chokonen warrior to live among the White Eyes. But if that was not to be his future, where would he spend his remaining years?

He no longer felt he belonged with his people. Reservation life had been miserable for him and undoubtedly would be even worse if he were to return to his people, now living on the reservation at San Carlos. And he refused to become a renegade like those who had bolted when the government of the White Eyes closed the Chiricahua Reservation.

The idea of closing their reservation and forcing the Chokonen to San Carlos sparked Nighthawk's anger once again. The White Eyes thought their new program of removal, to put all Apache onto one reservation, would make their job easier. Nighthawk made a sound of disgust. The White Eyes in Washington were fools. Either they weren't aware, or simply didn't care, that some Apache bands did not like or even trust one another and would never get along. Forcing them to live on the same reservation was sure to cause countless problems. Nighthawk feared the months ahead for his people would be troubled ones.

As usually happened when he considered the future of the Chokonen, his thoughts turned to Cochise and the man's final words. Just before his death, he told his people to live forever at peace with the White Eyes. Nighthawk had done everything he could to comply with that request, just as he'd followed the wishes of the Spirits. But he still had no idea what his future held.

Nighthawk drew a cleansing breath, then pushed thoughts of his uncertain future from his mind. He had to concentrate on his current responsibility, leading Mariah to where they'd make camp.

Since she wanted to begin her series of photographs with one of the entire town of Tucson, taken from the nearby mountains, he'd told her their first day on the trail wouldn't be a long one. And by early afternoon, the winding, gradually ascending path they'd followed ended at the destination he'd selected—a relatively flat stretch of ground at the mouth of a canyon.

"We will camp here," Nighthawk said, pulling his horse to a halt. "There is a spring deeper in the canyon and enough grass for the animals." He dismounted, tied the pair of mules to a small manzanita tree, then announced he was going to make a quick search of the area.

By the time he returned a few minutes later, Mariah had tied her two mules near the others and started unloading her gear. A large dome-shaped object sat on the ground by her feet.

He frowned at her. "You should have waited. I would have helped you with that."

"Thanks, but Screech goes everywhere with me, so I'm used to handling his cage. It isn't heavy, just awkward."

Nighthawk's frown deepened. "Cage?"

"Yes," she replied, untying the cloth covering the cage and slowly raising one side of the fabric. "This is Screech." She smiled at the occupant of the cage. "In the wild, he would be nocturnal, sleeping during the day and hunting for food at night, but he's adapted pretty well to living with—" She turned at the choking sound Ethan made.

Nighthawk couldn't believe what Mariah had revealed. His pulse raced. His breathing became labored. Squeezing his eyes closed, he shook his head to clear his mind of what had to be some kind of trickery. Then he opened his eyes and knew there was no trick. On a perch inside the cage, turning its head from side to side and blinking its huge yellow eyes, sat a bird. An owl. Another choked groan vibrated in his chest.

"Ethan, what's wrong?"

He heard Mariah, but he didn't answer. He couldn't. He just stared at the bird, fear clutching at his gut and rooting him to the spot. Then the owl gave a low whistle, jolting him from his paralyzing shock. He took a step back, then another, his gaze riveted on the bird.

Mariah's brow furrowed at his odd behavior. "Can you tell me what's wrong?"

Again he didn't reply.

"Ethan, talk to me. Please." She watched him turn and stumble across the campsite, then drop to his knees. Confused and concerned, she kept her gaze on Ethan while she spoke to her pet. "Sorry, fella. I'm going to have to cover your cage for a bit longer." She dropped the cloth back into place, then hurried over to Ethan.

She stopped beside him, wanting to touch him but afraid of his reaction. "Ethan," she said in a low voice. "Tell me what's wrong. Are you ill?"

He drew a shaky breath. "*Niishjaa,*" he managed to say in a croaking whisper.

"I don't understand. Tell me in English."

His throat worked with a swallow. "Owl."

"Yes, Screech is an owl. What about him?"

52

"*Ntui*—bad. Very bad." His shoulders convulsed with a shudder.

"Ethan, you're not making any sense. Are you saying owls are bad?"

"Yes," he said, sucking in another deep breath, then exhaling slowly. "Owls are greatly feared by all Apache. They"—he swallowed hard—"are ghosts of the evil dead."

Mariah stared at him for a moment, then smiled. "Ghosts again. I should have known." She chuckled, then said, "How do you come up with all this nonsense?"

The hot glare he leveled at her only added to her amusement and made her burst out laughing. "I can't believe a fierce, brave Chokonen Apache is actually afraid of a little bitty owl." She laughed even harder, her eyes filling with tears. "That's the funniest thing I've heard in a long time."

Nighthawk's face warmed with a flush of anger, the gut-wrenching fear he'd experienced at seeing Mariah's owl momentarily forgotten. "I speak the truth. From the time all Apache are small children, we are taught that seeing an owl, even hearing its call, signals something bad, even death."

Mariah's amusement slowly died. Wiping away her tears with the back of one hand, she studied him. She recognized anger in the tenseness of his features, in the way he held his clenched fists atop his thighs. But she also identified the genuine fear lingering in the depths of his dark eyes and remembered the way his body had trembled when she'd first approached him. She doubted anyone could fake such intense fear. "You truly believe what you said, don't you? Seeing

53

Screech is a sign that something bad is going to happen?"

His jaw muscles working, he bobbed his head in a curt nod.

"That's total nonsense," she said, taking the sting out of her words by gentling her voice. "I've had Screech for more than two years, and nothing bad has ever happened to me or to anyone else who's been around him." She flashed a sudden smile. "Well, other than Uncle Ned breaking his leg, but that was his own damn fault."

When he didn't react to her attempt at humor, Mariah fell silent, staring at him while trying to comprehend what she'd just learned. Only a few hours earlier she'd wondered what else this man would reveal about himself, and now she had another piece of the puzzle. Ethan actually feared owls, considered them harbingers of bad luck. Struck with the need to offer him comfort, she said, "Is there something you can do to . . . uh . . . reverse the . . . um . . . hex?"

Nighthawk looked up at her sharply, his eyebrows pulled together in a fierce frown. Expecting to find ridicule on her face, he was surprised by the concern he saw instead. Some of the tension in his muscles easing, he nodded. "I need to do a purification ceremony."

"Can I help?"

"No, I must do it myself." He got to his feet. "I will return soon."

Though Mariah wanted to witness the ceremony he spoke of, she didn't ask to go with him, sensing that whatever he planned to do must be done in private. After he retrieved a large buckskin bag tied behind his saddle and left the campsite, she tried to concentrate on something else, first by unloading the pack mules, then sorting through their supplies, and finally gathering firewood. But regardless of the chore she performed, her mind persisted in dwelling on one topic: Ethan Nighthawk.

What a complicated man he was proving to be. So much like American men in many ways—speaking perfect English, apparently well read, and displaying manners appropriate for even the fanciest of social clubs back East. Yet the deeply ingrained beliefs of his upbringing continued to play a prominent role in his life. Sophistication mixed with the well-honed instincts of an Apache warrior. A shiver of excitement rippled up her spine. What a sinfully fascinating combination.

# Chapter Four

As the minutes ticked by, Mariah's concern about Ethan grew. Nearly an hour had passed since he'd revealed his fear of owls, then bolted from their campsite to carry out what he called a purification ceremony. Several times she'd considering going to look for him, but each time she nixed the idea, instinctively knowing Ethan would not take kindly to her intruding on what he obviously wanted to be a private moment.

Then, just when she decided to take her chances at riling his anger, she saw him coming toward her. She ran her gaze over him, studying the way he moved. He appeared to be more relaxed, his long strides easy and graceful, his shoulders and back no longer rigid. When he stopped a few feet from her, she drew in a quick breath. Her lungs filled with the aromatic scent clinging to him, the aftereffects, she decided, of his purification rite. Forcing herself to breathe normally, she moved her gaze up to his face. His eyes looked calm, having lost the panic she'd seen earlier, yet the lines around his mouth and the tightness of his jaw revealed an inner tension. He may have his fear under control for the moment, but the battle was far from won.

She waited to see if he'd speak first. When he didn't, she said, "Are you all right?"

He nodded, then glanced around the campsite. Dropping his buckskin bag near the pile of boxes and satchels she'd unloaded, he said, "Chokonen women are expected to unload the pack animals and set up camp, but I did not expect you to do all the work."

"I didn't mind," she replied, noticing he avoided looking directly at Screech's cage. "I was worried about you and needed to keep busy to pass the time. I wasn't sure how your horse takes to strangers, so I didn't try to unsaddle him."

He glanced over at the pinto. "He is usually well mannered, but you were wise not to approach him."

She rubbed her hands on her skirt, then cleared her throat. "I ... uh ... want to apologize for laughing earlier."

"That is not necessary."

"Yes, it is. I had no idea anyone actually feared owls."

"You are not familiar with Apache beliefs."

"No, but that's no excuse. The way I behaved was still incredibly rude, and I want you to know I'm sorry. Will you forgive me?"

He met and held her gaze for several seconds, then said, "Yes."

"Good," she replied, the tightness in her chest easing.

He motioned toward the pile of supplies and gear. "Do you need help with anything?"

"The tent I use to develop my photographs has to be pitched, but"—she glanced over at Screech's cage—"there's something I need to do first." Although his possible reaction to what she had to say worried her, she couldn't wait any longer. "I need to feed Screech. I would've fed him while you were . . . uh . . . indisposed, but I didn't know how long you'd be gone, and I wasn't sure how you'd react if you returned while I was . . ." She massaged her forehead to ease the sudden pounding behind her eyes. "Anyway, I can't wait much longer, so if you'd rather not be here . . ."

She saw his back and shoulders stiffen, the rapid throb of the pulse in his neck.

He considered her statement, then said, "The horses and mules need to be watered, and later they should be picketed where there is plenty of grass. Or I could do both now."

She immediately understood his unspoken question and bit her lip to hide a smile so she wouldn't bruise his male pride. "Why don't you just water them for now. Screech doesn't eat much, and since I'm late with his feeding, he'll make quick work of his meal."

He nodded, his relief evident in the relaxing of his tight muscles. "I will unsaddle my horse, then take the animals to the spring."

As soon as Ethan led the horses and mules away from camp, Mariah dug through her supplies for Screech's food, then uncovered his cage. As she'd predicted, the small owl greedily attacked his meal. After he finished, he edged closer to the door of his cage.

"Sorry, Screech," she said, reaching inside the cage to stroke his whiskers—the long hairlike feathers around his beak—which always calmed him. "But I think you'd better stay in there today."

The owl's low whistle made Mariah smile. "Yes, I know, I always let you out. But we're going to have to change our routine, at least for a while. Can you believe someone is actually terrified of you?"

Screech blinked, then gave another whistle. She chuckled, stroking his whiskers again. "No, I can't either. But it's true." She touched the soft feathers on one of his ear tufts, then withdrew her hand from the cage. "The next few weeks should be interesting, Screech. Real interesting."

When Nighthawk returned to camp after watering the horses and mules, he found Mariah trying to dig a hole for a fire. He picked up an armload of the firewood she'd gathered and moved toward her. "Let me do that," he said, dropping the wood next to where she'd managed to scrape a small indentation in the hard ground with a stick.

Mariah rose and stepped aside. She watched him drop to one knee and bend to the task. The flex of his muscles caught her attention, his back and arms straining the fabric of his shirt. Her mouth went dry, her fingers tingling to touch those powerful muscles. Forcing her mind away from such tantalizing ideas, she moved to where she'd stacked her supplies and retrieved a box of matches.

After he finished arranging the firewood, he sat

back on his heels. When she held the matches toward him, he smiled and took the box from her. "Thanks." His smile fading, he stared at the box for a second. "Matches are one of the few reasons my people are glad the White Eyes came to our homeland. Lighting a fire with a match is much easier than using the Apache fire-making stick."

"Yes, I imagine it is," she replied, struck again by the difference between their cultures.

Later, after they'd pitched the tent she used as a darkroom, moved her developing supplies inside, and eaten supper, she poured each of them another cup of coffee. She handed one cup to him, then took a seat beside him. As she took a sip of coffee, she considered how to ask the question that had nagged at her all afternoon. Since he hadn't brought up the subject, she knew she'd have to, though she wasn't sure how to go about it. Deciding her normal practice of simply jumping in would have to do, she turned to him and said, "Now that you know about Screech, I hope you're not thinking of changing your mind about working for me."

Nighthawk leveled a scowl in her direction, wondering if his thoughts were that obvious or if she'd made a lucky guess. Shifting his gaze back to the fire, he mulled over his response. Since performing a purification ceremony to protect him from Mariah's owl, he'd considered doing exactly as she suggested. But memories of his last vision—especially the owl feathers—kept him from leaping onto his horse and riding away. And the more he thought about that vision and what had happened since, the more he was convinced the Spirits had deliberately brought both Mariah and her owl into his life. What reason the Spirits had for throwing together an Apache warrior, a white woman, and an owl, he couldn't imagine. But he knew they had, and, therefore, he shouldn't try to analyze the situation.

Mariah shifted beside him. He didn't look at her, but he sensed her growing exasperation with his silence. Still, he couldn't find the words to speak.

She finally heaved a sigh, then said, "Ethan, even if I'd known how you'd react to Screech, I didn't have any choice about bringing him with me. My uncle is the only other person who could've taken care of him, but with Ned nursing a broken leg, that wasn't possible."

Nighthawk lifted his cup to his mouth, surprised to see his hand shake, but this time not from fear. No one other than Father Julian called him Ethan, a name he hadn't wanted but had reluctantly accepted at the priest's insistence that he have a Christian name. He hadn't expected to like hearing Mariah saying the name, but each time she did, his pulse went into a wild cadence and a shiver of pleasure danced over his flesh.

He took a drink of coffee, then said, "You can stop worrying. I have not changed my mind." He frowned into his cup. "At least for now."

Mariah's smile of relief faltered. "What do you mean 'for now'?"

"Fearing owls has always been part of the Apache life-way. The only thing we fear more is ghosts. Apache parents tell their misbehaving children the owl will come and catch them if they are bad." He took another drink of coffee. "You must understand that ignoring what I have believed since I was a child cannot be done quickly. Being close to your owl will not be easy for me."

Her chin jutted forward. "It won't be easy for me either if you get spooked every time you see Screech and then have to do some self-purification ritual."

The corners of his mouth lifted in a half smile. "I cannot promise I will not get spooked, as you call it, but I will take every precaution to protect myself so I can continue working for you." His expression sobering, he lowered his voice to add, "That is the only way I will learn why the Spirits brought the two of you into my life."

Mariah's brow furrowed. "Brought us into your life? What do you mean?"

Nighthawk considered his answer carefully, uncertain if he should bring up a subject she'd clearly rejected the first time. Deciding to try again to tell her the truth, he said, "While I was in jail, I had a vision."

Mariah scowled. "So we're back to visions again?"

His lips flattened. "Yes. In that vision, I saw you and your owl."

Her eyes widened. "Let me get this straight. You actually saw Screech and me in a vision?"

"Not exactly. The Spirits did not show me your face. I saw only a woman with long, pale-gold hair. But there are few white women in Tucson and none I have seen with hair the color of yours. When you came to the jail, I knew you had to be the woman the Spirits told me I would meet. And while I did not see Screech, either, I saw feathers that I knew came from an owl."

She tipped her head to one side and studied him in

silence for a moment. "You weren't teasing me that first day, were you? You really do have visions."

He met her gaze. "Yes."

"But how is that possible?"

"It just is," he said with a shrug. "Many Apache experience visions. Some receive these messages from the Spirits while they are asleep, but they are not dreaming. For others, the visions come while they are awake. Some Apache only hear the Spirits speaking to them. Others also see images. Visions are something we learn about as children. Something we do not question but accept as part of the Apache lifeway."

Mariah could only stare at him, trying to grasp what he'd said. "You have no idea why you were told we would meet?"

"No," he replied, watching her tongue come out to wet her bottom lip. Struck with the sudden urge to replace her tongue with his, he jerked his gaze from her face. "The Spirits have not told me why they brought you into my life."

Mariah fell silent, turning to stare into the fire. If his claims of having visions could be believed—and, surprisingly, this time she'd found no reason not to— she and Ethan Nighthawk had been destined to meet. A slow smile stole across her face. He was like no man she'd ever met, and though her work as a photographer allowed no room for any man in her life, she realized she liked the notion that their meeting had been destined. She liked it a lot.

His voice pulled her from her musings. "I have answered your questions. Will you answer one of mine?"

She turned to look at him. "Sure."

"Why do you have an owl for a pet?"

"It wasn't something I planned. I found Screech while on a field trip in the mountains near Denver almost two years ago. He looked really young, and at first I thought he must have fallen out of a nest. But when I got closer, I discovered the problem. Somehow he'd hurt one of his wings and wasn't able to fly. I took him home, hoping his wing would heal so I could return him to the forest. But there was too much damage. Since he'd never be able to fly to hunt for food, I knew turning him loose would be a sure death sentence. I couldn't bear that, so I kept him."

"And you take him wherever you go?"

"Pretty much. He's really well behaved. I usually let him out of his cage part of the time, especially in the evening, but I . . . um . . . decided against it tonight after . . ." She drew a deep breath. "Anyway, if I ever settle in one place long enough, I plan to get a larger cage for him. He might not be able to fly, but he shouldn't be confined to such a small space."

"You do not tire of traveling?"

"Sometimes. But most of the time I love the excitement of seeing new sights, taking photographs of places most people will never get to see."

"Then you do not plan to settle in one place?"

She drank the last of her coffee, then said, "Probably not. At least not for a long time. There are too many places I want to visit. Too many photographs I want to take."

"Most women want a husband and children."

"I'm not like most women."

Nighthawk readily agreed but kept the thought to

himself. "Are you saying you do not want to get married?"

Her chin came up. "I've decided there isn't room in my life for a husband. I've worked too hard to get where I am to risk letting marriage jeopardize my future as a photographer."

He mulled over her answer for a moment. "You think any man you marry would make you give up your work?"

When she nodded, he said, "That is something I do not understand about the White Eyes. Why do they think people must stop being who they are when they marry? This does not make sense to me. When my people marry, the man and woman have new responsibilities, but otherwise each is the same person as before."

She gave him a thoughtful look. "Maybe Americans aren't as advanced as your people when it comes to marriage."

Before Ethan could respond, she got to her feet. "I'm going to wash the dishes at the spring, then I think I'll turn in."

He rose as well. "I will go with you."

When she opened her mouth, he held up a hand to silence what he knew would be an objection. "You do not know these mountains, or what animals could be hiding in the darkness. I will go with you to keep watch."

"I can take care of myself."

He released his breath in a huff. "That is not what I meant. Can you not stop being so sensitive about your independence and let someone else take care of you for once?"

Mariah swallowed hard, surprised to realize the idea of Ethan taking care of her appealed to her. "Okay," she said in a husky whisper.

As they made their way to the spring, she tried to convince herself she'd given in to his badgering because she knew he was right about her not knowing anything about the mountains, *not* because she liked the idea of him taking care of her. She tried to convince herself, but she wasn't sure she succeeded.

A while later, Mariah lay stretched out on her bedroll, staring up at the blue-black sky and the nearly full moon. Hearing Ethan's movements on the other side of the fire, she turned her head. In the moonlight, she could see him preparing his own bed. After he spread out his blanket, he moved closer to the fire pit, hunkered down, and dipped his fingers into the cold ashes at the edge of the fire. Using his fingertips, he rubbed the ashes on his forehead in the shape of a cross.

She rose up onto one elbow. "What are you doing?"

He moved back to his blanket and sat down before replying. "Protecting myself."

"From what?"

"Ghosts."

"Because of Screech?"

"Yes."

"I see." Though she found the idea laughable, she knew he was dead serious, so she kept her amusement to herself. "And that really works?"

He nodded. "An old shaman in my band told me using ashes at night is good medicine against ghosts."

"Well, then, you should be fine."

He stared at her long and hard, his gaze probing her moonlit face for signs of sarcasm. Finding none, he finally said, "Good night."

" 'Night," she replied, settling back on her bedroll. Though tired from lack of sleep the night before, her mind refused to slow enough for her to doze off. Her thoughts jumped from the photographs she would take the next day to the exhibit she planned to set up at the Centennial Exposition, to wondering about her uncle. Thank goodness she'd hired Señora Solares. Knowing the woman would look in on Ned and take him his meals eliminated one of her worries.

She still worried about getting her photographs to Philadelphia in time. She'd originally planned to have her exhibit ready when the Exposition opened, but she'd met with one delay after another. Finishing her last set of photographs had required more time than she'd anticipated, as did making the trip to Tucson. And then, right after arriving, Ned broke his leg, putting her even further behind. Thankfully, the Exposition ran through November, and the men in charge of the Colorado Pavilion had assured her they would hold a space for her exhibit. Contemplating the work ahead of her, she decided she could still take the photographs and get them to Philadelphia in time to be displayed for at least the last few months of the Exposition. She frowned up at the moon. She could do it provided Ethan didn't stop believing the ashes he smeared on his forehead protected him from Screech, prompting him to take off for points unknown.

She rolled onto her side, facing the banked fire and, on its opposite side, Ethan. He lay on his back, eyes closed, chest rising and falling in the slow, steady rhythm of sleep. The moon bathed his incredibly handsome face in silvery light, casting his profile in stark relief against the darkness of the night. Her gaze traced the line of his forehead, the slight hook of his nose, his full lips and strong chin. She smiled. Even in sleep, he bore the stamp of proud warrior. An emotion she didn't recognize plucked at her heart, making the simple act of drawing a breath nearly impossible.

As she rolled onto her back, a half sob escaped her tight throat. She couldn't allow herself to feel anything for Ethan Nighthawk. She had her life already planned—a plan that didn't include a man. She'd worked long and hard to reach her current level of success as a female in a male profession. Her photographs were beginning to be in demand by several publications back East, demand that could dry up in an instant if she allowed the distraction of a man to enter her personal life. As she'd told Ethan, she wouldn't risk jeopardizing her career by getting married. A husband wouldn't want her spending so much time on her photographic work. In fact, he would likely demand she quit altogether. She couldn't, she *wouldn't* do that.

A long time passed before her troubled mind allowed her to sleep.

Something awakened Nighthawk, something he couldn't immediately identify. Keeping his eyes closed, he didn't move but lay quietly, his senses straining to figure out what had pulled him from sleep. Then he heard it: a soft, rhythmic whisper of sound. He opened his eyes a slit and slowly turned his head. When he found the source of the sound, his eyes widened, his breath catching in his throat.

Mariah sat on her bedroll, her head turned away from him, a hairbrush in one hand. Her braid undone, she ran her fingers through the loose strands, then carefully used the hairbrush to work the snarls free. Each stroke of the bristles being pulled through the length of her hair made the soft whispering sound that had awakened him.

He stared in fascination, mesmerized by the sight of her hand moving the brush downward and the resulting waterfall of golden silk. An image formed in his head, an erotic fantasy of the silky strands brushing his bare chest, his belly, his hardened sex. His blood heating to a fever pitch, he clamped his lips together to hold back a moan.

He thought he'd managed to stifle the sound, but Mariah suddenly halted the brush in midstroke and turned to meet his gaze. Something leaped between them, a spark of awareness, a flash of desire so intense that the air between them seemed to crackle with it.

He dragged in a lungful of the charged air, surprised by the depth of desire singing in his veins. He couldn't understand why he wanted Mariah so strongly. It wasn't because he hadn't been with a woman recently—his frequent visits to the bordello where Carmen worked took care of his physical needs. Nor did his ego need the conquest of bedding a white woman. Being honest with himself, he couldn't deny that he desired Mariah sexually, but there was much more between them than physical need, an attraction he wasn't comfortable with and didn't comprehend.

Mariah watched the emotions flicker across Ethan's face. For once his usually stoic expression relaxed enough to reveal a little of what went on in his head. And unless she missed her guess, his thoughts, at least in part, mirrored hers. Surprise. Confusion. And desire, hot and potent. Needing to break the highly charged moment, she pulled her gaze away from his and cleared her throat.

"Sorry if I woke you," she said. "I was trying to be quiet."

Nighthawk squeezed his eyes closed for a second, willing the heat surging through his body to cool. "There is no need to be sorry," he replied, the remnants of his desire making his voice gravelly. He stirred the fire back to life, added more wood, then reached for the coffee pot.

As he got to his feet, he said, "I will fill this after I check on the horses and mules."

"Fine," she said, lifting her arm to resume brushing her hair. "After we eat, I'm going to decide where to set up my camera. Hopefully, by the time the sun is overhead, I'll be ready to take my first photograph."

Nighthawk watched the brush move through her hair, startled by the sudden urge to ask her to let him take over the task. Irritated by his inability to keep such wayward thoughts from entering his head, he felt his temper flare. "Whatever you say, boss lady." He turned on his heel and strode from camp.

Mariah stared after him, wondering what she'd done to earn the anger she heard in his voice, the fierce glare of his dark eyes. Pulling the brush through her hair a final time, she sighed. It was just as well. Whatever this—this *thing* was between them, she couldn't allow it to go any further. His anger would certainly make restraint easier.

Though she knew her reasoning to be correct—her work always had and always would come first—she experienced a tightening in her chest. A twinge of pain she recognized as regret for what could never be.

# Chapter Five

The first thing Nighthawk learned about photographers was the inordinate amount of time involved before they actually took a photograph. Mariah spent more than an hour prowling along the rocky ledge that overlooked Tucson far below, checking different angles for the exact view she wanted to capture, watching the play of sunlight and shadows on the dusty town.

Finally, she turned to him and said, "I'll take my first photograph from here. The light should be just about perfect by the time I get everything ready." She started toward their camp, waving him to follow. "I need you to carry my camera, so hurry up. I don't have all day."

Though her order might have rankled under different circumstances, Nighthawk merely nodded, then fell in step behind her. She obviously took her work seriously, an attribute he admired in anyone, even an outspoken white woman.

After he carried the strongbox to the spot she'd selected, he stood back while she set up the tripod and large camera with quick, efficient movements. Though he'd never had occasion to see photographic equipment, he had seen a drawing of a camera in one of Father Julian's books. But if he recalled correctly, the camera in the drawing hadn't looked as large as Mariah's.

"Are all cameras that big?" he said.

"No," she replied, adjusting the legs of the tripod. "The size of the camera determines the size of the photograph, and the smaller cameras simply can't do justice to landscapes." She glanced around at the cactus-studded mountains, the desert valley below. "For magnificent and vast scenery like this, I wouldn't use anything but this camera. It's heavier and more awkward to handle, but the results are far superior."

"What is in the rest of the boxes?"

"Chemicals, glass plates, and another camera. A smaller one. I always take two cameras into the field. Mostly as a precaution in case something happens to this one, but also to give me a choice. Most of my photographs are landscapes, but"—she eyed him silently for a moment, her gaze lingering on his face—"once in a while, I see something that should be photographed with a smaller camera."

Nighthawk absorbed her words, wondering at the look she gave him, then said, "Who taught you about photography?"

"A friend of Uncle Ned's back in Pennsylvania. From the moment I saw him take a photograph, I knew that's what I wanted to do. I used to hang around his studio, watching and memorizing his every move, soaking up all the knowledge I could. When he finally realized my interest in photography wasn't just a passing fancy, he offered to be my teacher." She frowned. "I was lucky. Most photographers wouldn't have taken on a young girl as an apprentice. Girls are only supposed to be interested in finding a husband, having children, and running a household." She huffed out a breath. "That's so unfair."

"There are many unfair things in life."

She met his gaze for a moment. "True." Turning her attention to her camera, she made one last adjustment to its placement, then said, "Ethan, I know this probably won't mean anything to you, and it certainly won't undo what's been done to you and your people, but I'm sorry for the way the American government has treated the Apaches."

He crossed his arms over his chest, his lips flattened. "You are correct. Your apology means nothing. You cannot undo the wrongs done to us. You cannot make the White Eyes stop hating my people and accept us among you. I learned the language of the White Eyes and live in one of their towns, but they do not accept me. The only place the Apache will be accepted is where the government of the White Eyes says we must live. But only until someone else wants *that* place. Then the White Eyes will force us to move again."

Mariah didn't know how to respond. She longed to offer him assurance that his statement wasn't true, that eventually his people would be accepted. But she knew the government's stand on Indians would take many years to change, if it changed at all. Finally she said, "I know what prejudice is like, being a woman who chose to work in a man's profession. But I can't begin to imagine what life has been like for your people. I hope one day it will change."

Nighthawk's jaw worked, the anger roiling inside him easing at her softly spoken words. Though he rarely believed anything a White Eyes told him, he did believe Mariah meant what she said. Shaking off his somber thoughts, he said, "What do you do next to take a photograph?"

Mariah started, disconcerted to realize something had momentarily distracted her from her work. Normally nothing interfered with her intense concentration while working. But then, nothing had been normal since she'd walked into the Tucson jail and met Ethan Nighthawk.

"I have to prepare a plate to put in the camera." She tilted her head to one side and looked up at him, then surprised herself by adding, "Would you like to see how it's done?"

He gave an affirmative response, a response he soon regretted. Preparing a plate had to be done inside the small canvas tent that he'd helped line with lengths of orange calico. The fabric, she'd explained, would help to keep out as much light as possible— an important part of the process. With the tent's six-foot-square interior already partially filled with boxes of her photographic supplies, they had just enough room to stand side by side. Such close quarters had a predictable and immediate effect on his body, but at least the near-darkness hid his aroused state. And thankfully, after she laid out an assortment of supplies on a makeshift table of wooden crates and began her explanation, his interest in the photographic process cooled his desire.

"Once a plate has been thoroughly cleaned and polished, this collodion solution," she said, picking up a bottle she'd already explained contained a mixture of guncotton and iodine of potassium, "is the next step." She held a plate by one corner, deftly poured the liquid onto the glass until the entire surface was coated, then let the excess run back into the bottle.

"As the solution begins to dry, a thin coating will be left on the glass. Then, while the plate is still wet, it's soaked in a bath of water and silver nitrate to make it light-sensitive."

As she carefully immersed the piece of glass in a flat wooden tray, Nighthawk's brow furrowed. "What does light-sensitive mean?"

"I'm not a chemist, so I can't explain the process in technical terms. But basically, when light strikes a sensitized plate through the camera lens, the image of whatever is being photographed adheres to the coating of chemicals. Does that make sense?"

"No," he said with a chuckle. "But I believe you."

Mariah's breath hitched in her chest, his deep chuckle creating a wild tingling of desire low in her belly. She inhaled a shaky breath, filling her lungs with his musky scent, which transformed the tingling into a throbbing ache between her thighs. She exhaled slowly, then said, "The . . . um . . . plate has to stay in the silver bath for"—she swallowed, hoping to ease the dryness in her throat—"for about five minutes."

As she shifted to check the time on the pocket watch she'd laid out with the other supplies, Nighthawk started to move out of her way. Each immediately shifted again but anticipated the other's move incorrectly and ended up moving in the same direction. She bumped against his chest with a soft thump and the whoosh of air leaving her lungs. He grunted, instinctively grabbing her elbows to steady her.

With her arms trapped between them, her fingers splayed over the hard muscles of his chest, Mariah could barely breathe, let alone speak. Staring up at him, she managed to say, "Sorry."

"My fault," he replied. The dim interior of the tent cast her face in heavy shadows, but he could make out her widened eyes, her parted lips. Though he knew he shouldn't, knew he'd probably regret his actions, he couldn't resist any longer. He had to taste her mouth just once.

He lowered his face until his lips touched hers. As he brushed his mouth over hers, he heard her soft gasp. And when he settled his lips atop hers and deepened the kiss, she moved closer. Slipping her arms around his neck, she pressed her full breasts more firmly against his chest and moaned into his mouth. Suddenly his body was afire with red-hot desire, the blood thundering in his ears, his sex engorged and throbbing.

Kissing was not completely unknown to the Apache. But in their life-way, kissing was generally reserved as a way for parents to show affection for their children. Even married Apache couples rarely kissed. So when Nighthawk moved to Tucson, he'd known little about kissing until he began frequenting one of the bordellos in town, much to Father Julian's shame. The priest had tried to convince him to control his baser instincts and stay away from Maiden Lane. But when Nighthawk refused to follow such advice, Father Julian finally resigned himself to praying to the White Eyes God to ask for Nighthawk's sins to be forgiven.

Nighthawk had learned a great deal from the women whose beds he'd shared, especially Carmen, who'd been more than willing to teach him not only all the intricacies of kissing but also the many ways to give pleasure to a woman.

Mariah fisted her hands in the long, silky strands of Ethan's hair and rose onto her toes in an effort to get closer. The rumble in his throat momentarily cleared her swamped senses enough for her to realize what was happening. Pulling her mouth from his, she dropped her heels to the ground. "We shouldn't be doing this."

He sucked in a deep breath. "I know."

But rather than release her, he lowered his face to nuzzle her neck, then her jaw. "We will stop in a minute, but first I—" His mouth pressed to hers muffled whatever he'd started to say. He ran his tongue over her full bottom lip, then gently suckled the swollen flesh.

Mariah groaned, pressing even closer against him, feeling the hard ridge of his arousal through the layers of her clothes. The place between her legs moistened, and the earlier throbbing gained intensity. She whimpered, desperately needing something from the man holding her, something she didn't completely understand.

Nighthawk slowly lifted his head, knowing they had to stop before the desire flaring between ignited

into a full-fledged inferno. When she groaned a protest, he dropped a quick kiss on her mouth, then
reached up to carefully free her fingers from his hair.
"Relax," he said in a crooning voice, rubbing a hand
up and down her back in a soothing motion. "Relax,
and the ache will go away soon."

She drew several deep breaths, removed her arms
from around his neck, then stepped out of his embrace. Hoping the lack of light would hide the blush
burning her cheeks, she forced herself to look up at
him.

"I . . . uh . . . I don't—" She swallowed hard. "I
don't know what came over me. I don't usually be-
have like . . . Anyway, I'm sorry."

He flashed a smile, lifting a hand to cup her chin.
"I am also to blame. Though neither of us should be
sorry for something we both enjoyed." His smile fading, he rubbed his thumb across her mouth, then
dropped his arm to his side. "But we should not allow
this to happen again."

"You're right. We shouldn't," she replied, though
agreeing sent a pang of disappointment ricocheting
through her chest. Remembering their reason for being in her darkroom tent, she frowned. "Drat, I forgot
about the plate." Glancing at the pocket watch, she
sighed with relief. "Good. Still a minute to go."

When the plate had soaked the requisite length of
time, she removed it from the wooden tray. "See how
the coating on the plate is a creamy yellow?" At his
nod, she continued with her explanation. "The excess
water is drained off the plate, then, while it's still wet,
it goes in this"—she picked up a rectangular box,
slightly larger than the glass plate—"plate holder,

which keeps light from striking the plate until after it's inserted into the camera and the slide is raised." She demonstrated how the plate holder's slide, the front panel, lifted to expose the prepared plate.

She pushed the slide down, then turned toward the closed tent flap. "Now we're ready to take this to the camera. Once the plate is prepared, it's important to take a photograph as quickly as possible. If the plate dries out, the image will be spoiled."

Nighthawk followed her outside and then to where she'd set up her camera. After she checked the angle of the sun and made a final adjustment to the camera's placement, she looked over at him.

"Okay, I'm ready to take the photograph." She moved next to her camera and indicated he should stand on the opposite side. "As I told you, the plate mustn't be allowed to dry out, so these last steps must be done quickly. First make sure the cap is on the lens, then insert the plate holder into the camera and lift the slide. The final step is removing the lens cap and allowing light to fall on the plate long enough for the image to adhere."

After she removed the cap, Nighthawk could see her lips move as she counted the passing seconds. When she reached her targeted passage of time, she replaced the cap over the lens, pushed the slide down over the plate, then removed the plate holder from the camera in quick succession.

She met his gaze and smiled. "Now it's back to the tent to develop the plate."

As they started back to the tent, he said, "How do you know how many seconds to count?"

"The length of exposure varies depending on the

amount of natural light and the subject of the photograph. It takes practice to learn the best exposure times."

She lifted the flap of the tent and stepped inside. Ethan followed her into the dim interior and closed the flap.

Once her eyes adjusted to the darkness, she removed the plate from its holder, then reached for another of the bottles she'd set out earlier. "This is pyrogallic acid," she said, pouring some of the solution over the plate's surface. "In a few seconds the image will begin to appear, only the light and dark areas will be reversed. The image on the glass plate is called a negative. When the actual photograph is made from the negative, the dark and light areas will reverse again and become a positive. The way they really look."

As the image on the negative became more distinct, Nighthawk watched with fascination. He could see the buildings of Tucson taking shape in the center and the mountain peaks in the background, though, as Mariah had explained, the dark and light areas were the opposite of how they were in reality. "Some of my people would call you a witch," he said in a soft voice, "because you can capture lifelike images with your camera."

Mariah smiled. "I've been called worse. But there is something magical about taking photographs. I guess that's one of the reasons I love being a photographer."

When the image on the negative had developed to her satisfaction, she washed the plate with clean water, then immersed it in a solution of hyposulfite of soda. "This is called fixing the plate," she said. "The hyposulfite will dissolve any remaining silver nitrate on the plate, then I'll rinse it again with clean water.

"Next, the fixed plate is carefully dried over a low flame. And the final step is applying a coat of varnish while the plate is still warm."

Nighthawk watched her complete the process, impressed with her skill and confidence. "The final photograph will be on paper?"

She nodded. "A specially treated paper. It has to be dipped in several chemical solutions so it will accept the image from the plate when laid atop the glass."

"When will you make the photograph from this plate?"

"Not until we get back to town. Then I'll make photographs from all the plates I've used while on this trip."

By midafternoon, Mariah announced she was finished for the day. She'd taken several other photographs—different views of the mountains with their assorted cactus: the short, heavily barbed barrel; the fuzzy but just as well-armed cholla; and, most spectacular of all, the majestic saguaro soaring to enormous heights toward the cloudless sky—until the light began to fade.

As they sat by their campfire that evening, Mariah contemplated her day's work. Satisfied with the photographs she'd taken and confident she would add equally good shots to her collection in the coming days, she hoped the incident with Ethan in her tent wouldn't be repeated. She didn't need that kind of distraction. Gazing over at where he lounged against his saddle, she felt her heart rate kick up and her lips tingle. All day she'd forced herself to keep her thoughts away from remembering the feel of his lips, the firm muscles of his chest, the hardness of his arousal. But now that she didn't have her work to occupy her thoughts, memories of their shared kiss filled her head. And, worse, she couldn't squash the wish for another chance to experience the wild thrill of passion his lips had sparked. His voice jerked her out of her daydreams.

"What do you want to do tomorrow?"

Mariah blinked, wondering if he'd somehow read her thoughts. Hoping the warmth flooding her cheeks wasn't visible, she said, "I'd like to take some photographs of the desert. Is there a place we can camp down there?"

"If there is enough water, I know of several places."

"How far's the closest one?"

"Half a day's ride, maybe longer with the mules."

"Good. We can set up my tent before dark. Then I'll survey the area first thing the following morning. And"— she took a deep breath—"I want to take your photograph."

Ethan's eyebrows rose. "What?"

Mariah couldn't believe she'd actually blurted out something that had been in the back of her mind for most of the day. "I said, I'd like to take a photograph of you."

"Why?"

She frowned, wondering exactly the same thing. She normally didn't do portraits, preferring to concentrate on her first love: landscapes. But ever since

her earlier realization that Ethan would make a wonderful portrait subject, she hadn't been able to shake
the thought. In fact, now that she'd given voice to the
idea, she realized she liked it even more.

She gave him a weak smile. "If you don't want to,
I'll understand. It's just that I thought . . ." She
couldn't bring herself to tell him what she really
thought, that the wonderful planes and angles of his
face appealed to more than her photographer's eye.
As a woman, she considered him the epitome of male
beauty—ruggedly handsome face, piercing dark eyes
beneath slightly arched brows, well-sculpted, muscular body. Even his proud, almost arrogant demeanor
added to his appeal. She cleared her throat, then said,
"Anyway, I hope you'll consider posing for me." Her
eyes went wide. "I mean, for a photograph."

His lips twitched with amusement at the expression
on her face and the splash of deep pink tinting her
cheeks. "I will think about it."

Mariah nodded, then looked at the sky. Barely
noticing the spectacular oranges and purples of the
sunset, she racked her brain for something to say. Recalling a statement Ethan made during an earlier conversation, she shifted her gaze back to him.

"Tell me about witches." When the only response
she received was a furrowed brow, she said, "While
I was developing a negative today, you said some of
your people would call me a witch because of what
I do."

His brow smoothed, but he didn't answer right
away. After drawing a deep breath and exhaling
slowly, he began speaking. "The Apache believe there
are two kinds of witchcraft. One is used to attract a

person of the opposite sex but is not considered a serious offense. The second kind is evil, used for a bad purpose against another person or the entire band. There is no charge against an Apache worse than being accused of using their power for evil witchcraft."

"What do you mean, their 'power'?"

Nighthawk bent one of his legs and draped a wrist over his updrawn knee. Normally he didn't discuss the Apache life-way with anyone, even with Father Julian, but unaccountably he wanted to with Mariah. Wanted her to understand the ways of his people. "As children, we are taught that power is the life force of our world. Everything around us—animals, insects, plants, the stars, even forces of nature—has power, which we can acquire and use for different purposes. Curing illness, confusing the enemy, finding lost objects. Some Apache use their power for only themselves or their family. Others use their power to help the entire band."

Mariah considered his explanation for a minute, then said, "So if a man with this power uses it to do bad deeds, he would be considered a witch?"

"Yes, but all Apache can receive power, not just men. A witch can be either man or woman. An accusation of practicing witchcraft is an extremely serious charge. If it is proven true, the punishment is death by fire."

"Fire?" she said in a whisper, repressing a shudder. Pushing such a horrible thought aside, she leaned back against her saddle. "You said power can be acquired. How is that done?"

"There are several ways. Confronting the source of the power directly. Receiving the power from another person. In a dream or in a vision. For some, the source of the power shows itself as a person. For others, the power source only speaks to them."

"Speaks! You're saying everything—animals, plants, stars, forces of nature—can transform themselves into people and talk?"

Had Nighthawk not spent the past two years living in Tucson, he would have taken offense at the doubt in her voice. But because of his growing knowledge of the ways of the White Eyes, he understood how odd some Apache beliefs must sound to them. "Yes. Ussen, the creator and Great Spirit of the Apache, gives all power sources the ability to change their appearance and speak."

"Ussen is like our Christian God?"

He nodded. "Once a person receives power, the source becomes his consultant and Spirit guide—what Father Julian would call a guardian angel."

Mariah thought about what he'd said for a moment. "Have you acquired power from something?"

"Yes," he replied, lifting a hand to finger the buckskin pouch hanging around his neck.

"Can you tell me how you acquired the power? Or is that something you're forbidden to talk about?"

"It is not forbidden." He changed position again, bending his other leg, then wrapping his arms around his knees. "I was hunting with two friends when a thunderstorm came over the mountains. Day became night. Rain fell so hard, I could not see. Fierce streaks of lightning blazed across the sky. As I ran to find shelter, one bolt struck so close, it knocked me to the ground." Pausing for a moment, he wondered how much to tell her. He drew a deep breath, then said,

"That is when I had my first vision. My friends also received visions from the Spirits."

He glanced over at her, expecting her to make a comment. When she merely lifted her eyebrows to encourage him to continue, he said, "We returned to camp and went to see Spotted Wolf, a shaman in our band. After we told him about the storm, each of us spoke to him about the vision the Spirits sent us. He said Ussen had protected all three of us from the thunderstorm, but because I was closest to where the lightning struck, I must have both lightning power and nighthawk power."

At Mariah's questioning expression, he said, "Thunderstorms are caused by the Thunder People, spirits who live in the sky. When the Thunder People are angry, their shouting is the thunder we hear, their arrows shooting across the sky are the streaks of lightning we see. The nighthawk is a bird with special power. It can dart and swoop so fast that my people believe it has the power to avoid being hit by lightning-arrows. Whenever a storm comes, my people seek shelter, but if we're caught in the open, we imitate the bird's call—*piishii, piishii*—to protect us from being struck by lightning."

"You did that when you were caught in the thunderstorm with your friends?"

He nodded. "Spotted Wolf said the nighthawk had protected me from harm, and that Ussen had given me a second power. That is when Spotted Wolf gave me a new name." He said the name in his native tongue.

"All that means *nighthawk*?"

He smiled. "No. Apache names usually are not just

one word. Our names usually describe something about us, or are given to us because of something we did or after an important occurrence in our life. My name means darts-through-lightning-like-the-nighthawk, but most refer to me by just the Apache word for *night-hawk*."

"What do you mean 'refer to you'?"

"Apache and White Eyes see names differently. To my people, a name is very valuable. As children, we are taught not to call people by their names when we see them. That is considered impolite."

"Your people never say a person's name to his face?"

"In times of war or if there is an emergency, it is done. Then, if a man calls another by name, he is willing to do anything for him."

Mariah mulled that over for a moment, then said, "How did you get the name Ethan?"

"From Father Julian. He thought I should have an American name. I did not want a White Eyes name, but after I lived here for several months, I finally agreed. I took the Christian name he suggested, Ethan, and made Nighthawk what he called my surname."

"Even though you don't like it."

"Apache words are not easy for White Eyes, so I understood part of Father Julian's reasons. Besides"—he lifted his shoulders in a shrug—"I knew it would please him. He was kind to me when others were not."

She nodded, unaccountably proud of his need to repay a kindness. She fell silent, staring off into the deepening darkness, thinking about what he'd revealed about himself. She mulled over one thing in particular, then turned her gaze back to him. "Can people acquire power from owls?"

She saw him flinch at her mention of the topic they'd avoided since the previous day.

He blew out a long breath before responding. "I have never known anyone with owl power, but, yes, it is possible."

"Interesting," she said, more to herself than to him, her gaze drifting to the cage across their campsite. "Very interesting."

# Chapter Six

Over the next several days, Mariah and Ethan settled into a routine. Each time they moved to a new campsite, he helped unload the mules and set up her tent, and she'd spend the remaining daylight hours scouting the area for potential views to capture with her camera. Then, on the following day, she watched the way the sun reflected off the mountains until she deemed the light to be perfect. Before the moment was lost, she worked quickly to prepare a plate, then took the photograph.

Though Ethan continued to accompany her into the tent while she prepared the glass plates, then again when she developed the negative, he took great pains to make sure they didn't brush against each other, for which Mariah was extremely grateful.

If he decided to kiss her again, she feared she wouldn't stop him. And, even more frightening, if he wanted more than a kiss, she doubted she'd be able to—or even want to—refuse him. Though the idea of such intimacy made her body tingle from head to toe, she knew the proper thing to do was eliminate temptation by keeping as much distance between them as possible. But inside the cramped tent, that distance shrank to mere inches. Such proximity caused her head to spin and her pulse to pound. With full awareness of the heat radiating from his body, of his musky masculine scent filling her lungs and titillating her senses when they stood side by side, maintaining her concentration became more and more difficult. With her normally unflappable attention wandering, she worried that her photographs wouldn't be up to her usual high standards. Somehow, she had to make sure her work didn't suffer because of her attraction to Ethan Nighthawk.

Because she could take photographs only during a few peak hours each day, she had a lot of free time. She filled part of those hours by making copious notes about the locale of each of the photographs she'd taken. When her exhibit opened at the Exposition, she planned for a small placard to be displayed with each photograph. The placards would contain a few carefully chosen words, a line or two describing the scene or some other interesting tidbit of information about the subject of the photograph. Though many of her photographs spoke clearly for themselves and needed no further explanation, she still liked providing the placards as a means to educate as well as enhance the enjoyment of those viewing her work.

She'd begun the practice of writing the text for her own work after a periodical published one of her photographs with a caption written by an overzealous editor. Because of the man's rambling, totally inaccurate description, she vowed from then on to provide the text for captions whenever she sold a photograph. She liked the results so much that she extended her writing endeavors to the placards she started displaying with her work.

Eventually, she hoped to be able to write essays to accompany the publication of her photographs—maybe even publish a book combining her photographic and journalistic efforts.

Though writing was hard work for her, she loved putting the words together, combining them into just the right phrase, creating the perfect description to add an extra layer of depth to a photograph. But the chore was much harder than taking photographs and consumed a lot of time. When she started writing and discovered how difficult it was for her, she'd hoped practice would make the process easier. Although she'd begun to see some improvement, she knew she'd never become as proficient at writing as she was at photography.

Still, she preferred struggling with the task herself rather than letting the job fall to someone who'd never been more than twenty-five miles from New York City, had no concept of the true magnificence of the scenery in the West, and, most important, had no idea what she wanted her viewing audience to know about each one of her photographs.

After more than a week into their field trip, Mariah and Ethan set up camp once again, this time in the foothills of another mountain range close to Tucson. She waited until Ethan left to water the horses and mules before she removed the cloth draped over Screech's cage.

Though she'd initially found Ethan's fear of owls totally absurd and still didn't fully comprehend how a mere bird could cause such intense fear in a full-grown man, she hadn't forgotten the look of pure terror on his face. She knew with a certainty that Ethan hadn't faked his reaction. She also knew she wanted to help him overcome his fear—a task she realized would be difficult, if not impossible. Unfortunately, she had no idea how to go about accomplishing such a feat, or if he'd even welcome her efforts. Until she figured out what to do, she would keep silent on the subject.

In the meantime, she continued with the unspoken arrangement they'd settled on regarding her pet: keep Screech out of sight as much as possible, and don't feed him until Ethan found an excuse, real or fabricated, to leave camp.

At times, Ethan seemed unaware that an owl shared their campsite, but every night before seeking his bed, he smeared ashes on his forehead. Though Mariah thought the practice ridiculous, the ritual appeared to ease his apprehension, so she kept her opinion to herself. But even with their precautions, there were times when a sudden whistle or hoot from Screech sent Ethan into a near panic. The first time the owl surprised him, he bolted from camp. She figured he probably went off to perform another purification ceremony. He didn't say, and she didn't ask.

After that he didn't flee, though she could tell staying went against his deeply ingrained instinct to get as far from Screech as quickly as he could. She knew the effort cost him and silently watched him struggle to control his bone-deep fear, a lump of sympathy clogging her throat for his obvious distress.

As she fed Screech, she wondered again how she could help Ethan overcome his fear. There had to be something she could do. By the time Screech finished his meal, she'd come up with an idea. Heading for her boxes of supplies, she dug through them until she found what she wanted. After moving Screech's cage to the center of the campsite, she opened the door. The small owl blinked his yellow eyes, turning his head from side to side, watching her every move. Then, with a soft hoot, he hopped from his perch to the cage door and then onto the second perch Mariah had placed outside his cage.

Screech ruffled his feathers, then leaned to the right and stretched his left leg and wing as far as he could. Shifting position, he did the same with his right leg and damaged right wing.

She smiled. "Feels good to be out of that cage, doesn't it, fella?" Her smiled faded. "Too bad I can't set you free."

Screech blinked several times. Ignoring her, he began preening, carefully cleaning and smoothing his feathers with his hooked beak. Mariah watched him for a moment, then turned to finish setting up camp. Though the nights they'd spent in the desert had cooled considerably from the blistering heat of the days, she knew from her first experience in the mountains that the nights would be even cooler. She pulled another blanket from one of the crates and threw it onto her bedroll.

She didn't hear Ethan's approach, but suddenly she

knew he'd returned. She could feel his presence. Turning from the task of sorting through their supplies, she saw him on the other side of the campsite. He stood frozen in place, his unblinking gaze locked on Screech, who returned his stare just as steadily.

Mariah slowly got to her feet. "Ethan," she said in a low voice. "It's okay. Just ignore Screech."

When he didn't respond, she took a step closer and said his name again, a little louder.

He flinched, then turned his head toward her.

"There's no need to be afraid," she said, keeping her tone soft and calm. "Come on." She waggled her fingers at him. "Come over here."

He glanced around, then brought his gaze back to her, obviously fighting the urge to run. She saw his throat work with a swallow before he took a tentative step in her direction, then another. When he drew abreast of Screech, he picked up his pace, then came to a halt a few feet from Mariah.

Nighthawk stared down at her, his heart thudding heavily against his ribs. Though still rattled by the discovery of her owl sitting outside his cage in the middle of the campsite, his mind-numbing fear had begun to ease. When the tightness in his chest allowed him to speak, he said, "Why?"

She knew there was no point in pretending she didn't understand his question. "Screech hasn't been out of his cage in more than a week, so I thought a few minutes wouldn't hurt. I meant to put him back inside before you returned, but I lost track of—" She frowned at the sudden arching of his eyebrows, then exhaled with a huff. "Oh, all right. I purposely moved his cage and left him out so you couldn't miss seeing him."

He crossed his arms over his chest, a muscle working in his jaw. "Why?"

Her lips pressed together, she lifted her chin and met his intense stare. "I wanted you to get accustomed to Screech. I thought maybe being around him more would help you get over your fear."

"My fear is not your concern. I have kept my word; I am still working for you."

"I know, but I don't want to see you ridiculed by anyone else." Seeing the surprise register on his face, she pulled her gaze from his, her cheeks warming with a blush. "If you're going to continue living in Tucson, you don't need to give the people there another reason to make derogatory comments. You've been subjected to enough of that kind of treatment."

He moved closer. Grasping her chin with one hand, he forced her to meet his gaze. He stared at her for a long moment. "I do not understand why you care what others think or say about me," he said in a fierce whisper. "But"—he drew a deep breath—"I am glad you do."

She blinked at his surprising statement, wet her lips with her tongue, then watched in fascination as the last of the fear in his eyes changed to something decidedly more dangerous. Desire.

Though she wanted to look away, she couldn't make herself do so. She placed a hand on his chest to prevent him from moving any closer. But rather than push him away, her fingers tingled at the hard muscles beneath her palm, a tingle that instantly drifted to places much lower on her body.

She watched his face come closer, knew he intended to kiss her, yet she couldn't summon the strength to move. When he stopped his descent, his mouth an inch from hers, she managed to find her voice. "I thought we agreed we shouldn't be doing this."

"We did," he said, then laved his tongue over her bottom lip.

She inhaled a quick breath, her fingers reflexively clutching at the fabric of his shirt, her body burning in places far from her mouth, as if his tongue had somehow touched all of them at the same time.

He brushed the tip of his tongue over her upper lip before settling his mouth atop hers. She froze for a moment. Then a groan worked its way up from her chest. Releasing her grip on his shirt, she wrapped her arms around his neck and leaned into him until their bodies met from breast to thigh.

He shifted, widening his stance so her belly nestled more snugly against his pelvis. Then he deepened the kiss, his tongue slipping between her opened lips. She wiggled her hips, instinctively rubbing her female mound over his hardened sex. He moaned at the intimate contact, his hips bucking against hers in reaction.

Mariah heard a whimper over the roaring in her ears and was shocked to realize she'd made the sound. Forgotten were the warnings she'd given herself about letting Ethan kiss her again or what might happen if he did. She forgot everything but the need to ease the throbbing heat building between her thighs.

Nighthawk hadn't meant to kiss Mariah, but when he touched her soft skin, inhaled her sweet scent, saw her eyes widen in awareness, his need to taste her mouth again took over. From the moment he'd met her, he'd lost the ability to think rationally—a disconcerting thought for an Apache warrior who prided himself on always being clearheaded. But as soon as Mariah entered his life, everything had changed. He'd wanted to kiss her, so he had, with no forethought given to the consequences. And when she recovered from her initial shock and pressed against him with an urgency that took him by surprise, concern about his loss of clear thinking faded. His thoughts centered on the woman in his arms and the desire spreading through him like wildfire.

Though aware of the danger if he continued kissing her, he couldn't make himself stop. Instead, he teased, tasted, then plunged his tongue past her lips, possessing her mouth the way he longed to possess her body.

He struggled to clear his mind, fighting to regain control of his soaring need and return to reality. Lungs burning, he finally managed to lift his head and suck in a deep, cleansing breath. Resting his chin on top of her head, he held her close, her ragged breathing warm on his neck. "I want you," he said in a rasping whisper. "I am sure you know that, since I cannot hide my body's response. But"—he dragged in another deep breath—"we have to stop before it is too late."

Mariah loosened her hold on his neck, then leaned back to look up into his face. She saw desire mirroring her own smoldering in his dark eyes and in the tenseness of his features, sending her pulse into an even wilder cadence. She didn't want to call a halt to the incredible sensations rushing through her, didn't care if it was too late, and for a moment she considered voicing her objection to his words. But as the haze of desire lifted and her senses cleared, she knew he'd made the right decision. Drawing a shaky breath, she pulled her arms from his shoulders and took a step back.

He let her move out of his embrace but kept his hands on her upper arms. "I must warn you," he said in a low voice, "if this happens again, I will not be able to stop at just a kiss."

She studied his face, noting the harsh line of his flattened mouth, the narrowed gaze boring into hers. Though certain he'd meant his words as a deterrent, she chose to view them as something else: an invitation to experience more than his kisses. The idea sent shivers of anticipation up her spine. Realizing he expected an answer, she took a deep breath, then said, "I understand."

He stared at her a moment longer. Apparently satisfied with her response, he grunted, released her arms, then turned and walked away.

While they ate supper that evening, Mariah said, "People often ask me how I can stand living like this"—she made a gesture with her fork to encompass their campsite—"for weeks at a time. I always tell them I don't mind. Sleeping on the ground and cooking over an open fire while on a field trip aren't so bad. But I don't tell them there's one thing I do miss. Taking a real bath." She sighed. "What I wouldn't give for a nice, long soak in a bathtub."

Nighthawk looked up from his plate. "There is a small pond upstream. You could bathe there. But the water will be cold."

Mariah flashed a smile. "A cold bath is better than none. Can we go there as soon as we finish eating?"

His mind suddenly filled with the image of the two of them sharing the pond. Knowing that wasn't what she meant, he resolutely pushed the enticing picture aside. Shrugging, he said, "If you want. But you will not be able to stay very long. As soon as the sun sets, wildlife will come to the pond to drink."

"That's okay. I only need enough time to scrub off a layer of trail dust and wash my hair. I'll be done in fifteen minutes."

Nighthawk's mouth went dry at the mention of her hair. Ever since the morning he'd awakened and watched her pull a brush through her long, silky hair, he'd had more fantasies about those golden strands. Fantasies that left him hard and throbbing with need. He reached for his coffee cup, trying to shake off those erotic memories before his body reacted in predictable fashion.

A few minutes later, Mariah gathered up what she needed for her bath, then followed Nighthawk away from their campsite.

When they arrived at the pond, he said, "I will wait and take you back to camp. I will not be far, so call when you have finished." At her nod, he retraced his steps down the barely visible path.

She stripped off her clothes, then stepped into the water and moved to the center of the small pond. As she eased to a sitting position, she gasped at the coldness of the water, her skin erupting in gooseflesh. Working her cake of soap into a lather, she clenched her teeth to keep them from chattering. Still, the coldness of the water was a small price to pay for a chance to get her entire body wet. For one day at least, she wouldn't have to bathe using only a cloth and a pan of water.

Nighthawk stayed close to the pond, behind a stand of trees. He'd selected the spot so he'd be within calling distance, forgetting he would also be able to hear her bathing. As the sounds filtered to him, his brain conjured explicit mental images to go with them. Closing his eyes, he could see Mariah in the pond, arms raised in the task of shampooing her hair, water lapping at her full breasts, their twin tips tightened into hard, rosy peaks.

He opened his eyes, disgusted with himself for not being able to control his thoughts or his reaction to Mariah. He'd never imagined wanting a woman as much as he wanted the White Eyes splashing in the pond behind him. Lifting his face to the sky, he offered a prayer to Ussen, asking the Great Spirit for the strength to keep him from going to Mariah, pulling her from the water, and pressing his mouth to— He clenched his hands into fists, frustration and anger filling him. He couldn't even seek the sanctuary of prayer without Mariah's intrusion into his mind.

He inhaled a deep breath, then exhaled slowly, forcing his muscles to relax, his mind to clear. When he'd regained his composure, he opened his eyes, his thoughts turning to the visions sent to him by the Spirits. Though he could do nothing to summon a vision, he hoped the Spirits would send one soon. He needed to know the reason for Mariah's entry into his life. He needed to know before he made what could be a grave mistake.

A few minutes later the voice of the woman at the

center of his confusion startled him out of his reverie.

"Ethan, I'm done."

Nighthawk escorted Mariah back to their campsite, trying not to think about the peaked nipples visible through her blouse or his urge to lap up the bead of water resting in the hollow of her throat.

As soon as they reached their campsite, he glanced up at the sky. "There is still time for me to bathe before sunset. I will not be long." After fetching what he needed from his belongings, he headed back to the pond, hoping the water would be cold enough to extinguish the desire sizzling in his veins.

By the time he started back to camp a second time, he felt relaxed and in control once again, his tension having been washed away by the invigorating chill of his bath.

When he reached the clearing and spotted Mariah sitting on a large rock beside the dying fire, he stumbled to a halt. His sharply indrawn breath hissed through his clenched teeth. She sat with her head turned away from him, her nearly dry hair spread across her shoulders like a cape of golden silk.

He fought the wild pounding of his heart, the instantly rekindled heat building in his groin. He achieved only partial success. How his desire could flare to life so quickly and with such intensity astounded him. He'd never had trouble controlling his reaction to a woman. Not until he'd met Mariah Corbett.

The realization that he found a white woman attractive was shocking in itself, since he'd spent nearly half his life hating all White Eyes. And even after he'd decided to follow Cochise's dying request to live at peace with the White Eyes, none of the few white women he'd seen had sparked even a flicker of sexual interest. Which made the depth of his desire for Mariah even more difficult to explain. And to add to his confusion, she appealed to him as more than a potential source of sexual pleasure. He'd never considered a relationship with a woman as anything other than a means to appease his physical needs, and though he desired Mariah more than he could have thought possible, deep inside he knew a physical relationship wouldn't be enough. He wanted more. A lot more. Halting the direction of his thoughts before they crept into even more dangerous territory, he started forward.

Mariah caught movement from the corner of her eye and turned. Smiling at Ethan, she said, "Didn't the water feel—" Her smiled faded, his expression setting off an alarm in her head. "Is something wrong?"

He shook his head, then moved to the shrub where she'd spread out her towel to dry.

She frowned, watching him drape his towel next to hers. His movements seemed forced, not the usual fluid ease she'd become accustomed to. "Are you sure?"

He swung around to face her. "Yes," he said more sharply than he intended, shoving a strand of damp hair off his face with an impatient gesture.

Mariah's eyes widened, but she didn't comment on his curt reply. "Would you like to borrow my hairbrush?"

He blinked at her change of subject. "What?"

"I asked if you'd like to borrow my hairbrush."

When he didn't respond, she said, "Or I could brush your hair, if you'd like. I used to love it when Uncle Ned brushed mine."

He stared at her long and hard, the expression on his face telling her that some kind of battle raged inside him. After a few moments, she saw his chest rise and fall with a deep breath, and he moved closer.

Without saying a word, he took a seat on the blanket at her feet, his back toward her.

As Mariah pulled her brush through his hair, Nighthawk closed his eyes against the unexpected rush of sensations careening through him. His scalp tingled at the stimulation of the brush bristles. The tension seeped from his body, leaving his muscles pleasantly relaxed. Yet deep inside a flame of need flickered to life, growing hotter and stronger with each stroke of her brush.

After several minutes, he could bear no more of the sweet torture and reached up to still her hand. "Enough," he said in a rough voice.

When he turned, he found her staring at him through widened eyes, the throbbing of her pulse visible at the base of her neck. Brushing his hair had obviously affected her as well.

She licked her lips, then swallowed hard. "Did I hurt you?" she said, her voice not quite steady.

He shook his head.

"Then why—"

He pressed a finger to her lips. "Do not talk." He took the hairbrush from her and tossed it aside. Rising onto his knees, he cupped her face with his hands. "I should have known better," he murmured, brushing his mouth over hers in a gentle kiss. "No matter what

104

I do"—he touched the corner of her mouth with his tongue—"I cannot stop wanting you." He nipped her bottom lip with his teeth. "You have become a fever in my blood."

Mariah's heart accelerated. "Did you"—she drew in a shaky breath—"did you mean what you said earlier?"

He pushed his fingers into her hair until he cradled the back of her head, then moved his lips to her jaw. "I do not remember what I said. I cannot think clearly when we are this close."

"You said if we kissed again, you wouldn't stop at just a kiss."

"Yes, I meant that." He ran the tip of his tongue around the rim of her ear, smiling at her startled gasp and the quiver rippling over her body.

"But, you won't"—she swallowed hard, her eyes drifting closed—"you won't change your mind, will you?"

He straightened. Taking care not to pull her hair, he eased his hands from the back of her head. Gently gripping her shoulders, he held her at arm's length, his gaze locked on her face. "Do you want me to?"

# Chapter Seven

Mariah opened her eyes and met Nighthawk's stare. Realizing the importance of her next words and how they would affect her life, she took a moment to consider her response. Was she truly ready for the intimacy promised by the dark gaze of the man kneeling in front of her—the man who had somehow burrowed his way into her heart? Her breath lodged in her throat. *Oh, my God, I'm actually falling in love with him!* She certainly hadn't meant to, not when she'd decided long ago that there was no place in her life for a man. Nor did she think Ethan had purposely set out to win her love and that she'd fallen neatly into his trap—she doubted he wanted a permanent relationship any more than she did. But as she'd just discovered, the workings of the heart required neither her permission nor her cooperation.

As she lifted a hand to brush a strand of silky black

hair off his temple, she shifted her gaze to skim over his face. He really was a beautiful man, though she doubted he'd appreciate her saying so. Biting her lip to hide a smile, she ran her fingertips over an arched eyebrow, then down across a high cheekbone before tracing the firm line of his upper lip. Certain she'd made the right decision, she finally said, "No, I don't want you to stop."

Nighthawk didn't realize he'd forgotten to breathe until her response registered. As he drew a relieved breath, his lips twitched beneath Mariah's fingers; he was surprised that her candor appealed to him, though he shouldn't have been. He found so many things appealing about the fascinating woman he held.

In the back of his mind, he knew his earlier misgivings about an intimate relationship with Mariah were still valid. But after hearing her clearly state her willingness and having his desire blaze even hotter, he no longer had the strength to do the right thing. Accepting defeat, he kissed her fingers, then ran the tip of his tongue across her palm, "I do not intend to stop," he said.

She jerked her hand away, her eyes going wide, the flush on her cheeks deepening. He smiled at her reaction. "See how you respond to me?" he murmured. "We will be good together."

Mariah repressed a shiver, his softly spoken words intensifying the firestorm simmering low in her belly. Taking a deep breath to calm the wild racing of her heart, she leaned closer. "Then I think"—she nipped his chin with her teeth—"we should get started. Don't you?"

He winced at the momentary sting of her teeth raking his skin; then unexpected laughter rumbled in his chest. "Yes, I do," he replied, totally enchanted by the frank banter of the temptress staring at him through eyes glowing with a mixture of humor and passion. Something besides laughter vied for a place in his chest, a warm ache he didn't recognize. But he couldn't take the time to analyze and identify the odd sensation. He had more pressing matters that required his immediate attention.

Nighthawk got to his feet, pulled Mariah up beside him, then led her to his bedroll. He removed his shirt, then reached for the row of buttons on the front of her blouse. Though the urge to hurry was great, he forced himself to free the buttons with slow, methodical movements. When the last one slipped through its buttonhole, he pushed the garment off her shoulders and down her arms. Her skirt soon joined the growing pile of clothing at their feet, leaving her clad in only a chemise and pair of drawers.

Mariah resisted the instinct to cover herself, feeling his hot gaze through the thin fabric of her underclothes as surely as if he'd touched her breasts, her belly, the throbbing flesh between her thighs. Staring at the buckskin pouch tied around his neck, her hands itching to explore the smooth expanse of his chest, she nervously waited for him to finish his visual examination. She'd never given any thought to her physical attributes as a woman; she simply didn't care how men viewed her. So the realization that she actually cared what Ethan thought, that he might find her lacking in some way, came as a shock.

When he lifted his gaze and met hers, the unmistakable heat blazing in his eyes eased her unexpected fears. Closing her eyes for a second, she eased out a relieved breath.

Nighthawk dropped down onto his bedroll. After pulling off his moccasins, he braced himself with one forearm and stretched out on his side. When he patted the blanket in front of him, she didn't hesitate to accept his invitation. Gathering her hair at her nape, she pulled it over one shoulder before lying down next to him.

He brushed the stray wisps of hair off her face with a gentle touch of his hand. "I have never wanted anyone as much as I want you," he said, surprised to hear himself make the admission aloud.

"Me either," she replied.

He swallowed. "I will try not to hurt—"

Her fingers stopped his words. "Shh," she said, sliding her arms around his neck. "No more talk."

His heart hammering in his chest, he leaned over her, closing the distance until his lips touched hers. When she immediately opened her mouth and allowed his tongue entrance, he groaned, his hips rocking forward. Pressing his hardened flesh against her thigh, he continued kissing her, using his lips, his tongue, his teeth. She moaned, her fingers digging into his back, her hips lifting off his bedroll.

He lowered one hand to her waist. She flinched at his touch, then immediately relaxed. As the tension left her muscles, he found the tie of her drawers and slowly loosened the ribbon. His hand slid beneath the fabric, his fingertips skimming over the silken skin of her belly in a gentle caress, slowly inching lower.

His mouth still crushed against hers, he pushed his fingers through the soft curls between her thighs and

109

found the damp folds of her sex. As he opened the delicate flesh and touched her most sensitive place, he groaned, his already burning need leaping even higher. She was so hot, so incredibly slick with arousal.

He wrenched his mouth from hers, fighting for the strength to control his need a little longer. His breathing labored, he glanced down at the rapid rise and fall of her breasts, their tips already peaked, beckoning him through their sheer covering. Lowering his head, he nuzzled between her breasts, inhaling the scent of her soap and the faint musk of female before settling his mouth over one fabric-covered nipple. He rolled his tongue over the tightened bud, then suckled, his fingers still working the nubbin of flesh between her thighs.

Mariah gasped, the pull of his mouth and the steady rasp of his fingers nearly more than she could bear. "Ethan," she said in a breathless whisper. "Ethan, please."

He released her nipple, then lifted his head and stared down into her flushed face. "Be patient," he said, his own voice thick with passion. "I will give you what you need." Using one knee, he pushed her thighs apart, holding them in place with the weight of his leg, then slid his hand lower. As he eased one finger into her warmth, he had to clench his teeth against the nearly overwhelming urge to forget his words to her and take his own pleasure.

He might have done so with another woman, but not Mariah. Making sure she achieved satisfaction was just as important—maybe more so—than seeking his own.

He pressed a quick, hard kiss on her swollen mouth, then lifted his head so he could watch her face. He began moving his finger, sliding in and out with slow, easy strokes, the pad of his thumb rubbing her sensitive bud. She moaned deep in her throat, then caught his rhythm and lifted her hips off the bedroll in perfect timing.

Mariah thought she might die if the pleasure-torture Ethan was inflicting didn't end soon. She'd never been so mindless with need, yet relief remained elusive. Her breathing ragged, her fingers curled into tight fists, the spiraling heat continued to build between her thighs. The pressure intensified with each stroke of his knowing fingers.

"Ethan," she managed to say between breaths. "I can't . . . I can't take anymore."

He leaned closer. "Yes, you can, Mariah," he murmured into her ear. "You are almost there. Give in to it. Let it come."

"No, I—" She inhaled sharply, her eyes popping open.

He saw the surprise flash in their depths before her eyelids drifted shut. Another moan vibrated in her throat. Her hips moved faster and faster, thrusting frantically against his hand; then the tension holding her captive abruptly snapped. Sobbing his name, she arched up one final time, then collapsed on the bedroll, limp and breathless.

Nighthawk carefully eased his hand away from her, then watched her eyelids flutter open. She blinked several times before her dazed eyes focused on him.

"Are you all right?" he said.

She stretched, a lazy smile curving her lips. "Um, yes. I'm wonderful."

He returned her smile. "I agree." Giving in to temptation, he reached for her hair, lifting the heavy mass to rub against his cheek. The pale strands as silky as he'd imagined, he couldn't help wondering if his other fantasies about her hair would also prove true. Opening his fingers, he watched the cascade of gold spill back onto her breast, the pale color so unlike his own.

All at once the differences between them came into sharp focus, his doubts about his actions resurfacing. His smile faded, his brows drawing together in a frown. How had he let himself get involved with a White Eyes?

He knew the answer, of course. A vision from the Spirits had foretold he would meet a woman with yellow hair. But the vision hadn't revealed if his relationship with Mariah would become intimate. That he had accomplished on his own.

Beginning with the moment he first saw her, he'd been attracted to her, an attraction that quickly escalated into desire more potent than any he'd ever experienced. A searing desire that had come within a hairbreadth of shattering his self-control.

From the time his training to become a warrior had begun, he'd been taught the importance of controlling himself—not just while fighting the enemy, but in all aspects of his life. Hunting game, taming a wild horse, or seeking physical pleasure with a woman. Throughout his adulthood, he'd never had trouble doing so. And even after going to Tucson and discovering the pleasures to be found on Maiden Lane, he'd never come close to losing control. Mariah was the only woman who made him forget everything he'd been taught, who made him want her so much, maintaining his control bordered on the impossible.

He closed his eyes, unsure how the Spirits would view his shameful behavior. If only they would send him another vision so he'd know what—Mariah's voice jerked him back to the present. Releasing his breath in a huff, he opened his eyes and looked down at her. "What?"

She searched his face for several seconds. "I asked what you were thinking," she said, running her fingers over his furrowed brow. "You look so serious. Almost angry. Did I do—"

"No," he replied, pulling her hand from his face. "It is not you." He rolled away from her, then reached for his moccasins.

She pushed herself up onto her elbows. "What are you doing? You said you wouldn't stop."

"I changed my mind," he replied, pulling on one of his moccasins.

"Ethan, I don't understand." She watched him pull on his other moccasin, then get to his feet. "What about you? You didn't . . . um . . . finish."

He swung around to face her, the corners of his mouth lifting in a humorless smile. "That is true. I am still as hard as stone. But I will survive," he said, his temper flaring to life. Glaring down at her, he rubbed a hand over the prominent ridge beneath the fly of his trousers in a crude gesture. "Or I can take care of this myself. In fact, it would probably feel just as good."

Even in the last remnants of daylight, Mariah could

see the harsh glint in his eyes before he looked away. In stunned silence, she watched him snatch up his shirt, then stalk from their campsite.

She didn't move for a long time, trying to figure out the reason behind Ethan's abrupt change. He'd been a willing and eager participant, a considerate lover, making sure she achieved her release. Her cheeks warmed in remembrance of his unselfishness. Then suddenly he'd pulled away, no longer interested in finishing what they'd started in spite of still being physically aroused. Instead, he'd become angry and turned his temper on her. What had he been thinking just moments before his sudden transformation? And why had he felt the need to make comments he obviously intended to be cruel? She drew a shuddering breath, wishing she knew the answers.

Nighthawk headed deeper into the mountains, paying little attention to his surroundings, not caring where he went. When he realized he was trying to run from himself, he stopped. Still aching with need, aroused to the point of pain, he considered doing as he'd suggested to Mariah. He moved his hand to the fly of his trousers and touched himself. He was so close, so near the release he craved, that just a stroke or two of his hand would—Grunting with disgust for even considering such behavior, he jerked his hand from his hardened flesh.

Now that he knew how Mariah responded to him, her passion blazing hotter than the sunbaked desert, he wanted her to be the one to quench his need. But he'd ruined his chance for that by letting his anger intervene, and the pain of unslaked desire was a just punishment.

He sat down on the ground, wincing at the tightness across the front of his trousers. Ignoring his discomfort, his mind replayed what had happened with Mariah. He couldn't believe what he'd done. Losing his temper had been bad enough, but what he'd said to her was far worse. Remembering the shock on her face at his crude gesture and cutting words, bile rose in his throat. How could he have treated her with such cruelty? She'd done nothing to earn his ire, yet he'd directed his anger at her.

Shamed by what he'd done, he squeezed his eyes closed for a moment, waiting for the knot in his stomach to ease. When he opened his eyes, he looked out across the rock-strewn mountains, his mind jumping from thoughts of Mariah to his concern for the future of his people, to what his own future would hold, then unerringly back to Mariah. He sat in that same spot for a long time, unmoving, staring into the night, searching for, but not finding, the answers he sought. As darkness began to fall, he knew he should head back, though he had no idea what he would say to Mariah. Blowing out a weary breath, he got to his feet.

By the time Mariah heard Ethan return to camp, she still hadn't solved the mystery of his strange behavior. But during his absence, she had made one decision. She wasn't going to pretend what happened hadn't taken place. She deserved an explanation, and she intended to get one.

She sat on her bedroll, arms wrapped around her updrawn knees, watching him cross the campsite, drop an armload of firewood beside the fire pit, then move to his bedroll. She gave him several minutes to be the first to speak, but he neither glanced at her nor did anything else to acknowledge her presence. Though she'd never had trouble charging into a verbal fray without any forethought, for once she took the time to think through what she wanted to say before opening her mouth.

Finally, she said, "Since you apparently aren't going to talk about what happened, I will." She swallowed, struggling to remain calm. "Are you going to tell me what that was all about?"

He sat down on his bedroll, then looked over at her, the darkness hiding his expression, but he didn't respond.

"At the very least," she said, her voice taking on a sharp edge, "I think I deserve to know why you thought you had to insult me."

She watched his shoulders lift, then lower, heard the air leave his lungs in a sigh. Again he remained silent.

"Ethan, did I do something to make you angry?"

"No," he said in a low but fierce voice, "you did nothing."

"Then talk to me, so I can understand."

"Even I do not understand." Another long silence passed. Finally, he ran a hand over his face and began speaking. "During my thirteenth summer, my father and my older brother were killed by the treachery of soldiers from the White Eyes fort. That day I felt hatred for the first time. It filled my heart and my belly.

"For Apache, the killing of a family member demands revenge. As I trained to become a warrior, I had one thought—avenge the deaths of my father and brother by killing as many White Eyes as I could."

"Is that what this is about? The color of my skin? Do you hate me because I'm white?"

"No, I do not hate you. One of the things Father Julian taught me is that hatred causes nothing but pain, that it breeds only more hatred. At first I did not want to listen to him. Did not want to believe what he said. I finally realized he was right, and I have tried to follow his teachings. But forgetting the hatred that has burned inside me for half my life has not been easy. Sometimes I still feel it."

He paused to gather his thoughts. "The reason I pulled away from you is complicated. I was frustrated because I do not know why the Spirits brought you into my life. I was confused by how much I wanted you. I was shocked that I had nearly lost control. I did not know what to do about all of those emotions battling inside me, so I reacted the only way I could. I became angry."

He drew a deep breath before continuing. "Maybe I am not supposed to want you. Maybe I should not have touched you. Maybe the Spirits have another purpose for bringing us together." He shook his head. "I do not know the answers. I will not know until the Spirits speak to me again."

She got to her feet and moved to his bedroll. Sinking onto her knees beside him, she said, "Have you ever done something without the Spirits telling you to?"

"Of course. They do not send visions about everything in my life."

"Would you ever go against their wishes?"

"I have always tried to follow the Spirits' directions. I never had a powerful reason not to. So I cannot answer whether I would go against their wishes."

"But you might, if you felt strongly enough about something you wanted to do?"

"Disobeying the Spirits would mean risking their punishment. But, yes, if I felt strongly enough about something, it is possible I would go against their wishes." He stared at her for a moment, then added, "Why are you asking me these questions?"

"I'm just trying to get to know you better. To understand how you think and why you acted the way you did a while ago." She paused for a few seconds, then said, "If I've understood you correctly, you were overwhelmed by all the emotions you were experiencing, didn't know what to do about the situation, and reacted in the only way you knew how. With anger, which you directed at me. Do I have that right, or did I miss something?"

He glanced at her. Dusk had given way to full darkness, so he couldn't see her expression, but there had been no censure in her voice. He swallowed to ease the sudden tightness in his throat. "You missed nothing."

Though he longed to move closer to her, to touch her, he didn't. Instead, he said, "Mariah, I never should have lost my temper, and directing my anger at you was worse. There is no acceptable excuse for that, or for the insulting things I said to you, but I am sorry. Will you accept my apology?"

Mariah stared at him for a full minute before responding. At last she said, "Yes, but there's one more thing I have to ask you." She cleared her throat, uncertain how to phrase the question. Deciding to plunge in, she took a deep breath and lifted her chin. "Did you do what you said you were going to? Did you . . . um . . . take care of yourself after you left me?"

Nighthawk blinked at her, not immediately understanding her question. Then a chuckle rumbled in his chest. "No, I did not. Doing as I suggested goes against Apache beliefs. I should not have said such careless words. If they hurt you, I am sorry for that also." Unable to resist touching her any longer, he held his arms out to her. "Come here. Let me hold you."

Mariah moved willingly into his embrace, letting him adjust their positions so that she sat within the circle of his arms, her back against his chest. Once they were settled, he began speaking in a low voice.

"As soon as I left camp, my temper started to cool, but not my desire. That took much, much longer. I admit, I briefly considered self-gratification, I believe you would call it, even though it goes against what I was taught. But I did not. Because of my own foolishness, I turned away from the most desirable woman I have ever met and gave up a chance to be with her. There was no acceptable alternative for me, and I deserved to suffer the painful consequences."

She leaned to one side and tilted her head so she could see his face. "But you're okay now?"

He chuckled again. "Yes. I am fine. I was uncomfortable for a very long time, but that eventually passed." He sobered, staring down at her for several seconds. "I do not know what the Spirits have in store for me, for us, but I will try to keep better control of my temper." He lowered his head and pressed a light kiss on her lips. "I want to spend whatever time we have together enjoying each other. Not arguing."

"Me, too," Mariah managed to say around the lump in her throat. As she considered what would happen in the coming weeks, a dull ache gripped her heart. She would finish her photographic work, prepare for her trip to Philadelphia, then leave Tucson. And Ethan Nighthawk. The last increased the ache surrounding her heart until she could barely breathe.

She pushed away her painful thoughts, determined not to think about leaving any sooner than she had to. Resettling herself against Ethan's chest, she let her head fall back onto his shoulder and released a contented sigh.

After a long silence, she said, "We'll have to go back to Tucson soon. I need to get another box of plates. I have only enough left for two or three more days."

"Two or three days," Nighthawk murmured. "Not enough time."

"Enough time for what?"

"I have been thinking about taking you to the homeland of my people. I want you to see the mountains. They are beautiful like these but also very different. I think they would make a fine photograph for your exhibit." She felt his chest rise, then fall with a deep breath. "But you need more supplies for such a trip."

"You could take me there after we pick up more supplies in Tucson, couldn't you?"

Nighthawk didn't immediately reply but took a moment to reconsider his offer. He hadn't been back to the Chokonen ancestral home since the government of the White Eyes closed the Chiricahua Reservation and relocated his band to the north at San Carlos. Though he knew returning to the area where he had spent most of his life would bring back painful memories, he realized taking Mariah there was more important than his own reaction. For reasons he didn't want to examine, he wanted her to see and walk the land where he'd lived. He wanted the chance to view the wild beauty of the rugged mountains and wide valleys through the freshness of her eyes.

At last he said, "Yes, I will take you."

"Good," she replied, nestling closer, rubbing her cheek against his chest. Encountering the buckskin pouch he wore, she reached up and touched the small bag through his shirt. "I noticed this the first time I saw you, but I've never asked what it is."

He pulled the small pouch through the neck of his shirt. "This is my medicine bag. I wear it to protect me."

"From what?"

"Lightning, evil, sickness."

"Sounds kind of like a rabbit's foot."

"A rabbit's foot? I do not understand."

"It's a custom, probably centuries old. People who believe in carrying a rabbit's foot say it will bring them good luck."

"Apache have a belief much like that. For protection, we carry a piece of the blue stone that is sacred to us. The White Eyes call the stone turquoise."

When she made a snorting noise, he said, "You do not believe it is possible for those things to bring good luck or protection?"

"No, not really." She shifted position so she could

reach up and touch the bead on one of his earrings. "Is this also made of turquoise?"

"Yes. The stone is used for decoration on many things."

As she snuggled back against his chest, she said, "Do all Apache wear a medicine bag?"

"We all wear something for protection. Some wear a medicine bag around their neck like mine, others tie the bag to a cord at their waist. Some wear necklaces made of beads or animal teeth. I know Apache who wear a piece of leather decorated with painted symbols that hangs from a strip of rawhide tied around the neck."

"So what's inside your medicine bag?"

"What an Apache keeps in his medicine bag is personal. The items chosen all have special meaning."

"Like what?"

Nighthawk smiled. "All right, to satisfy your curiosity, I will tell you. There is a piece of turquoise, a piece of root from the plant that prevents sickness, and, because of my power against lightning, a piece of wood from a tree that was struck by lightning. Apache who have received power always wear or carry something that is a link between them and the source of their power."

She traced the zigzag pattern on the buckskin with her finger. "Is that why you painted this symbol?"

When he nodded, she said, "Is there anything else in the bag?"

"There is one more thing. A feather from the nighthawk."

"Because of your nighthawk power?"

"Yes."

Mariah nodded, then fell silent for a few moments. At last, she said, "Can you add more things to your medicine bag?"

"If there is a reason."

"Hmm, I see," she replied, tucking away that bit of information with the others she'd already collected.

# Chapter Eight

Mariah awoke with a start, stunned to find herself lying beside Ethan, her back pressed to his chest, his left hand draped over her left hip. She blinked several times, searching her memory for how she'd ended up sharing his bedroll. She remembered Ethan pulling her into his arms and the conversation they'd had afterward. He'd told her about the medicine bag he wore, but that was where her memory ended. Apparently she'd fallen asleep while still in his embrace, and he'd chosen not to move her to her own bedroll.

Her heart leaped at the notion that he'd wanted her to sleep beside him. Forcing herself not to jump to any conclusions, she shifted, carefully rolling onto her back. The movement repositioned his hand from her hip to her belly, his little finger just inches from touching—His hand twitched, the action moving his fingers even lower and causing her breath to catch.

Forcing herself to breathe normally, she slowly turned her head toward him. When her gaze met his heavy-lidded stare, her eyes widened in surprise.

She swallowed, then managed a raspy, "Morning."

He didn't speak but continued staring at her, an unreadable expression on his face.

She tried to smile, hoping to lighten the mood, but wasn't certain her lips had cooperated. "I slept like a log. How about you?"

He blinked; then the corners of his mouth quirked. "How does a log sleep?"

This time she managed a real smile. "Actually, I don't know. Uncle Ned used to say that all the time. But I guess it means not moving, sleeping really soundly."

"Ah, now I understand," he replied, hoping she'd forget he hadn't answered her original question.

After she'd fallen asleep against his chest, he held her for a long time, enjoying the weight of her leaning against him, the scent of her soap, the silk of her hair brushing the underside of his jaw. And even after shifting their positions so they lay side by side, he'd remained awake well into the night. His mind refused to quiet, spinning with thoughts of Mariah, his longing to find a place where he belonged, and what his future might hold. Though he had learned to clear his mind and fall asleep quickly wherever the opportunity arose—often a necessity when traveling with a war party—his training had been of no value the previous night.

He watched her lick her lips, clamping down on the urge to lean closer and press his mouth to hers. After all the thinking he'd done while the night slipped by, he hadn't reached any conclusions regarding his attraction to Mariah. What should have been an easy decision had turned out to be anything but. Knowing he had to get away from her before he did something to further complicate matters, he said, "Go back to sleep. I will see to the fire." Then he rolled away from her and got to his feet.

Mariah swallowed her disappointment. She'd been sure he wanted to kiss her, had held her breath in anticipation that he would. Then, in the next instant, he'd pulled away from her, the distress in his eyes telling her he didn't like being so attracted to her.

She watched him move around the campsite, wishing she could read his mind. Then maybe she could find a way to ease some of his inner turmoil. She closed her eyes, knowing she'd never be a mind reader and fearing Ethan would never allow their relationship to go any further. The strong possibility of the latter caused a painful tightening in her chest. Certain that going back to sleep was out of the question, she rose and headed away from camp to take care of her personal needs.

For the next two days, Mariah took photographs using the last of her glass plates. Though Ethan continued to fulfill his duties as her assistant, moving her camera and carrying anything too heavy for her, the rest of the time he was a totally different man. He no longer accompanied her into the tent while she prepared her plates, didn't sit beside her, didn't share his bedroll at night. In fact, he only came within arm's length of her when he had no other choice. And to add to the strain between them, he seldom spoke.

His changed behavior made her heart ache. She

considered trying to make him talk to her, but she didn't, sensing he had to work through the problem himself.

In spite of his withdrawal, she felt his gaze following her around, even caught him staring at her a time or two, which gave her hope that all was not lost. But when she told him she'd used all her plates and they needed to head back to town, she saw the relief cross his face before his usual impassive expression slid back into place.

The following morning, they secured everything on the pack mules, then started their return trip to Tucson. As usual, Nighthawk rode in the lead, keeping his gaze trained straight ahead. Although he didn't turn to look, he knew if he did he'd find Mariah staring at him, a look of confusion and pain on her face. He wished he hadn't put that look there, hadn't hurt her with his coldness over the past several days. But he'd had no other choice.

In spite of how he'd treated her, he suspected she would still be his champion. He could almost hear her brain working, trying to figure out the reason for his behavior so she could make everything right for him. That thought brought a smile to his lips, and a warmth settled around his heart. When he realized what he was doing, his smile disappeared as quickly as it had come. He had to keep his mind away from what he liked about Mariah. He had to concentrate on what he should do about their mutual attraction and the desire that ignited so easily between them.

In order to come up with a solution, he had to keep a clear head, which meant not allowing her to dominate his thoughts. An impossible task with her constantly so close to him. Once they reached Tucson and were no longer in such proximity, perhaps he'd finally be able to put everything in perspective, then make a sensible decision.

Ned Corbett ran a hand through his hair, then checked his pocket watch for the third time in five minutes. Señora Benita Solares had never been late in all the times she'd come to his hotel room since Mariah hired her two weeks earlier, so he didn't know why he kept checking the time. But for some reason, the pending arrival of the pretty widow with huge dark eyes and smooth brown skin filled him with nervous anticipation. He fidgeted with the collar of his shirt, wiped his suddenly damp palms on the legs of his trousers, then checked his watch again.

"Damn. What the hell's wrong with me?" he muttered, shifting in his chair. "I ain't never acted like this. God a' mighty, ya'd think this was the first time I ever had a woman caller." He snorted, totally disgusted with his antsy behavior.

Just when he was about to reach for his watch again, a knock sounded at the door. "It's about damn time," he said under his breath, then louder he said, "It's unlocked. Come on in."

The door swung open, and Benita Solares swept into the room. "*Buenos dias,* Señor Corbett," she said, her around face glowing with a bright smile. "It is a beautiful morning, *sí?*"

An enormous lump in Ned's throat prevented him from speaking, so all he could do was nod in reply. Looking at the woman who'd filled his thoughts all morning, he felt his heart pound so hard he feared it might leap from his chest. And in those moments he made a shocking discovery. He loved her. How he—a bachelor who'd never felt even a twinge of love for a woman in all his forty-four years—had managed to fall in love with a woman he'd known for only two weeks, he couldn't imagine. But he knew the truth: He had fallen in love with Benita Solares. As he watched her set down his breakfast tray, then remove the rebozo she always wore over her hair when she went out, he realized another truth. Hell, he'd been a goner from the moment he first saw her. No doubt about it, he hadn't stood a—Her voice snapped him out of his daydreams.

"Señor. Señor, are you unwell? You are not looking so good."

He cleared his throat, then said. "I'm fine, just thinking is all. And I thought you agreed to call me Ned."

A blush spread across her cheeks. "*Sí,* I did. Ned."

He smiled at her, silently cursing his broken leg. How he longed to go to her, to pull her petite body against him, to cover her rose-colored lips with— Jerking his mind away from thoughts he had no business thinking, he nodded at the cloth-covered tray.

"What'd ya bring me for breakfast?"

"Everything you like. Eggs, ham, biscuits, and very strong coffee," she replied, picking up the tray and carrying it toward him. "But they may not be so hot by now."

"It'll be just fine." He held his breath while she settled the tray on his lap, curling his fingers around the arms of the chair to keep himself from giving in to his urge to touch her.

129

Once she moved away from him, he blew out a relieved breath. Several seconds passed before he felt steady enough to reach for his coffee cup.

He'd just taken a big sip of coffee, when she said, "While you eat, I will get everything ready for your bath."

Ned choked, nearly spewing his coffee down the front of his shirt. He swallowed, wiped his mouth, then turned to look at her. "Bath?" He frowned, his eyes narrowing. "I can't get into a bathtub with this leg. And you sure aren't strong enough to pick me up."

She gave him another of her blazing smiles, sending his heart into a second around of wild pounding. "*Sí*, I know," she said. "That is why I have decided to give you a sponge bath."

His eyebrows shot upward, then crunched into a deep scowl. "Ya don't have to go to all that trouble. I can bathe myself just fine, like I been doin'."

"It is no trouble. And you will feel so much better after I wash the places you cannot reach."

At the thought of her washing *any* place on his body, desire shot through him like fire devouring a pile of dry leaves. He gave his head a fierce shake. "No, absolutely not."

"But why? You will—"

"It's not a good idea, that's all."

She stared at him for a few seconds, her gaze moving over his face. "I did not think a man such as you would be modest," she said, a dimple appearing in one cheek.

His scowl deepened. "What are you talking about, a man such as me?"

"A man who has traveled to so many places, who has seen so many wonderful things, has to have been with many"—she dropped her gaze, clasping her hands at her waist—"beautiful women."

Ned's mouth dropped open, shocked by the conclusion she'd drawn from what he'd told her about his life. He cleared his throat, then said, "Yeah, I've traveled a lot, and I've seen a lot, but yer wrong about me being real experienced with women. There haven't been all that many, and not one of 'em was anywhere near as pretty as you."

She lifted her head, her gaze seeking his. After a moment, her bosom rose with a deep breath. *"Gracias,"* she said in a low voice. Tilting her chin, she gave him a pointed look. "Now eat your breakfast while I go downstairs to fetch hot water."

"But I just told you, I—"

*"Sí, sí.* I heard what you said, but I have not changed my mind. Eat before your food gets any colder."

When he opened his mouth to protest, the expression on her face halted his words. He sighed and reached for his fork, wondering how he'd be able to get any food down his dry throat.

A few minutes later, Ned wasn't sure how a woman as small as Benita Solares had managed it, but he found himself sitting on a towel-covered stool in the center of the room, wearing nothing but a second towel draped over his lap.

He couldn't remember ever feeling so self-conscious, or so damned exposed. Hell, most of the time when he'd been with a woman, he hadn't even taken off all his clothes. The only reason he stripped down to his skin

131

was for a bath, and there sure as hell had never been a woman present. The fact that he'd fallen ass over teakettle for the woman about to bathe him made the situation even more uncomfortable.

The sound of water sloshing pulled him from his musings. He turned his head to see Benita ringing out a cloth over a pail of hot water. As she rubbed a cake of soap on the washcloth, she straightened, then moved closer.

"You are ready, señor?"

"Ned," he replied in a strained voice. "You agreed to call me Ned, and"—he swallowed hard—"yeah, I reckon I'm as ready as I'm ever gonna be."

As she reached toward him, he held perfectly still, mentally preparing himself for her touch. When the washcloth and her fingertips finally touched his cheek, he managed not to flinch, but he couldn't stop an indrawn breath from hissing through his teeth. He squeezed his eyes closed. Lord, have mercy. How in the world was he gonna survive this?

While she rubbed the washcloth over his face, she said "I will work quickly so the water does not get too cold." She washed his neck, then moved the cloth to his chest. "When I finish, I will let you wash your private parts."

Ned's eyes snapped open. One of the parts she mentioned twitched in response to her nearness and the smell of roses that always clung to her. He drew a shallow breath, trying to keep his mind from thinking about his body's reaction to Benita's touch and her scent, or how much he wanted to kiss her. He succeeded for a few minutes, but then she leaned closer, one full breast pressing against his arm. The twitch in his groin changed to a full-blown throb. Shifting on the stool to ease the ache, he bit back a groan. He didn't dare look down for fear of finding the towel over his lap peaked like a tent.

He tried to concentrate on Benita's constant chatter, hoping each time she paused for his response he filled the silence with a coherent reply. Though he had to admit having his back scrubbed felt wonderful, he wasn't sure those few moments of enjoyment were worth the price. He didn't consider himself a religious man, but he prayed a lot during the next few minutes, promising just about anything in exchange for an immediate end to his agonizing bath.

He didn't realize his prayers had been answered until Benita gave his arm a shake.

"Ned, are you all right?"

He blinked several times. When her face came into focus, he nodded, licked his dry lips, then said, "Are you done?"

"*Sí.* Now it's your turn. Take this"—she held the washcloth toward him—"and finish. I'm afraid the water is no longer hot."

He shifted his gaze from her hand to her face, then back to her hand. Seeing no way to refuse, he finally said, "That's okay, I don't mind." He took the cloth from her but made no move to use it.

"What are you waiting—" She gave a startled gasp. "Oh, of course." A flush creeping up her neck and cheeks, she turned her back and busied herself by wiping up the water that had splashed onto the floor.

Ned closed his eyes for a second, relieved she'd

understood his need for privacy without his having to tell her.

By the time he finished his bath and tossed the washcloth into the pail of water, the toll for what he'd been through during the past few minutes hit him full force. Both mentally and physically exhausted, he gripped the sides of the stool to keep from toppling to the floor. Damn, he felt like he'd been pulled through a knothole pecker first.

If not for Benita's help, he doubted he could have dressed himself or moved back to his chair by the window. Once she got him settled, his splinted leg again resting on the stool, she smiled at him.

"You feel better, *sí?*"

He managed a weak smile. "Yeah, but not for long. It's not even noon, and it's already hot. Looks like the day is gonna be a scorcher."

"*Sí*, the desert can be very hot this time of year." She brushed a lock of hair off his forehead. "How long must you wear the splints?"

"I'm hopin' not much longer," he replied, his skin still tingling from her touch. "But it'll probably be another week before I can get rid of 'em. I'll find out later today when Doc Handy comes by."

"San Juan's Day is next week. There will be a fiesta with much food, music, and dancing. Perhaps by then you will be able to go. I think you would enjoy it."

"I'll have to wait and see what the doc says, but"— he reached for her hand and squeezed her fingers— "if you're there, I know I'd enjoy it."

"You make me feel like a schoolgirl, not a middle-aged woman who has been a widow for fifteen years."

"Yer husband musta robbed the cradle, cuz you sure don't look middle-aged to me."

She smiled. "I will be thirty-eight on my next birthday, and taking a bride of seventeen cannot be called robbing the cradle."

"You've been alone a long time," he said, rubbing his thumb over the back of her hand. "Didn't ya ever think of marrying again?"

"*Sí*, I have thought of it. But I never met anyone I wanted to marry." She shrugged. "And my sister needed help with her family, so I moved in with them. When her husband decided to come here and open a freight company a few years ago, they asked if I'd like to join them. There was no reason for me to stay in Chihuahua, so I agreed."

"I'm sure glad you did," Ned said in a low voice.

She smiled again. "*Sí*, so am I."

Mariah followed Ethan into Tucson late the following afternoon. She brought her horse to a halt next to his pinto in front of Smith's Corral, then dismounted. Though exhausted from two long days in the saddle and the extreme heat, she helped Ethan unload the mules.

When they finished, he said, "Do you want me to take your equipment to the hotel?"

"No, I'll get one of Mr. Smith's men to load everything into a wagon and haul it over to the Palace."

Ethan nodded. "Then, unless you need me to do something else . . ."

"No, go ahead. There's nothing more to be done here." When he started to walk away, she said, "Wait.

I don't know how to contact you in case I need to . . . um . . . talk to you or . . . something."

He stared at her for several seconds, a muscle ticking in his jaw. Finally, he said, "Ask Father Julian at San Agustín Church. He will know where to find me."

At her nod, he turned to leave. He'd taken only a step or two when she called his name. He stopped but didn't turn around.

"If you're interested in watching, I plan to start printing photographs from my negatives tomorrow."

"I will be busy tomorrow."

She stared at his back for several seconds. "Oh. Well, maybe some other time."

"Maybe," he replied, then took several hesitant steps. When she didn't stop him, he increased his pace.

Mariah watched him walk down the street until he disappeared from view, wondering again at the reason for his deliberate change in behavior. Maybe he was right to pull away. Maybe there shouldn't be anything between them. But how would she stop the love growing in her heart? Wishing she knew the answer, she heaved a weary sigh, then turned and started toward the stable.

Nighthawk spent the following day as well as the next helping Father Julian. Late in the afternoon of his second full day back in Tucson, the two men worked together to replace a door hinge. Normally Nighthawk enjoyed working with the priest, but Father Julian's endless questions about Mariah's photographic work made him sorry he'd told the man about her before he'd left town. He knew the questions stemmed from nothing more than curiosity—the priest was an educated man with a constant thirst for knowledge, something Nighthawk understood. Even so, he couldn't help thinking the priest had joined a conspiracy against him—a conspiracy to make sure Mariah remained in his thoughts.

After a lengthy lapse in their conversation, Father Julian said, "Ethan, you know I would never pry into your private life. But I think I know you well enough to tell when something is bothering you."

Nighthawk looked at the man who had befriended him when no one else in town would give him the time of day. Though Father Julian nearly matched him in height, the priest was thinner, with dark brown eyes and hair and a full but closely cropped beard. Nighthawk didn't reply but shifted his gaze back to the door hinge.

"I'm not asking you to confide in me, Ethan, but I would like to help if I can. Sometimes simply talking about a problem can ease the burden."

Again Nighthawk remained silent.

"Does it have anything to do with Miss Corbett?"

Nighthawk's head snapped up. Though he tried to hide his reaction, the back of his neck burned at the priest's calm regard.

"Ah, I hit a nerve," Father Julian said, a brief smile lifting the corners of his mouth. "I suspected as much."

Nighthawk narrowed his eyes. "How?"

"Every time I said her name, you tensed. And when you talked about her, there was something in your voice I've never heard before." When Nighthawk made no comment, he said, "As I just told you, talking about it might help."

Nighthawk continued staring at the priest in stony silence, surprised by the man's perception. Though, on second thought, he shouldn't have been. Father Julian had told him once that part of being a good priest was the ability to read those in his flock. He took a deep breath and released it slowly. Maybe Father Julian was right. Maybe talking would help.

Finally, Nighthawk spoke. "Mariah Corbett is unlike any woman I have known. Ever since I met her, I have been able to think of little else. She constantly fills my mind."

"Perhaps you have come to care about her."

Nighthawk stiffened. "I cannot allow myself to care about a White Eyes."

"But it troubles you that you may already care for Mariah Corbett?"

Nighthawk clenched his teeth, trying to convince himself that there was no truth to Father Julian's suggestion. Finally accepting defeat, he gave a curt nod.

"You cannot continue blaming all whites for what was done to your people."

Nighthawk snorted. "The White Eyes blame all Apache for what was done by a few."

The priest's mouth curved into a sad smile. "I know, and that is also wrong. We've discussed this before, Ethan. The only way there can be peace among people is for both sides to stop placing blame and for the hatred to end."

When Nighthawk didn't reply, Father Julian said, "You still want peace, don't you?"

"Yes. I know the only way the Chokonen can survive is to live at peace with the White Eyes. I am trying to follow your teachings, but forgetting the hatred inside me for what has been done to me and my people"—he drew a shuddering breath—"what continues to be done to us, is not easy. That is what I told Mariah."

"You told her why you hated all whites?"

Nighthawk nodded. "I told her about the soldiers killing my father and brother and how I tried to avenge their deaths. She asked if I hated her because she is a White Eyes."

"You don't hate her, do you?"

"No. I am not sure what I feel for her, or what I am supposed to feel, but I do not hate her."

Father Julian fell silent, mulling over their conversation. Something about Nighthawk's last statement struck him as odd. After several minutes, he said, "Did your Spirits send you a vision about Mariah Corbett?"

When Nighthawk first became friends with Father Julian, he'd told him a great deal about himself but purposely omitted his visions. As their friendship grew, he realized the priest would not judge him, no matter what he revealed about himself. Being a man of God, Father Julian accepted Nighthawk's account of having visions without a qualm, viewing the phenomena as religious experiences.

"Yes," Nighthawk replied, "I had a vision the night before I met her. But the Spirits have not spoken to me since, so I do not know their reason for bringing her into my life."

"The ways of God—or, in your case, the Spirits— can be a mystery to us mortals. But this time, perhaps the Spirits haven't sent you another vision because they're waiting for you to do something."

"Me?" Nighthawk replied, shaking his head. "But their last vision did not tell me what to do."

Father Julian rubbed the sweat off his brow with a forearm. "Maybe it did, and you just aren't aware of it." Seeing Nighthawk's confused expression, he continued. "My guess is that the Spirits brought Miss Corbett into your life knowing how you would react to her. And now they're waiting for you to take the next step. Do you think that's possible?"

Nighthawk blinked. "I do not know." He thought about Father Julian's theory for a moment, then said, "Perhaps it is possible."

As the two men finished their work in silence, Nighthawk's mind spun at the notion that Father Julian might be correct. Did the Spirits expect him to be attracted to Mariah, expect him to desire her? Were they waiting for him to take the next step? If the answer to those questions was yes, one important piece of information still had to be filled in.

What was that next step?

# Chapter Nine

The sound of feminine laughter followed by a much
deeper male chuckle drifted to Mariah's bedroom
from the parlor of the hotel suite. She shook her head,
still having trouble believing the change in Uncle
Ned. As soon as she returned to Tucson three days
earlier and asked how he'd gotten along with Señora
Solares, he'd blurted out his love for the woman. His
sudden announcement had come as such a complete
shock that for a moment she hadn't been able to reply.
When she finally found her voice, she'd demanded to
know who he was and what he'd done with her uncle.
Though Ned burst out laughing, and her laughter soon
joined his, she didn't tell him she hadn't meant the
question entirely as a joke. The man who declared
he'd fallen in love couldn't be the uncle she'd lived
with for the past fourteen years.

The Ned Corbett she knew had never taken a romantic interest in a woman. Not that there hadn't been women in his life—though, of course, she hadn't let on that she knew the exact nature of those relationships. But he'd certainly never behaved like the love-struck man now sitting in the parlor with the object of his affection. Although Mariah had initially had her doubts about his claim of falling in love, they fled the moment Benita Solares walked into the room. She recognized the look on Ned's face—she saw the same one every day in the mirror.

In the days since she and Ethan had returned to Tucson and parted company at the corral, she had searched her heart long and hard. The conclusion she'd reached was irrefutable. She loved Ethan Nighthawk.

She hadn't wanted to fall in love, any more than she suspected her uncle wanted to, and she definitely didn't need the complication in her life. However, that didn't alter the facts; she and Ned had each done the unthinkable and allowed themselves to become entangled in love's complicated net. They both had been happy with their lives: Ned, a confirmed bachelor, content working as her assistant, and she, a willing candidate for spinsterhood, determined to let nothing get in the way of her success as a photographer. But their contentment with life hadn't kept either of them from being struck by cupid's arrow. And even though she'd fallen in love with Ethan and would have to deal with the consequences of such foolishness, she had no plans to change her life. Unfortunately, she couldn't be so certain about her uncle's future.

Mariah had always known that eventually she would have to face the time when she and Ned no longer worked together. But in her mind, that wouldn't have happened until they were well into their dotage. Now the need to move up that timetable was a real possibility. Though Ned hadn't mentioned his intentions toward Benita Solares, Mariah figured marriage was the next logical step. And a newly married man would not want to be away from his wife for weeks at a time.

"Then what will I do?" she said aloud. The answer wasn't one she cared to contemplate. Hiring a new assistant would be a time-consuming and difficult process, but the alternative—giving up photographing spectacular landscapes in remote places and opening a studio, where her work would be limited to portraits—would be far worse.

*At least Ethan's still working for me.* Her spirits lifted at the thought, then immediately sagged. As soon as they concluded their next field trip, his tenure as her assistant would end. Then she would leave for Philadelphia and never see him again. The last thought hit her like a physical blow. She squeezed her eyes closed, biting her lip to hold in a sob. *How could I have done something as stupid as fall in love?*

Several minutes passed while she collected herself. She released a long sigh, then opened her eyes. Deciding a walk might chase away her melancholy, she reached for her hat and quickly pinned it in place.

After letting Ned and Benita know her plans, she hurried downstairs and out onto the street. The day was hot and windy, not a cloud in the deep blue sky.

Mariah looked up and down Meyer Street, undecided about which direction to take. She should find Ethan to make sure he still planned to leave for their second field trip the following day. On the ride back to Tucson, they'd agreed to stay in town five days. He'd wanted to catch up on his work for Father Julian, and she'd needed to develop the photographs she'd taken and replenish her supplies. Deciding that looking for Ethan could wait until her mood improved, she started walking with no particular destination in mind.

She strolled through the main section of town, occasionally going into one of the stores but just as content to window shop. As she neared the Lord and Williams Store, she nodded and smiled at a woman standing in front of the door.

The rail-thin woman nodded, loosening the auburn hair piled haphazardly atop her head. Then, as Mariah got closer, the pleasant expression on her deeply lined face abruptly changed. The warmth in her washed-out blue eyes turned icy, her thin mouth puckering as if she'd just swallowed the vilest of medicines. Mariah wondered at the reason for such odd behavior but kept walking. She'd taken a couple of steps when the woman spoke.

Mariah stopped and turned. "I beg your pardon?"

"I said," the woman replied in a venomous tone, "ain't you that lady photographer?"

Mariah stepped closer. "I'm Mariah Corbett, and yes, I'm a photographer. What can I do for you, Mrs. . . ."

The woman tucked a strand of hair behind one ear. "Dean. Wilma Dean. And there ain't nothin' you can do for me. I don't want anythin' from the woman who's been traipsin' all over creation with one of them heathen Injuns."

Mariah curled her hands into fists. "Ethan Night-hawk isn't a heathen. And I would appreciate it if you wouldn't refer to him as an Injun."

"Oh, ya would, would ya? Well, aren't you little miss high-and-mighty, tellin' me what to say." Her narrow face twisted with rage. "You didn't have yer wagon attacked by them red devil Apaches. You didn't see yer own brother shot dead right in front of yer eyes. If ya had, you'd be calling them a lot worse than Injuns."

Mariah clenched her teeth so tightly, her jaw ached. "You're right, Mrs. Dean. I didn't experience those things. But there's still no need to blame every Apache for the crimes of a few."

The woman took a step forward. "Why don't you get on a stage and get outta town. We don't need the likes of you around here. Yer nothing but trouble."

"I'm not trying to cause trouble. I'm just trying to point out that Ethan shouldn't be held accountable for everything—"

"Ethan, is it?" Mrs. Dean said with a sneer. "Have ya spread yer legs for him? Is that why yer so quick to defend his kind?"

Mariah's hold on her temper snapped. Shrieking her outrage, she leaped at the woman. She grabbed a handful of hair and yanked until Mrs. Dean's face was just inches from hers. "How dare you speak to me that way?" she said. "I demand an apology, and I want it now!" She gave the woman's hair another yank for good measure.

Mrs. Dean yelped and wrapped her hands around Mariah's wrist, the smarting of her scalp bringing tears to her eyes. "I ain't gonna apologize to no Injun-lover!" she yelled. "Let go of me!"

The two continued struggling in front of the store, Mariah keeping one hand fisted in her opponent's hair while repeating her demand for an apology. Mrs. Dean repeatedly refused to apologize while unsuccessfully trying to free herself from Mariah's grasp.

Someone shouted something from the door of the store, and soon there was a sound of boots pounding on the hard-packed ground. Mariah didn't pay any attention; she had never been so blinded by anger in her life. Her fingers still curled in Mrs. Dean's hair, she pulled back her other arm, intent on socking the woman square in the nose if she didn't offer an apology.

Just as she prepared to smash her fist into its target, a voice penetrated the red haze of her anger. Breathing heavily, she turned her head enough to see the sun glinting off something shiny on a man's chest. *Drat. The marshal.*

"Dammit, did you hear me, Miss Corbett?" the marshal said in a harsh voice. "I said, let go of Mrs. Dean."

Mariah lifted her gaze to stare at the lawman's scowling face. Reluctantly, she relaxed her grip on the woman's hair. Mrs. Dean jerked away so quickly, she stumbled backward and nearly fell.

When the woman regained her balance, she straightened the bodice of her dress, then turned a sugary smile on the marshal. "This woman attacked me for no reason, and I want her—"

"No reason?" Mariah said in a near shout. Lowering her voice, she said, "Marshal, Mrs. Dean said some terrible things about Eth—er—Mr. Nighthawk and me. She insulted both of us, calling us horrible—"

"I was just offerin' you my opinion," Mrs. Dean said in a haughty voice. Pasting another smile on her face, she turned her gaze on the marshal. "Everyone's entitled to an opinion. Ain't that right, Marshal? So she had no call to attack me." She lifted a hand and gingerly touched her scalp. "She nearly pulled my hair out by the roots."

Mariah glared at the woman. "You were doing more than offering your opinion, and you damn well know it. You deserve a whole lot worse than having your hair ripped from your—"

"All right. All right," the marshal said. "That's enough from both of ya." He turned to Mariah. "Mrs. Dean said you attacked her. Is that right?"

"Yes, and I told you why," Mariah replied, lifting her chin.

"Yeah, I heard what you said. Mrs. Dean insulted you. That don't break no laws. But you physically attacked a person. Now that there is a different breed of cat."

"But—"

"Mrs. Dean," he said, holding up a hand to silence Mariah, "do you want to press charges?"

"I most certainly do."

"Well, then," the marshal replied, turning his gaze back to Mariah, "I got no choice, Miss Corbett. I'm placing you under arrest." He cupped a hand around her elbow. "You'll have to come with me."

In a daze, Mariah let the marshal escort her down the street. Taking a last look over her shoulder, she saw the satisfied smirk on Wilma Dean's face, heard her demented cackle of laughter. Her temper rising again, she longed to drag the woman down into the dirt and pound the smirk off her face. Instead, she gave the woman a final glare, then turned to stare straight ahead, her chin held high.

Nighthawk sat on the bed in the small room Father Julian had assigned him when he started working for the priest. At first, Nighthawk hadn't been certain he could sleep inside a building, but eventually he'd become accustomed to the confinement of the room. The sparseness of the furnishings suited him, since the Apache placed no value on material things. But the room had one thing in abundance: books.

Father Julian had not only taught Nighthawk to read, he'd also instilled a thirst for knowledge that rivaled his own. Pleased by Nighthawk's love of the written word, he'd immediately offered him the use of his personal library. From then on, Nighthawk's room always contained a stack of books on a variety of subjects.

Nighthawk lifted his gaze from the volume in his hands, his concentration broken by a sound coming through the open window. He closed the book, waiting, listening. A few seconds passed before the sound came again; a soft whistle. Setting the book on the bedside table, he rose. He gave an answering whistle out the window, then moved across the room, opened the door, and waited.

A man left the shade beneath a tree and came toward where Nighthawk stood in the doorway. When the man reached him, he spoke in the Apache language. "It is good to see you."

"It has been a long time," Nighthawk replied.

The two embraced, then Nighthawk stepped aside to let Whitehorse enter the room. Nighthawk closed the door, then studied his lifelong friend.

Whitehorse wore buckskin trousers, a shirt of brightly patterned calico, a headband made from a strip of white cloth, and knee-high moccasins nearly identical to Nighthawk's. He looked well, though Nighthawk could see that the grief Whitehorse had suffered over the loss of his wife and child had left its mark. Shadows of the pain he'd endured still lingered in his dark-brown eyes.

When Whitehorse made no offer to explain his presence, Nighthawk said, "Why are you here?"

"I came to Tucson for supplies and to see you."

"You are going on a journey?"

Whitehorse nodded, fingering one of his earrings, a habit Nighthawk remembered from when they were boys.

Nighthawk stared at his friend for a moment, then said, "The Spirits have spoken to you in a vision? Told you to make this journey?"

"Yes." He glanced around the room again. "How is life for you?"

"It is good," Nighthawk replied. Apparently Whitehorse didn't want to discuss the vision the Spirits had sent him, a decision he would respect. Leaning a shoulder against the door, he folded his arms over his chest and said, "You know I like working for Father Julian."

"Yes, and you also like"—he nodded toward the bedside table—"reading his books."

Nighthawk smiled. "It is true. You should have Father Julian teach you to read. There is much to learn in his books. About other people, other places. Things our mothers and fathers, even the shaman in our band, could not teach us."

"I have no need to read," Whitehorse replied. "I do not care about other people and places. I care only about horses and this land, the land of our Chokonen grandfathers."

Nighthawk nodded. "I also care about the Chokonen homeland, but there is much beyond where we have lived all our lives. Much more than I could have imagined."

"You plan to go to these places?"

"I make no plans," Nighthawk said. "I do as the Spirits tell me." Though the notion of seeing some of the places he'd read about had crossed his mind, he'd never seriously considered actually doing so. He'd always let his visions control the direction of his life. But the more he thought about the idea, the more it appealed to him. Especially since Mariah would be leaving Tucson soon, and he would need a distraction to help him forget her. But perhaps the Spirits had other plans for him—plans they had yet to reveal. If only he knew what—

Whitehorse's voice pulled him from his musings.

"You have done nothing more than work for the priest?"

Nighthawk narrowed his gaze, noticing that a sparkle had chased the shadows from his friend's eyes. "I think you already know that answer."

Whitehorse grinned. "From the time we were boys and played our first arrow game, I never was good at hiding anything from you." He moved to the bed, tested the mattress with his hand, then sat down. "You like sleeping on such a soft bed?" When Nighthawk nodded, he said, "Perhaps living like a White Eyes has made you soft as well."

A smile flickered around Nighthawk's mouth. "I speak the truth when I tell you living here has not made me soft."

Whitehorse gave him a thoughtful stare, his fingers again playing with the bead on one of his earrings. "I do not agree. You must be soft to let a white woman defend you."

"What white woman? And what do you mean, defend me?"

"The White Eyes called Mariah Corbett. I saw her on the street before I came here."

"And?" Nighthawk said, trying to control his impatience.

"Another white woman said bad things about you. This Mariah Corbett became angry and tried to defend you, but the other woman would not listen and said bad things about her, too. That is when she started the fight."

"Mariah started a fight?" Nighthawk unfolded his arms and pushed away from the door. "Was she hurt?"

Whitehorse's gaze narrowed. "Ah, your heart cares for this woman. I wondered. Your hatred of White Eyes has always been strong, so I did not think—" He shrugged. "I was wrong. Does her heart care for you?"

"Answer my question."

"I think, yes," Whitehorse replied, answering his own question while ignoring Nighthawk's menacing glare. "Why would she start a fight because of something someone said about you, unless her heart—"

"Stop playing games."

"—cared for you. She would make a fine warrior. Fierce. Unafraid. A man would be proud to have such a woman fight for him." When Whitehorse saw Nighthawk's lips flatten into a harsh line, his hands curl into fists, he flashed another grin. "You know I cannot resist teasing you. But you can relax, my friend. She was not hurt. When the marshal arrested her, she was still angry but unharmed."

Nighthawk's eyes widened. "Mariah was arrested? Are you sure?"

"It is true. I heard the marshal say she was under arrest and he had to take her to jail."

Whitehorse saw Nighthawk's shocked expression, but he noticed something else as well, an emotion he'd never seen on his friend's face. Nighthawk had never given his heart to a woman, but Whitehorse suspected the White Eyes called Mariah Corbett might have changed that. He waited, hoping Nighthawk would volunteer some information. When he didn't, Whitehorse said, "Are you going to tell me about her?"

Nighthawk drew a deep breath, exhaled slowly, then nodded. He wanted to go to Mariah, to see for himself that she was unharmed, but first he knew he owed Whitehorse an explanation. He took a seat on the room's only chair and rubbed a hand over his face while he collected his thoughts. A few seconds passed before he began speaking.

"I met Mariah Corbett when I was in jail." He saw the surprise on Whitehorse's face, but before his friend could ask any questions, he said, "That story will wait for another time."

Whitehorse nodded, then indicated Nighthawk should continue.

"Mariah and her uncle came to Tucson so she could take photographs of the mountains. Her uncle, who is also her assistant, broke his leg soon after they arrived. She needed to find someone to take his place. That is why she came to see me at the jail."

"How did she know you were there?"

He frowned. "I do not think she said. Someone must have suggested me for the job and told her where I was."

"And you agreed to work for her," Whitehorse said, shaking his head. "That is what I cannot believe. Maybe she bewitched you."

"She did not use witchcraft," Nighthawk said with a laugh, then immediately sobered. "I agreed because the Spirits sent me a vision the night before I met her."

"Ah, now I understand," Whitehorse replied. "Your hearts care for each other because the Spirits said it would be so."

Nighthawk scowled. "I saw only a woman with yellow hair. The Spirits did not tell me *why* I would meet a light-haired white woman or what I would feel for her." He exhaled heavily. "They have not spoken to me since."

Whitehorse still thought he hadn't misinterpeted

the actions of the Corbett woman or what the Spirits foretold in Nighthawk's vision. But he would wait to speak his thoughts. "Tell me more."

Nighthawk told Whitehorse about his first field trip with Mariah—omitting the intimate details—and concluded with his offer to take her to the Chokonen homeland on their second trip. A trip that was supposed to begin on the following day.

After he finished, Whitehorse mulled over everything Nighthawk had told him, then said, "I think your heart does care for her. If it did not, you would not want to take her to see our homeland."

Nighthawk didn't immediately reply. He'd done a lot of thinking since his conversation with Father Julian about Mariah the day before. He'd finally come to the conclusion that the priest's theory about why he hadn't yet received another vision was correct. The Spirits were waiting for him to do something. And he planned to oblige them.

As he thought about the decision he'd made, he wondered if Whitehorse's conclusions were also correct. Had his heart already started caring for Mariah? Did he feel more than desire for her? Unfortunately, he couldn't answer those questions with any certainty.

But he did know there was no future for an independent white woman and an Apache warrior caught between two worlds. He had nothing to offer her, no means of supporting them. Therefore, allowing his heart to become involved in his relationship with Mariah would be a grave mistake.

Mariah sat on the edge of the jail-cell bunk, her spine stiff, her hands clasped together in her lap. Though her temper had cooled, her irritation with the marshal continued to grow. In spite of her near pleading, he had yet to send anyone to the Palace Hotel to deliver a message to her uncle. She'd left the hotel first thing that morning, and with late-afternoon fast approaching, surely Ned was worried about her.

She stood and moved to the bars of her cell. Raising her voice to be heard beyond the closed door to the office, she called for the marshal. When the door opened almost immediately, her heart sped up. Maybe this time, he'd do as she asked. But instead of the scowling marshal, her gaze landed on the solemn face of Ethan Nighthawk.

She blinked, certain her eyes were playing tricks on her. No, Ethan really was standing in the doorway.

As he moved closer to the cell, the same cell he had occupied the first time they met, her heart rate increased even more.

"How did you know I was here?" she said, surprised by how breathless she sounded.

"Someone I know saw what happened and told me you had been arrested." He searched her face for signs of injury. Though he found none, he couldn't resist touching her to reassure himself she wasn't hurt. Reaching between the bars, he ran the backs of his knuckles across her cheek. "Are you all right?"

She nodded, staring into his eyes. Her lips curved in a crooked smile. "I'm fine, just thoroughly miffed at the marshal for not sending someone over to the hotel to tell Uncle Ned where I am."

"I will go see him when I leave here."

"Thanks. That's a big relief."

He ran his fingers over her cheek one more time,

then withdrew his hand. "I cannot decide whether I should be angry with you for feeling the need to come to my defense—again—or if I should thank you."

"Thanking me would be the best choice. I'm already angry enough at myself for what I did." Seeing something flicker in his eyes, she reached through the bars and laid a hand on his arm. "Not for defending you. That mealymouthed biddy had no call saying the things she did about either one of us, and she deserved a lot more than having her hair yanked a few times. I'm angry at myself because I allowed her to goad me into a fight. If I hadn't lost my temper, I wouldn't have ended up in jail."

His lips twitched. He leaned closer and lowered his voice. "Want me to break you out?"

She stared at him for a moment, then burst into laughter, the last of her self-directed anger fading away. "Probably not a good idea," she replied. "Likely we'd both just end up back in here."

"I might not mind being in jail," he said with a smile, "if we could share a cell. Of course, there is not much to do in there, so we would have to find ways to pass the time. I would enjoy that." He brushed his thumb over her bottom lip. "What about you?"

Her eyes went wide at the implication of his words. She ran her gaze over his face, looking for assurance that his coldness toward her had ended. He was a hard man to read, but the smoldering heat in his gaze told her she hadn't misunderstood him.

She drew a deep breath, then said, "Yes, I would like that, too."

The heat intensified in his dark eyes, lighting a responding fire low in her belly.

"So when do you get out of here?" His softly spoken question stirred the fire hotter.

"As soon as I pay my fine. Eight dollars or a night in jail." She swallowed, dropping her gaze. "I ... uh ... refused to pay the fine on general principle. Mrs. Dean should be in here, too, for the awful things she said."

Nighthawk shook his head. "When are you going to learn that people always have and always will say things about me that you do not like?" He placed a hand under her chin and forced her to meet his gaze. "My prickly Mariah," he said in a soft voice, his fingers caressing her jaw. "Always trying to make things right."

She could barely breathe, let alone speak. His touch, his possessive reference, had stolen the air from her lungs.

He smiled at her, then said, "You do not want to spend the night in there. The bed is very uncomfortable." He dropped his voice to a whisper. "What if I pay your fine, then we go somewhere more private?"

She gulped, then said, "I need to talk to Uncle Ned first."

He nodded, gave her jaw one last stroke of his fingers, then stepped back.

Before he turned away, Mariah saw the promise blazing in his eyes and had to grab the cell bars to keep herself upright. Her heart thundering in her ears, she watched him disappear through the door to the outer office.

# Chapter Ten

By the time the marshal came to unlock Mariah's cell, she had regained her composure, though her body still hummed with anticipation at the prospect of being somewhere private with Ethan.

A few minutes later, she left the marshal's office, hoping she never had reason to set foot inside again— as either a prisoner or a visitor. Walking beside Ethan, her arm looped through his, she pointedly ignored anyone who gave them even the faintest look of disapproval. She didn't care what people thought. After all, what she did was her business and no one else's. Still, keeping herself from speaking her mind required every ounce of her willpower.

With silent amusement, Nighthawk watched Mariah restrain her temper, his chest nearly bursting with pride. Never had he thought to meet a white woman he would truly like, let alone one he would be proud to be seen with. He was finally beginning to realize the full extent of how his life had been turned upside down by the woman at his side. And although he knew their relationship couldn't become permanent, he no longer felt the need to stay away from her. In fact, he planned to get a whole lot closer as soon as possible. His blood heated at the thought.

As they entered the Palace Hotel, Mariah turned to smile at Vincent Pomeroy, the desk clerk. The man's reaction to Ethan was clearly visible on his thin face and made her smile disappear. Stopping in front of the desk, she leveled an icy glare on the bespectacled clerk. "Is there a problem, Mr. Pomeroy?"

Pomeroy started to reply, then apparently thought better of it and snapped his mouth shut. Swallowing hard, he shook his head, flipping a lock of dark red hair onto his forehead.

"I certainly hope not," Mariah said in a no-nonsense tone. "I'd hate for the hotel to lose my business because you or anyone else working here doesn't approve of the company I keep." She paused to let that statement sink in, then added, "Have I made my position clear?"

The clerk's pale face changed to a red that nearly matched his hair, and his Adam's apple bobbed with another swallow. In a choked voice, he managed to say, "Yes, ma'am."

Ethan remained silent until they were well up the staircase. Then he leaned closer and said, "I thought getting arrested taught you a lesson about using that sharp tongue of yours."

"I thought so, too," she replied. "But bigots like that fool Pomeroy make me so angry, I can't see

159

straight." She drew a deep breath, released it with a sigh, then flashed Ethan a grin. "Guess I forgot there for a minute, huh?"

"Yes, you did," he replied, returning her smile. "The clerk should be glad you fought him with only words. If you had started another fistfight, I would have had to step in to keep you from hurting him." He chuckled. "Can you imagine the color of his face if I had been the one to save him?"

She stared up at Ethan for a moment, then burst into laughter. "That would be priceless—a bigot having his sorry hide saved by the object of his prejudice."

Though Mariah knew Ethan had meant to lighten the mood with his teasing, she also knew how deeply the sting of bigotry must hurt him. She'd suffered the pain of prejudice firsthand, but what she endured as a female working in a male-dominated profession didn't begin to compare with the hatred heaped on Ethan for simply being alive. Her heart ached at the thought that he might well have to endure a lifetime of such bias.

As Ethan opened the door of the hotel suite and stepped aside to let her enter first, she made herself a promise. Before leaving for Philadelphia, she would do all she could to make the people in Tucson see beyond the color of Ethan Nighthawk's skin. Remembering her recent jail stay, she amended her promise a bit. She'd do everything she could short of running afoul of the law.

Mariah spotted her uncle sitting near the window, holding the crutches Dr. Handy had left on his last visit. As she started toward him, she said, "Uncle Ned, I'm—"

A gasp followed by a cry of *"¡Madre de Díos!"* brought Mariah to a halt. Turning toward the direction of the voice, she saw Benita Solares standing in the doorway of her uncle's bedroom, a hand pressed to her bosom, her eyes wide with fight.

Ned turned in his chair. "Benita, what's wrong?"

Benita didn't respond. She simply crossed herself, her lips moving in silent prayer.

"Benita," Ned said, holding a hand toward her, "come here."

The woman hurried to Ned's side and grasped his hand.

Nighthawk closed the door, then moved to stand next to Mariah. "I think I frightened the señora," he said.

Mariah nodded, then said, "Señora Solares, there's no need to be afraid."

"That's right," Ned said, squeezing Benita's fingers. "This is Ethan Nighthawk, the man Mariah hired to take my place. He won't hurt you. Isn't that right, Mariah?"

"Yes. I promise you, señora, Ethan's far more civilized than most of the men in this town."

When Benita still didn't respond, Ned said, "Benita, talk to me, darlin'."

She flushed at the endearment, drew a shaky breath, then managed a weak smile. "I am fine now." She shifted her gaze to Ethan. "I am sorry, Señor Nighthawk. I was not expecting to see a wild"—her flush deepened—"an Apache, and I was startled for a moment. I hope you can forgive me; I did not mean to embarrass you."

Nighthawk smiled at the woman. "There is nothing to forgive, señora."

Once everyone had recovered from the uncomfortable moment, Mariah said to her uncle, "Have you been practicing with your crutches?"

"Yeah. Benita and me were just gettin' ready to go out. Thought we'd find a cool spot to sit for a spell, then go to a restaurant for an early supper."

"Are you sure you can manage the stairs?"

Ned nodded. "I'll just take my time. Besides, Benita will be right beside me in case I need help." He smiled at the woman next to him. "Won't ya, darlin'?"

When Benita bobbed her head in agreement, Ned shifted his gaze back to Mariah. "Would you two like to join us?"

"Thanks, but I . . . uh . . . I'm not hungry," Mariah replied, her pulse increasing with the knowledge that she and Ethan would soon be alone. She tried to keep her expression bland when she looked up at Ethan. "How about you?"

"No," he said. Though his response contradicted what she saw in his eyes, she knew his hunger had nothing to do with food.

She swallowed, pulled her gaze from Ethan, then said, "You two go ahead. Ethan and I need to . . . um . . . discuss . . . uh . . . things."

If Ned noticed anything strange, he gave no sign. Instead, he gave her a nod, then turned his attention to his crutches and got to his feet. Mariah released her held breath, relieved he hadn't noticed the slight tremble in her voice or seen through her stammered excuse.

As soon as Ned and Benita left the suite, Nighthawk crossed his arms over his chest and turned to Mariah. "What are these things we need to discuss?" he said, amusement gleaming in his eyes.

"You know I made that up," she replied, taking a step toward him. "Finding out we were going to have the suite to ourselves took me by surprise, and that was the best I could come up with. It's a good thing Uncle Ned is so smitten with Benita, otherwise he would've known I was lying through my teeth."

Nighthawk chuckled. "It was pretty obvious." He uncrossed his arms, then reached to remove her hat. Tossing it aside, he worked his fingers into the pile of hair atop her head, searching for, then removing, the hairpins. "You did not tell him why you were gone so long."

"In case you didn't notice, he didn't exactly look worried when we got here," she said, holding out a hand to take the hairpins from him. "I doubt he even realized how long I was gone. Love certainly has changed him."

Ethan's probing fingers sent a tingling sensation up her spine and stirred her simmering desire. Her entire body aching with need, she closed her eyes for a moment, stifling the urge to groan aloud. "Besides, it's probably just as well that I didn't tell him. If he knew I'd been arrested, he might've stayed in to lecture me."

"Then we would not be alone," he said in a soft voice, handing her the last hairpin. "And that was not what we wanted, was it?" He tunneled his hands into her hair, sending the heavy mass tumbling down her

163

back, the pale strands curling around his fingers in a silky caress.

He stared down at her, his pulse pounding heavily against his temples. "And I could not do this." Moving his hands to cradle the back of her head, he bent and brushed his mouth over hers. Once, twice, then a third time.

She groaned and tried to lean closer, but he held her firmly in place.

He murmured something she didn't understand, then ran the tip of his tongue over her bottom lip before capturing her mouth in a kiss.

He tipped her head slightly, changing the angle to give him better access to her mouth. He pushed his tongue past her lips, exploring, tasting, nearly devouring her with the skilled onslaught of his kiss. His tongue teased hers in a sensuous dance, sending white-hot heat careening through her body to settle between her thighs.

When Ethan finally broke the kiss, Mariah drew a deep breath to clear her reeling senses. Her hairpins still clutched in one hand, she placed her other hand on his chest to steady herself. In a ragged whisper, she said, "I . . . I think we should lie down."

The rumble of his laughter vibrating beneath her palm, he carefully removed his hands from her hair. "I agree," he said, lifting her into his arms. "Where is your bedroom?"

Ethan carried her into the room she indicated, set her on her feet next to the bed, then reached for the buttons of her blouse. Before he could free one button, she wrapped her fingers around his wrist to halt his efforts. He lifted his head, skimming his gaze over her face. "Have you changed your mind?"

She shook her head. "I'm absolutely sure this is what I want. But"—she swallowed—"are you?"

He stared at her for a moment, understanding her need to ask. After his conversation with Whitehorse earlier that day, he'd reconsidered his conclusion that the Spirits were waiting for him to take the next step. But despite the possibility that his friend might be correct—that his heart cared for Mariah—he hadn't changed his mind about proceeding with his plan. He couldn't endure another day without experiencing her passion completely. He'd wanted her from the moment he first laid eyes on her, and he intended to have her.

Finally he said, "Yes, I am sure."

She smiled, releasing her hold on his wrist. Her voice thick with growing passion, she said, "Then please continue."

Mariah wasn't sure how Ethan accomplished it, but she soon found herself divested of her clothes and lying naked on her bed, her gaze glued to him while he undressed.

He pulled his shirt off over his head and tossed it aside, removed his moccasins, then reached for the fly of his trousers. She watched him peel off the tight buckskin, her breathing suddenly erratic, a warm flush spreading over her body. She must have made some sort of sound, because his hands abruptly stilled in their task. When he lifted his gaze to meet hers, she could see desire blazing in his dark eyes.

He stared at her for a moment, then finished undressing. After stepping out of his trousers and kicking them out of the way, he brushed his hair off his shoulders and stood perfectly still. As her gaze drifted downward, her breath caught in her throat. Ethan Nighthawk was the most blatantly masculine, perfectly formed man she'd ever seen. The muscles of his arms and chest bulged beneath his gleaming copper skin. His stomach was flat, his hips narrow, and that most male part of him proudly erect. She swallowed, then once again met his gaze.

When he didn't move, she licked her lips and said, "Aren't you going to join me?"

"If you have finished looking at me." His voice held a hint of amusement.

"For now," she replied with a smile. "Come here." She patted the mattress beside her.

He placed a knee on the bed, then stretched out next to her and pulled her into his arms. He lifted a trembling hand to brush a wisp of hair off her face. "What have you done to me?" he whispered. "I am shaking with my need for you."

Before Mariah could think of a reply, he pressed his mouth to hers. What began as a gentle kiss soon became hot, demanding. He used his lips, his teeth, his tongue, to coax an equally heated response from her. She pressed closer, grabbed a handful of his hair, and pushed her hips forward to trap his straining erection between their bodies.

Nighthawk moved a hand down her back, his finger skimming over her silken skin, tracing the ridges of her spine, then splaying over her bottom and tugging her more firmly against him. His throbbing manhood brushed the soft curls between her thighs, wrenching a groan from deep in his throat.

The need to push her onto her back, shove her legs

apart, and bury himself deep inside her grew stronger with each heartbeat. He fought the urge, wanting to make sure she was ready to take him. Loosening his grip on her bottom, he rolled her onto her back, then eased his mouth from hers. He silenced her moan of protest by moving his hand to her belly and gently stroking her.

She opened her fist, let his hair slide through her fingers, then dropped her arm to the bed. Her breathing harsh, she opened her eyes and stared up at him.

Nighthawk knew he'd never tire of looking into her eyes, especially when her passion darkened them to a green so deep it was nearly black. As he slid his hand lower, her breathing caught on a gasp. And when his fingertips reached the pale hair covering her sex, a second gasp ended with her moaning his name, her hips lifting in a silent plea for his intimate touch.

He complied, opening the damp folds, finding the sensitive nubbin of flesh. As he stroked the bud, her eyes drifted shut, her hips catching the rhythm of his hand. He bent his head, ran his tongue around the tip of one breast, then pulled the nipple into his mouth. He gently suckled the hardened peak into a tighter knot before shifting his attention to her other breast.

Her sudden sharp gasp and the increased thrusting of her hips told him her release was near. He wouldn't deny her, but he'd already held his own need at bay too long to continue waiting.

He carefully inched his hand away from her, shushing her protest with a gentle kiss. "Be patient. I will see that you are satisfied." In quick, efficient movements, he shifted position. "But first, I must have you." Bracing his weight on one forearm, he pushed her legs apart, then guided his straining sex to her.

As the blunt tip of his manhood brushed against her slick flesh, he bit back a groan. She was incredibly hot and wet, ready for their joining. He clenched his jaw, praying for the strength to control his raging need. Flexing his hips, he eased forward, pushing inside her.

At first her inner muscles protested the invasion. He stopped, waiting for her body to adjust to his presence. Her muscles remained unyielding for several seconds, then abruptly relaxed, allowing him access.

He waited another second, then pushed forward to slide completely into her tight passage. "Bend your knees," he whispered.

She complied, the movement forcing him deeper. Resting his forehead on hers, he fought for self-control. Never had he experienced such a feeling of oneness, such an overwhelming sense of rightness. Never had he been so close to exploding so quickly.

"Ethan? Ethan, are you all right?"

Mariah's voice finally registered. He lifted his head and stared down at her. Seeing her worried frown, he managed a weak smile. "I am fine." He dropped a brief kiss on her mouth. "I needed a minute to regain my control."

"Then you aren't planning to stop?"

"No," he replied, his smile widening. "That is not my plan." To prove his point, he lifted his hips to partially withdraw, then immediately thrust forward, burying himself fully in her heated depths. Her gasp mixed with his groan. He repeated the motion of his hips, again and again, each stroke faster and harder than the last. Clutching the pillow on both sides of her head, he bent closer and ran his tongue along her neck. In a ragged voice, he murmured Apache words in her ear.

Mariah locked her legs around his waist, lifting her hips off the bed to meet his thrusts. She wished she knew what he'd said to her, but as quickly as the thought came, it fled. The coil of heat in her belly made her forget everything but the need for completion. The pressure between her thighs increased with each powerful stroke of his body until she thought she couldn't stand another moment of the pleasure-torture.

"Ethan!"

Her breathless call cleared the fuzziness from Nighthawk's mind. He whispered words of reassurance against her throat, and, shifting his weight to one forearm, he slipped his other hand between their sweat-dampened bodies, his fingers unerringly finding the swollen nub of flesh just above where they were joined. When he touched her, she gasped. With a few more strokes of his fingers, she arched up, sobbing his name over and over.

As the first spasm of her release rippled through her body, her inner muscles gripping his sex, he could no longer hold back. He removed his hand from between them, then slid his arm around her waist to hold her more firmly against him. He pounded into her with faster and faster strokes until his climax crashed over him in wave after wave of sweet ecstasy. Clenching his jaw to hold in a shout of victory, he rejoiced in the flood of incredible sensations rushing through him until the last of the tremors faded away.

Several minutes passed before he stirred. When he started to push himself up onto his knees, Mariah's voice stopped him.

"Not yet."

"I am too heavy," he replied, kissing the side of her neck, then drawing her unique musky scent into his lungs.

"No, you're fine." She lifted a hand and rubbed his back.

"I like touching you."

He chuckled. "I like that, too. But it is too hot to stay like this."

"I know. Just a little longer, okay?"

He nodded, then propped himself up on his elbows. Brushing damp locks of hair off her forehead, he stared at her. Not sure how to broach the subject, he finally said, "You were not untouched."

Though his words sounded more like a statement than a question, Mariah knew what he was really asking.

"No, I wasn't a virgin," she said, carefully choosing her words. "A few years ago, I decided it was high time I found out what it was like to be with a man."

His eyes widened. "You selected a man at random?"

Mariah chuckled at the horrified look on his face. "No. Give me credit for a little more discretion than that. He was a close friend, someone I'd known a long time. In fact, I might have married him if circumstances had been different. But I didn't want a husband, and I knew he didn't want a wife who travelled as a photographer. So, after a few weeks, we stopped seeing each other."

Her lips twitched. "And, in case you're wondering, you're a much better lover than he ever was." Before he could respond, she said, "Now I have question for you. Are all Apache men like you?"

His brow furrowed. "What do you mean?"

"Are they all as skilled in intimate matters? In how to please a woman?"

"Ah," he replied, a smile pulling at the corners of his mouth. "Apache parents teach their children not to pay attention to the opposite sex. Boys are kept busy learning how to become worthy hunters and warriors. Girls spend all their time learning the skills they will need when they become wives and mothers. There is little opportunity to experiment with sexual relationships. Not that it does not happen on occasion, but such behavior is discouraged."

"Then how did you become so talented?"

He chuckled. "I was not so talented, as you put it, before I came to Tucson."

"Oh. Then you learned from the women on Maiden Lane? Like the one you were with when you were arrested?"

Nighthawk thought he heard a hint of jealousy in her voice, but he couldn't be certain. "Yes, Carmen. She taught me much more than any of the others."

Mariah thought about his answer for a moment, swallowed, then managed a smile. "Well, I guess I owe Carmen a thank-you."

Nighthawk blinked, then chuckled. Running the backs of his knuckles down her cheek, he said, "Mariah Corbett, you are a most unique woman."

"Well, I should hope so," she replied, her eyes

171

alight with amusement. "I'd hate to go through life as just plain ordinary."

He shook his head and chuckled again. "No one could ever call you ordinary," he said, pushing himself to his knees, then moving to sit on the side of the bed.

Her gaze landed on the puckered skin just above his waist on the right side of his back, the scar she'd noticed the first time she saw him. Reaching out to touch the spot, she said, "How did this happen?"

"I was shot by Mexican soldiers."

"Why would the Mexican Army attack you?"

"We were returning to our camp after raiding a Mexican village, and the—" Mariah's gasp made him turn to look at her. The expression on her face clearly revealed her thoughts.

His good mood dissolving, his back stiffened. "You should not judge me or my people."

"You wouldn't have been shot," she said in fierce whisper, "if you hadn't been raiding in the first place."

The censure in her voice didn't surprise Nighthawk, but how much her words stung did. The muscles in his jaw working, he glared down at her. "You know nothing about the Apache life-way. I was taught to be a warrior. To raid for food, to fight and kill the enemy when necessary."

"Raids, war—they're both the same."

"They are not the same. For Apache, war is for survival. Raiding became necessary to feed our people. Once the White Eyes came to our homeland, game became scarce, and our people were in need. We had to raid for food and supplies."

Mariah held his gaze for several seconds. Finally, she blew out a deep breath and said, "You're right. I shouldn't have judged you." She lifted a hand and pushed a strand of his hair over his shoulder. "But that doesn't mean I approve of raiding, even when the reason is to help those in need. To me raiding is nothing more than stealing from innocent victims. I hope you can understand why I feel that way."

He continued glaring at her, lips flattened, teeth clenched. A full minute passed while he considered her statement, wondering again about the Spirits' motives. What purpose could there be for bringing the two of them together—two people from totally different backgrounds? Realizing he was no closer to finding an answer, he said, "I understand the Apache life-way is much different than the ways of the White Eyes."

"That's true," she said. The rebuke in her eyes suddenly cleared, replaced by a bright twinkle. "And that's also one of the reasons I find you so fascinating."

Her statement caught him off guard, making him forget his lingering anxiety about his future. "You find me fascinating?" At her nod, he said, "What are the other reasons?"

"Maybe that's for me to know"—she flashed a secretive smile—"and you find out."

He frowned. "What does that mean?"

"Never mind," she said, sitting up and pressing a kiss on his shoulder. "We'd better get dressed. Uncle Ned might get tuckered out using his crutches and decide to come back early."

# *Chapter Eleven*

The following morning, Mariah and Ethan set out on their second field trip. The day started out cool, but the temperature rose quickly, and by late morning the heat shimmered off the hard-packed desert floor in undulating waves.

Though Mariah found the heat oppressive, she ignored the discomfort. Instead, she concentrated on enjoying her surroundings and being with the man she loved. After the night before, she no longer had any doubts about her feelings for Ethan Nighthawk—she'd fallen in love with him. She knew allowing herself to love him was a mistake, but as she'd also recently discovered, she had little choice in the matter. Without her permission, her heart had led the charge, refusing to listen to common sense and leaving her only one option: to hang on for the ride.

She cast a quick glance toward the man filling her

thoughts and couldn't help wondering what he felt for her, aside from the obvious desire. Pressing her lips together, she chastised herself for letting female pride barge into her thoughts. Ethan's feelings toward her didn't matter. Since their relationship was temporary, she should just enjoy the time they had together. Then she would go her way, and he would go his. Even though she knew that was what she should do, she couldn't stop a tiny part of her from wishing he would return her love.

Because of the intense heat, Nighthawk said they would stop for several hours to avoid the worst of the day's scorching temperatures. He led them to a dry arroyo with several large cottonwood trees.

"There's no water here," Mariah said after looking around.

"None that you can see," Nighthawk replied.

Her brow furrowed. "There's water here that I can't see?"

Nighthawk smiled at her dubious tone. "Yes," he said, kicking his feet from the stirrups and sliding off his horse. "Come with me, and I will show you."

She dismounted, tied the gelding near his pinto, and followed him to one of the cottonwoods.

He dropped onto his knees at the base of the tree and began digging. "These trees only grow where there is water," he said while he worked. "By digging a hole near the tree, you will find water."

Mariah watched Ethan make the hole deeper. "How far do you dig?"

"Until you feel moisture in the dirt. Like this." He held up a handful of damp earth. "Now we wait," he said, tossing the dirt aside and sitting back on his haunches. "The water will seep from the ground and fill the hole."

Mariah stared at the hole Ethan had dug. A slow trickle of muddy water had already collected in the bottom. She wrinkled her nose. "Are we going to drink that?"

"No. There should be enough in our canteens to last until we make camp tonight. This is for the horses and mules." He flashed her a smile. "They are not as particular."

Mariah frowned. "I suppose I wouldn't be either, if that's the only choice I had."

Nighthawk's smile faded. "That is what my people have been forced to endure," he said in a low voice. "Having no choice in where they live or the food they are given."

"Do you see your people often?"

"No. I no longer belong with them."

"Then you're planning on staying in Tucson?"

He stared out across the desert for a moment, then said, "I do not know. I do not feel I belong there either."

Mariah's heart cramped at the pain she heard in his voice. She could only imagine the agony of being caught between two cultures, neither offering a sense of belonging.

She finally said, "Have you considered living somewhere besides Tucson? Somewhere where people won't care about your heritage?"

"Are there such places?" His tone said he didn't think so.

"Of course. In the East, people of all races live together, and they get along fine. Well, for the most

part. I doubt anyone would care that you're Apache.
In fact"—she flashed a grin—"I can imagine how the
ladies would react. If you walked into one of their
fancy parlors, they'd take one look, then flip open
their fans and wave them frantically to cool their
flushed faces. Some might even swoon."

Nighthawk narrowed his gaze. "Swoon?"

"I wouldn't be surprised. You do have an overwhelming effect on women."

"I do?" he said, getting to his feet and moving toward her.

She nodded, licking her dry lips.

He stopped in front of her. "Is the way I affect
you"—he placed his hands on her shoulders, then
bent to run his tongue across her bottom lip—"another of the reasons you find me fascinating?"

She sucked in a lungful of air, her pulse thundering
against her ears. "Um, yes," she managed to say in a
strained whisper before looping her arms around his
neck and pressing her mouth to his.

Once again Nighthawk forgot everything except the
woman in his arms, the taste of her mouth, the scent
of her skin. Losing himself in the passion that flared
so easily between them, he widened his stance, pulled
her flush against him, and rubbed his hardened flesh
against her belly. He had never wanted a woman as
much as he wanted Mariah. She was a fever in his
blood. He'd thought once he had her, his need would
cool. But, in fact, the opposite was true.

One of the horses nickered, then stomped a hoof,
jarring Nighthawk back to the present. He pulled his
mouth from Mariah's, lifted his head, and cast a quick

glance around the arroyo. Finding nothing amiss, he eased her away from him.

"I burn for you," he said, running his thumb over her moist lips. "But this is not the time or the place."

"How about later, after we make camp tonight?"

Nighthawk smiled. "Yes, a much better time and place. And it will be cooler then."

"Mmm, that's true." She ran a hand over the muscles of his chest, smiling when his shoulders rippled with a shiver. "Your fire will keep me warm though, won't it?"

Something flashed in his eyes, a dangerous, predatory gleam. In one swift motion, he hauled her against him and captured her lips in another kiss. He plundered her mouth, inundating her senses until she clutched at him in desperation.

As quickly as the kiss began, he jerked away from her and held her at arm's length. "Does that answer your question?" he said between deep breaths.

She nodded, wrapping her fingers around his forearms to keep herself upright. When her breathing evened out, she said, "I'm definitely going to have to thank Carmen personally. Your kiss packs quite a wallop."

"A what?"

"Wallop. A punch. Your kiss left me reeling, like I'd been punched."

His brow cleared, and he chuckled. "I could say the same about your kiss. But there is no reason for you to thank Carmen. We never kissed that way."

"Really?" she replied, enormously pleased by his admission. Removing her hands from his arms, she

178

smiled up at him. "I'm glad to know she isn't responsible for all your skills."

He chuckled again, then turned to see to the animals.

They stayed in the arroyo until the sun had passed its zenith and started its downward journey in the western sky. As Mariah rode her horse from the shade of the cottonwoods, a blast of hot, dry air struck her, the glare of the sun so bright it nearly blinded her.

The desert was a glorious but unforgiving place—a place one had to respect in order to survive. Yet she realized she loved the arid land. The spectacular giant saguaro, the beautiful surrounding mountains, the bluest sky she'd ever seen, even the blazing heat—she loved it all. Glancing at Ethan, she wondered if her love of this land was an extension of her love for him.

A lump formed in her throat at the thought of leaving him and his homeland behind. Her eyes burned with the threat of tears, and an ache gripped her chest. She swallowed, then blinked several times, annoyed with herself for being so emotional. She'd never behaved so pathetically. But then, she'd never been in love before. That thought only increased the ache in her chest.

Nighthawk pushed them hard, wanting to cover as much distance as possible before darkness settled over the desert. By the time he finally called a halt to their ride, the last of the sun's light was casting their surroundings in heavy shadow.

Mariah helped unload the mules by rote, weary from the long day in the saddle. As soon as she set Screech's cage on the ground, he whistled.

"Yes, I know you're hungry," she said, pulling the

cloth off the cage. "It's been a long day for you, too."

As she turned to fetch his food, she nearly ran into Ethan. "Oh, sorry," she said, giving him a tired smile. "I was just going to feed—" She grabbed his arm to stop him from turning away. "Wait. I think you should stay. You could even feed Screech if you'd like."

The near-panic on his face prompted her to add, "Okay, maybe it is too soon for that. But I still think you should stay while I feed him."

His gaze moved from her to Screech's cage, then back to her. She saw his throat work with a swallow.

"Ethan, please do this for me. Nothing will happen to you. I give you my word."

Several seconds passed before he said, "I will stay."

She squeezed his arm, realizing that his agreeing to stay went against a lifetime of fear and the resulting deep-seated urge to flee. As she fetched Screech's food, she couldn't help wondering if Ethan had agreed because of his feelings for her. Chastising herself for allowing her thoughts to stray again into territory best left unexplored, she turned her attention to feeding her pet.

Nighthawk kept his word, staying in camp, though he stood at what he obviously considered a safe distance from Screech's cage, arms crossed over his chest.

"What do you feed him?" he said, watching her give pieces of food to the owl.

"A mixture of dried meat, flour, lard, and molasses. In the wild he would catch mice and insects, maybe even small birds. Since he can't hunt and I can't provide live food for him, this is the next best thing."

"He seems to like it."

"He does now," she replied with a smile. "When I found him, feeding him was my biggest concern. I talked to an old man living in the mountains near Denver who knew a lot about owls. He suggested feeding Screech this—what he called pemmican—because it contains meat and keeps well. The first time I tried giving it to Screech, he didn't quite know what to make of his new food or of me trying to hand-feed him. After several frustrating tries, I think he finally got too hungry to keep refusing to eat." She gave the owl the last piece of his meal, then smiled again. "It took us a while to get used to each other, but now we get along great. Don't we, boy?" she said, running her fingers over the whiskerlike feathers around his beak. "Just goes to show how adaptable we can be when we set our minds to it."

Nighthawk watched her close the cage door, then turn and start toward him, his mind lingering on her last statement.

A few minutes later, Mariah and Ethan sat down to eat their own meal. Every time she looked up, she found him staring at her. She waited for him to speak, but when he didn't, she finally said, "You're awfully quiet. Is something wrong?"

He started, then drew his eyebrows together in a frown. "What?"

"I asked if something was wrong. Every time I look up, you're staring at me."

"Nothing is wrong. I was—" He dropped his gaze, then shrugged. "I was thinking."

Mariah studied him for a few moments. The firelight flickering on his face made it difficult to determine his expression. Giving up, she looked away with a sigh. Whatever the reason for his introspection, he didn't want to share it.

After they finished eating, Ethan went to make a final check on the horses and mules, then gather more wood to use in the morning.

While he was gone, Mariah cleaned up after their meal and spread out her bedroll. She wasn't sure where he wanted his, but in his absence she decided to put his bedroll where she wanted him to sleep— eventually. Thinking about what would happen before either of them fell asleep, she smiled.

Ethan returned to camp to find Mariah sitting on her bedroll, unbraiding her hair. He watched her fingers separate the sections of her thick braid, fascinated by her expert movements and how the pale strands caught the light from the dying fire with each flick of her wrist.

He dropped the firewood he'd gathered, brushed his hands on his trousers, and moved closer. Noticing his bedroll next to hers, he lifted his eyebrows slightly but didn't comment.

"Can I do that for you?" he said, easing down beside her.

She turned her head and met his gaze. "Thanks, but I—" The look on his face caused her heart to race. She swallowed, then said, "Yes, I'd like that." She shifted so she sat with her back toward him.

He lifted the plait of hair off her neck and carefully began unweaving the rest of the braid. When he finished, he ran the brush she handed him through the silky hair until it fell down her back in shimmering golden waves. He'd never thought of a woman's hair as provocative; in fact, he'd rarely given any thought to a woman's hair at all. And he certainly hadn't expected to find the simple task of unbraiding and brushing it so arousing. Yet, like so many other facets of his life, everything was different with Mariah.

Mariah turned around and took the brush from his hand. She smiled, lifting her gaze to meet his. "Thank you. That felt won—" The smoldering gleam in his eyes made her breath catch. Certain she hadn't misinterpreted that look, she tossed her hairbrush aside, then rose to her knees and moved closer.

"Make love to me, Ethan," she said in a raspy whisper, watching his face to gauge his reaction. He looked startled by her bold request; then his eyes darkened even more, his nostrils flaring.

With a moan, he wrapped his arms around her waist and pulled her against him. Pressing his mouth to her neck, he whispered her name.

She shivered in response, her body on fire for his touch. Pushing away from him, she started jerking at her clothes. "Drat," she muttered, her fingers fumbling with the buttons of her blouse.

Nighthawk chuckled at her clumsiness. "Slow down," he said, placing a hand atop hers. "We have all night."

Her head snapped up, her gaze meeting his. The heat in his eyes made the blood pound even harder in her ears and created a wild throb between her thighs. Drawing a deep breath, she released it slowly, then managed a shaky laugh. "I don't know why I'm suddenly all thumbs." She dropped her gaze, afraid he'd see the truth reflected on her face—that her unusual nervousness stemmed from her love for him. Since theirs couldn't be a permanent relationship, she saw no purpose in letting him know she loved him. In fact, admitting her love might push him away, and she wasn't ready to give him up. Not until she had to.

When her second effort to unbutton her blouse met with success, she spared a quick glance at Ethan. "Aren't you going to undress?"

He gave her a lazy smile, then pulled his shirt up and over his head. The flexing of his arm and chest muscles made her mouth go dry. She licked her lips, then drew a steadying breath before resuming her task.

After more fumbled attempts to undress, Mariah got to her feet and finally wrestled off her clothes. Naked and breathless, she turned to find Ethan already stretched out on his bedroll. He lay on his side, braced on one elbow, his gaze holding hers for a moment before sliding lower. She stood quietly while he looked his fill.

Nighthawk had never known a woman more beautiful or more desirable than Mariah. He raked his gaze down her body to her feet, then reversed direction for a more leisurely return trip. Moving up her well-shaped legs, he lingered on the nest of golden curls for a moment before continuing his upward visual journey. His gaze passed over her belly and narrow waist to her full breasts. He watched them rise and fall with her breathing, their tips already tightened into hard peaks.

His desire surged even higher. An increasingly familiar warm ache filled his chest, then wrapped around his heart. A possible cause of the mysterious sensation crossed his mind, but he quickly shoved it aside. He wanted no distractions from what was about to take place.

Though he still didn't know why the Spirits had brought Mariah Corbett into his life, he did know one thing. He could look a lifetime and never find a woman like her. He owed his thanks to the Spirits for bringing them together, but offering a prayer would have to wait.

He shifted his gaze to her face, then said, "Come here, Mariah. I want to kiss you."

The huskiness of his voice sent a tingle up her spine. She gulped in another deep breath, then sat down on the bedroll and stretched out beside him.

He ran the backs of his knuckles down her cheek before lowering his face and pressing his mouth to hers.

Mariah moaned, wrapping an arm around his neck and pulling him closer. The scent of his warm skin, the taste of his mouth, blurred everything except her need for his kisses, his touch, the joining of their bodies.

He continued kissing her, caressing the inside of her mouth with his tongue, sucking on her bottom lip while his hand explored her back, her rib cage, her breasts. He gently pinched a nipple, then trailed his fingertips over her belly.

She lifted her hips in anticipation. When his fingers skipped over where she longed for his intimate touch and settled on her inner thigh, she moaned a protest, her hand fisting in his hair.

He chuckled into her mouth, then broke their kiss. "You are so greedy," he said, nuzzling the underside of her jaw. "We will have to work on teaching you to be patient."

"That could take a while," she replied in a breathless whisper.

"Hmm, yes, maybe a lifetime," he said against her neck, another chuckle vibrating in his chest. Then, as he realized what he'd said, that he wanted to spend a lifetime with Mariah, his amusement fled. He lifted his head, angry at himself for allowing such an impossible thought to enter his mind.

She opened her eyes to look at him. "Is something wrong?"

"No," he replied, tamping down his anger and forcing his lips to curve in a smile. "Everything is fine." He moved his hand to cup her feminine mound.

As his fingers stroked her sensitive flesh, her eyes widened. "Yes," she managed to whisper. "Yes, it is."

He leaned closer and ran his tongue across her bottom lip. "Touch me," he said, nipping at her mouth with his teeth. "I want you to"—he grasped her wrist and pulled her hand down to his erection—"touch me." He tightened her fingers around his hardened flesh, then removed his hand and slipped it back between her thighs.

As she followed his whispered instructions on how to move her hand, his breath hissed through his teeth, and his hips bucked forward of their own accord. Maybe having her touch him wasn't such a good idea. Much more of her hot hand stroking him, and his control might snap. Hoping to take his mind off his own soaring desire, he concentrated on giving Mariah pleasure.

He settled his mouth atop hers while his fingers

186

carefully opened the folds of her sex. Rasping his thumb over the swollen bud, he slipped a finger inside her. She moaned, her hips lifting off the bedroll with each stroke of his hand.

He continued kissing her. His initial gentle brushing of lips quickly deepened to a mind-spinning, breath-stealing melding of their mouths. She matched his efforts, mimicking what he did with his lips and tongue, driving him nearer to the edge. When he suckled her tongue, she groaned, then returned the favor with incredible skill.

The combination of the pull of her mouth on his tongue and the stroking of her hand pushed Nighthawk even closer to the brink. Knowing he was only seconds away from exploding in her hand, he wrenched his lips from hers. "Enough!" he said with all the strength he could muster.

Mariah opened her eyes and stared up at him. "Did I do something wrong?"

A corner of his mouth lifted. "No, you did everything too right."

Her brow furrowed. "What?"

"Nothing." Wrapping an arm around her waist, he said, "Roll with me."

She followed his instructions and soon found herself lying atop him. Propping herself up on her elbows, she smiled down at him. "Ah, this is nice." She wriggled her hips, causing his erection to jerk against her belly. She moved again to see if she got the same reaction. When she did, her smile widened. "Does this mean I'm in control?"

"For the time being," he replied, lifting a strand of

187

hair off her face and tucking it behind her ear. "What are you going to do?"

She pursed her mouth in a thoughtful frown. "I'm not sure."

His lips curved into a lazy smile. "Do what feels good."

She stared at him for a moment, then gave a quick nod. She kissed the corner of his mouth, then slid down his body so she could kiss his chest. As she touched her lips to the smooth expanse of skin, she felt the muscles bunch beneath her mouth, heard his sharply indrawn breath. She smiled against his chest, reveling in his physical response to her. Her new-found sense of power surged through her like a narcotic, leaving her dizzy and desperate to join their bodies.

Not sure how to accomplish her goal, she shifted until she sat straddling his hips, then wrapped her fingers around his manhood. His skin was hot and as soft as velvet. Moving her hand the way he'd shown her, she heard him moan, saw the tightening of his jaw.

She stroked him several more times, then, groaning with frustration, lifted herself off him. His hands came up to grasp her waist, helping her position their bodies. As he held her steady, she lowered herself with slow deliberateness.

Nighthawk fought the urge to flex his hips upward, battled the need to sheath himself inside her in one quick stroke. Squeezing his eyes closed, he allowed her to continue the torturous pace, though he wasn't sure how much more he could stand. Apparently she wasn't content with her progress either, because she abruptly finished her descent in one swift movement.

As she took his hardened flesh into her completely, she gave a soft gasp, followed by a long sigh. Seeing the pinched look on his face, she touched his cheek. "Are you all right?"

He moaned, then opened his eyes. "I do not know," he said in a raspy whisper. "I think I may have passed to the Spirit World."

She smiled. "No, you're alive." She rotated her hips, making his manhood jerk in reaction. Her smile broadened. "Very much alive."

"Good," he replied with a growl, tightening his grip on her waist. He began moving his hips in a thrusting motion, holding her firmly in place when he thrust upward, then lifting her until he nearly withdrew when he dropped his hips.

She splayed her hands on his chest for balance and let her head fall back. Catching his rhythm, she moved as one with him. Nighthawk had never seen anything more sensuous, more breath-stealing, than Mariah sitting astride him, naked, full breasts thrust forward, head thrown back, hair falling past her hips to brush the tops of his thighs. He clenched his teeth, knowing he'd soon be unable to hold back his release. But he didn't want to make the journey alone.

He released her waist with one hand and slipped his fingers down to the delicate flesh between her thighs. Rubbing the swollen bud, he continued the motion of his hips.

A few seconds later, Mariah's sharp gasp told him she had reached the peak. As her climax began, she gave a high, keening cry and dug her fingers into his chest, pushing against him faster and faster. When the spasms of her release slowed, she moaned his name, pushed against him a final time, then went limp.

She swayed and would have fallen forward if he hadn't steadied her by again clasping her waist. Digging his heels into the bedroll, he thrust into her as far as possible, nearly withdrew, then thrust again. He repeated the movements several more times, then a burst of light flashed behind his closed eyes and a roaring filled his ears. Pushing his hips up once more, he groaned as his climax crashed over him in one pulsing throb after another.

When the cloudiness in his brain cleared, he loosened his hold on her waist and eased her down onto his chest. He was shocked to realize his muscles were actually shaking from the intensity of his release. Smoothing her hair away from her face, he kissed the top of her head, his heart once again aching with the strange warmth he hadn't experienced until he'd met Mariah. This time when the probable cause came to mind, he didn't shove it aside. Instead, he forced himself to seriously consider the possibility.

The conclusion he reached greatly disturbed him, but he knew there was no other answer. Father Julian and Whitehorse had spoken the truth. His heart cared for Mariah. He loved her.

# Chapter Twelve

Nighthawk kept walking down the road that stretched out before him as far as he could see. Piishii. Piishii. He stopped, turned to look in all directions, but didn't see the bird whose call had broken the silence. When he swung back to face the road in front of him, he found it had divided. He waited, knowing the nighthawk would show him which path to follow.

He heard the bird call again, closer this time. Turning his head, he saw the speckled bird flying toward him. When the nighthawk drew even with him, it stopped, hovering in midair.

"Look for the bridge," the bird said before resuming its flight and veering down the left fork in the road.

Nighthawk followed the same path, increasing his pace to try to keep up with the bird's flight. But as quickly as the bird had appeared, it vanished from *sight. Then he spotted something farther down the road. When the image began to take shape, he slowed, then stopped. A short distance away stood a woman with long yellow hair. Mariah. He had no doubt about her identity this time. The face of the woman who'd captured his heart was clearly visible. As he watched, an owl suddenly appeared, perched on a stick Mariah held. She stroked the owl's feathers, then turned to look at him. Smiling, she made a gesture for him to follow her. Without waiting for his response, she turned and started walking toward the distant mountains.*

*Nighthawk blinked at the distinctive rocky peaks that hadn't been there just moments before. His eyes widened with recognition. There was no mistaking the mountain range as one of those in the Chokonen homeland. As he stared at the mountains, Mariah called to him. He strained to hear, but he couldn't make out her words.*

*He started running. "Wait!" he shouted. When she didn't stop, he called again. "Wait for me."*

Nighthawk awoke with a start. His heart racing, he lay still, keeping his eyes closed.

"Ethan," Mariah said, placing a hand on his arm. "Are you all right?"

He opened his eyes and turned to find Mariah lying beside him. In the pale predawn light he could see the concern on her face. He swallowed, then nodded.

"You were yelling at someone to wait for you. You must have been dreaming."

Nighthawk lifted a hand to smooth the lines on her forehead. "No, not dreaming. A vision."

"Really?" Her eyes went wide. "Can you tell me about it?"

He slipped an arm under her shoulders and pulled her against him. Running a hand over her hair, he took a deep breath, then exhaled slowly. "It began like the others," he said in a low voice, then told her all he remembered. He concluded with, "I called for you to wait, but you did not stop."

"That's when I woke you." She tipped back her head to look into his face. "I'm sorry if I interrupted your vision. I thought you might be having a nightmare."

He smiled. "You did not interrupt my vision. If the Spirits had more to show me, they would have made it harder for you to awaken me."

"Good," she replied, resettling her head on his shoulder. She ran her fingers over the smooth expanse of his chest, glad he hadn't put on his shirt after they'd made love. She loved the feel of his skin and— she pressed her nose against his chest and drew a deep breath—the scent of him. A shiver raced up her spine.

"Are you cold?" Before she could answer, he pressed her body more fully against the length of his, then pulled the blanket up over her shoulders. "Is that better?"

"Hmm, yes," she replied, deciding he didn't need to know her shiver had nothing to do with being cold.

After a few minutes, she said, "What do you think it means?"

He didn't respond for a moment. Picking up a lock of her hair and rubbing the silky strands between his fingers and thumb, he said, "The Spirits approve of my taking you to the Chokonen homeland."

"That makes sense," she replied. "But what about looking for a bridge? Do you know what that means?"

His chest rose and fell with a deep breath. "No, that part I do not understand. I saw no bridges in the vision."

"Maybe the Spirits aren't referring to a man-made bridge. Maybe they mean a natural bridge, like one made of rock that arches over a ravine or a creek."

Nighthawk frowned. "I know of such a bridge in the mountains of my homeland, but I cannot think of a reason the Spirits would tell me to look for it."

"Well, maybe the bridge isn't around here at all," she said with a yawn. "Maybe it's somewhere you'll go after we finish our field trip."

"Maybe," he replied, dropping her hair and smoothing the lock back into place.

Mariah yawned again. As she drifted into sleep, she went lax against him, a hand curled on his chest, her nose tucked against his neck.

Nighthawk smiled, tightening his hold on her. He knew he should try to sleep as well, but he couldn't stop thinking about his vision. He went over every detail again, looking for clues he might have missed, trying to decipher the message the Spirits were trying to give him about a bridge. When his contemplation turned up empty, he changed the direction of his thoughts to a more enjoyable topic: the woman sleeping in his arms.

Mariah was truly an incredible woman. Intelligent. Ambitious. Dedicated. Passionate. He smiled. Yes, definitely passionate. No wonder his heart had fallen for a woman with such a fine combination of attributes.

His smile faded. It would be better if his heart did not love Mariah, since there could be no future for them. But he knew he couldn't change what he felt for her, so he'd have to make the best of the situation. He would enjoy their remaining time together, and when that came to an end, she would leave, taking his heart with her. And then he would have to figure out how to live the rest of his life with a hole in his chest.

Two days later, Nighthawk called a halt to their journey at midday along the banks of a river that cut through a broad valley between two mountain ranges. Huge cottonwood trees lined the riverbank, providing plenty of shade, a welcome reprieve from the blazing heat of the sun.

After dismounting, he indicated the mountains to the east. "We are going there. I spent much of my life in those mountains. The White Eyes call them the Dragoons."

Mariah moved to stand beside him, gazing at the sun-drenched mountains. In the center of the range were several jagged peaks, tall, sheer-sided bluffs of sand-colored rock jutting into the clear blue sky.

She shifted her gaze to Ethan. "I'd like to take a photograph from here, if we can stay that long."

"We can stay," he replied, then turned to begin unloading the supplies she would need.

They spent several hours at the river. Then, once Mariah had taken the photographs she wanted, they repacked her gear and resumed their journey.

As soon as they left the river, Marian noticed a change in the terrain. The ground began a gradual ascent toward the base of the mountains. The valley became a lush grassland, broken by mesquite trees, ocotillo, prickly pear cactus—a few still sporting bright yellow blossoms—and the sharp-pointed agave.

They reached the foothills of the mountains late that afternoon. Ethan led them through a maze of huge boulders, clusters of oak trees, and enormous piles of rocks to the mouth of a narrow canyon. As they worked their way along a winding trail farther into the canyon, Mariah looked with wonder at the spectacular rocky outcroppings high above them.

The narrow canyon eventually opened onto a valley deep in the mountains. A stream ran through the center of the valley, fed by a nearby spring. In a clearing beneath a stand of oak trees, Nighthawk pulled his pinto to a halt.

Mariah halted her gelding not far from his horse. As she looked around them, she gave a soft gasp, her eyes wide with surprise. "Oh, Ethan. This is beautiful."

He looked at their surroundings, nodded, then dismounted. "I spent many summers here. This was one of my band's favorite places to make our camp."

"I can see why," she replied.

He led two of the pack mules to the opposite side of the clearing and started unloading their supplies.

"Tomorrow," he said, "I will take you deeper into the mountains so you can see if there is anything you want to photograph."

"I'm sure there will be." Anticipation at the prospect made her forget her saddle-weariness. She never tired of the excitement of seeing new places, the thrill of finding another of nature's wonders to capture with her camera. With renewed energy, she helped unload the mules and set up camp.

Later that evening, Mariah sat beside Ethan in front of a blazing fire. The temperature in the mountains, already considerably cooler than the desert, had dropped even more once the sun set, yet Mariah found the coolness invigorating. Or maybe her exhilaration had more to do with the man sitting beside her than the air temperature.

Nighthawk added more wood to the fire, then said, "What will you do when the Exposition closes?"

She stared at him for a moment, then shifted her gaze to the dancing flames. "I'm not sure. There are a number of options, but which one I pursue depends on how well my photographs are received at the Exposition. I sank every cent I could spare into this trip, hoping my efforts will pay off by landing me a job working for a railroad or one of the periodicals back East."

"Railroad? Why would a railroad need a photographer?"

"Owners of railroads often hire photographers to make a visual record of their construction. Or sometimes they want photographs to use in their company brochures. I met a man in Denver who once worked as the authorized photographer for a railroad. He said the company paid for his room, board, and transportation, and he was allowed to travel anywhere on their rail line. All he had to do was provide the railroad with a certain number of photographs from each negative he made. He got to keep all the negatives and could sell any of the other photographs he took."

"And you would like to be one of those authorized photographers?"

"Sure, if the opportunity comes along. Pictures of what the folks back East call the Wild West are always in high demand, so there's definitely excellent potential to make a good living as a railroad photographer. Plus we'd get to travel to all kinds of new and exciting places."

"That would be a good opportunity for you and your uncle," Nighthawk said. "You will do well in whatever job you choose."

"That's kind of you," she replied, an enormous lump forming in her throat. She'd momentarily forgotten that Ethan wasn't the other half of the *we* when she spoke of traveling for a railroad. Thankfully, he wasn't aware of her slip, thinking she meant Uncle Ned. But that did little to ease the ache in her chest. Swallowing hard, she said, "I'm really tired. I think I'll turn in."

Though Nighthawk longed to reach for her, he forced himself to remain still. She'd given him an excuse to put some distance between them, and he meant to do so. Getting to his feet, he said, "I need to check on the animals. Sleep well."

She gave him a weak smile. "You, too."

The following morning, Nighthawk led Mariah from the valley through another canyon, then up a steep, twisting trail to a narrow pass hugging the edge of a cliff. As her horse picked its way along the rocky ledge, Mariah's heart pounded with a combination of fear and excitement. She now understood Ethan's concern about the horse he'd selected for her at the stable.

After making their way over the pass, they followed an equally twisting trail down to another mountain valley, this one larger than the first. They rode a short distance into the valley before Ethan pulled his horse to a halt.

"This is where I was born."

"Really?" Mariah said, pulling back on the reins of her gelding and looking around. "How can you be sure?"

"The place where a Chokonen is born becomes holy to his family. Whenever their band travels near the area, the parents take their child to the birthplace and roll him on the ground to renew his spirit."

She stared at him for a moment. "Are you serious?"

When he nodded, her gaze swept over the valley again. "Your parents brought you here?"

"Several times."

"And they rolled you around on the ground to . . . um . . . renew your spirit?" She had to bite her lip to keep her amusement from bubbling out in laughter.

He nodded again.

Mariah cleared her throat. "I see." Though she longed to say that what he'd just told her was almost as bizarre as his fear of ghosts and owls, she kept the comment to herself. When the urge to laugh passed, she said, "It must feel good to be back in your homeland."

He frowned, shifting his gaze to stare off into the distance. "I thought I would be glad to return, but"—his frown deepened—"that is not what I feel."

Mariah reached over and placed a hand on his arm. "What are you feeling?"

He exhaled heavily. "This is part of the homeland of my Chokonen ancestors. Both my father and his father were also born in these mountains. I spent much of my life here. But now"—his voice dropped to a whisper—"this land has been taken from us. It is no longer my home."

The anguish she saw on his face, the despair she heard in his words, sent a piercing pain into her heart. She squeezed his arm. "Ethan, I'm so sorry."

He shook off her hand and jerked the pinto's reins to move the horse away from hers. "I told you before," he said, a sudden fury blazing in his dark eyes, "I do not want your pity." He pulled his gaze from hers. Then, after a moment, the harshness left his features. He released a long sigh. "Forgive me. I am not angry with you."

"I know. You're angry at the American government for what we've done to your people, for making them move from here, for taking away your home."

He nodded. "That is true. But now I wonder what good can come from allowing myself to remain angry. The old ways are gone forever. I cannot change that."

The hopelessness in his voice tugged at Mariah's heart. Though she wished she could tell him he was wrong, give him some reassurance that the old ways would survive, she feared his words were completely accurate. She hadn't given much thought to the treatment of Indians prior to her trip to the Arizona Territory. But since her arrival, the shocking policy of the American government—undoubtedly created by

200

some nincompoop politicians in Washington—had become all too clear. How anyone could treat their fellow human beings with such callous dis—

Ethan's voice jerked her from her mental ranting. "We will camp there." He pointed to a stand of trees fifty yards ahead of them. "Water is close by if you want to bathe. And there are good views of both the mountains and the valley for you to photograph."

She nodded, thankful one of them hadn't forgotten the reason for their trip.

After they unloaded the mules, set up camp, and pitched Mariah's tent, she surveyed the area for potential scenery to photograph. Ethan went with her, showing her the places he thought would provide the best views. After determining the perfect locations for setting up her camera, they started back.

"You were right," she said. "This is a wonderful place to make our camp. The views of the mountains are magnificent."

He nodded but didn't speak.

She stared at him thoughtfully for a moment, then said, "Ethan, you have a good eye for visualizing what the camera will see. That's a special talent. Some people take years to learn what comes naturally for you. I think you'd make a fine photographer."

When he made no comment, she said, "I could teach you, if you'd like."

His jaw tightened. "What would an Apache do with such knowledge? You will leave soon, taking your cameras, so what is the point in teaching me to use them?"

His matter-of-fact statement about her leaving struck her like a fist in the stomach. He was right, of course; teaching him was pointless. She never should have brought up the subject. But for a few minutes she'd forgotten she and her uncle would be leaving Tucson soon, forgotten Ethan would remain behind. She squeezed her eyes closed and tried to compose herself. "I'm sorry. I didn't think." Striving for a non-chalance she didn't feel, she shrugged. "I just hate to see natural ability go to waste."

He responded with a grunt.

She stole a quick glance at him, wondering if he'd heard the slight tremble in her voice. Seeing nothing in his demeanor to indicate he had, she eased out a relieved breath.

When they arrived at their camp, Mariah went to Screech's cage and removed the cloth cover. The owl blinked at her, then gave a soft whistle. "I'll be right back with your supper," she said, then turned to fetch his food and nearly bumped into Ethan.

"Holy Joe!" she said, pressing a hand to her bosom. "You scared the daylights out of me."

He chuckled. "Sorry. I was bringing Screech's food to you." He handed her the pemmican. "Who is Joe, and what are daylights?"

She grinned. "I don't know who Joe is. That's just an expression of surprise. One I probably picked up from Uncle Ned. And daylights are . . . my wits, my . . . um . . . mental soundness. But they weren't lit-erally scared out of me. That's another old saying."

"Ah, I think I understand," he replied. He watched her break off a piece of the dried meat mixture and give it to her owl. "I thought I knew English well. Now I am finding out there is a lot Father Julian did not teach me."

This time Mariah chuckled. "I doubt Father Julian, or anyone else, knows all the quaint expressions people use. I never thought about it before, but I guess English is a pretty complicated language." She smiled at him. "I think you know it very well, if my opinion means anything."

"Yes, it does," he replied, returning her smile.

Mariah's breath hitched in her chest. She tried to concentrate on feeding Screech, but her thoughts kept straying to the man whose smile had the power to make every nerve ending in her body throb with need.

After she managed to pull herself together, Ethan's proximity to Screech finally registered. Though uncertain of his reaction to her observation, she decided to broach the subject anyway. "Ethan, since you're this close to Screech, would you like to give him the last of his food?"

When he didn't respond, she glanced over her shoulder at him. He stood in the same spot, his gaze riveted on the owl. The tenseness of his features revealed he hadn't yet conquered his fear, but she saw none of the terror she'd previously seen in his expression—definitely a good sign.

"Ethan?"

He shook his head, crossing his arms over his chest.

"Okay. Maybe some other time." Hiding her disappointment, she gave Screech the final piece of his meal, then closed the cage door.

As she turned and met Ethan's gaze, she decided the time was right to say something else. "There's no reason for you to fear owls, because I think you have owl power."

He blinked, his eyebrows knitting in a scowl. "What do you know about power?"

"Only what you told me, but that's enough for me to decide you must have owl power." Before he could comment, she reached out and placed a hand on his arm. "Ethan, think about it. Why would the Spirits show you an owl in your visions? Why would they have you meet me and Screech? Why has nothing bad happened to you since meeting us?" She paused to let her words sink in, then said, "The only answer that makes sense is that you've been given owl power."

She watched his face closely, saw the hope flicker in his dark eyes, then quickly change to confusion.

After a moment, he shook his head. "I do not—"

"I know this is probably hard to accept, but just think about what I said." She gave him an encouraging smile. "Please."

A few minutes later, as Nighthawk gathered firewood, he did think about Mariah's claim. He had to admit he couldn't fault her logic, especially since he had no better explanation to offer for his escape from harm despite his frequent encounters with her ominous bird. But he still couldn't make himself accept her conclusion—that he'd been given owl power. He'd never known anyone with owl power, so the notion that he had been selected to possess such power was simply beyond belief.

When he returned to camp, he found Mariah sorting through one of her satchels. Glancing up, she said, "I'm going to take a bath before supper." She found what she wanted, then got to her feet. Sending him a sizzling look, she said, "Care to join me?" then headed in the direction of the pond.

His mouth hanging open, he watched the gentle sway of her hips until she disappeared from sight. Snapping his mouth shut, he tossed the firewood to the ground, retrieved a towel from his belongings, then started after her.

By the time he reached the pond, Mariah stood with her back to him, naked, arms raised to pin her braid atop her head. As he hurried to remove his clothes, he never took his gaze off her. She stepped into the pond and moved to the center, where the water reached her knees, then turned and met his gaze. She smiled, then motioned for him to join her. His heart hammering against his ribs, he stepped out of his trousers and tossed them aside.

Mariah watched Ethan move closer. He was fully aroused, the heated desire glittering in his eyes making her forget the coolness of the water.

He stopped in front of her, then held out a hand. "Let me bathe you," he said in a rough whisper.

She couldn't get a word past the tightness in her throat. Swallowing, she handed him her washcloth and cake of soap.

As he bent to wet the soap and cloth, he paused long enough to whorl his tongue around the tip of one of her breasts. She gasped at the erotic rasp of sensation, her nipple tightening even more.

When he straightened, he worked the soap into a lather, then began slowly rubbing the cloth over her body. As he bathed her, he didn't say a word. The only sounds were an occasional splash of water and the soft moans Mariah wasn't able to hold in. When he washed between her thighs, she had to grip his shoulders to keep from falling.

"Ethan." His name came out in a quavering whisper. "I can't take much more of this."

He chuckled, rinsing off the last of the soap. After tossing the soap and washcloth onto the bank of the pond, he pressed a kiss to the side of her neck. "I have only begun." He nibbled on her earlobe. "Let me enjoy you, *shijei*," he whispered into her ear.

She shivered, but not from a chill. She wanted to ask what he'd said in Apache but couldn't form the words. Not with her senses so overloaded, her skin tingling, the insistent throbbing between her thighs.

As Nighthawk moved his mouth lower, he dropped to his knees. He licked a bead of water off her left breast, then bent his head to nip her waist with a light graze of his teeth. Wrapping an arm around her legs, he kissed her belly, then slid his mouth lower to nuzzle the triangle of hair between her thighs. She jerked in reaction and tried to pull away, but he wouldn't release her.

"I want to taste you," he said. "I *have* to taste you." He opened her with his fingers and touched his lips to her sensitive bud. She gasped, the throbbing in the place beneath his mouth intensifying a hundredfold. Before she could recover from the shock, he ran his tongue over her. She gasped again, her hips bucking forward.

She grasped his shoulders, certain her knees would collapse. He held her steady while his tongue and lips continued their intimate assault.

Her vision blurred, the pressure between her thighs increasing. "Ethan, I—" She sucked in a sharp breath and tightened her grip on his shoulders. "Oh, my God, I—" Her voice rose in a joyous cry, her release sweeping over her so quickly she thought she might faint. Barely hanging onto consciousness, she felt the wild spasms rack her body until she clung to Ethan, weak, dazed, and panting.

He got to his feet, keeping an arm locked around her. He held her against his chest until the trembling in her legs stopped and her breathing slowed. Easing her away from him, he looked down into her flushed face.

"Can you stand?"

She wet her lips. "I . . . I think so," she said, her voice little more than a croak.

"Dry off and get dressed while I bathe." He started to turn away, but her hand on his arm stopped him.

"Wait." She glanced down at his erection. "What about—"

He removed her hand from his arm, then pressed his lips to the backs of her fingers. Releasing her hand, he smiled. "Do not worry about me. There will be time later, and the wait"—his smile widened to a grin—"will make the moment that much sweeter."

He spun her around to face the bank, then gave her bottom a playful slap. "Go get your towel, then throw the soap to me."

# Chapter Thirteen

Mariah lay on her bedroll beside Ethan, staring up at the nighttime sky. A thousand stars twinkled against a background of velvety black. She sighed, knowing she would never tire of looking at the spectacular sight. Just as she would never tire of the man lying next to her.

She turned her head to look at him. He was also staring at the sky, the light from the fire casting his profile in stark relief. He was such a complex man. Proud. Fiercely loyal. Intimidating. Trained to be a ruthless warrior, yet better educated than many men of her acquaintance. A gentle, considerate lover one minute, then wild and demanding the next. Her love for him swelled in her chest, rising to clog her throat. How would she survive leaving him? Never again to know his touch, taste his kiss, experience his passion. Never again see his face.

She swallowed hard. At least there was something she could do about seeing his face. If he agreed. "Ethan," she said, trying to keep the hope out of her voice. "Have you decided whether you'll allow me to take your photograph?"

He glanced at her, then turned his gaze back to the night sky. "If you still want to, I will allow it."

She smiled. "Great. We'll start tomorrow."

As Mariah drifted off to sleep, her thoughts centered on the photographs she wanted to take of Ethan. She hoped he wouldn't object to her wanting to take more than one. In fact, she wanted to take an entire series. Aside from the fact that she wanted a photograph of the man she loved, she also recognized him as an ideal subject for her work. Someone whose striking good looks and proud demeanor her camera would capture perfectly.

The following day, she took the photographs she wanted of the surrounding landscapes, then set up her smaller camera to take Ethan's picture. When she asked him to pose for a second photograph, his eyebrows arched slightly, but he complied.

Then, when she prepared for a third, he balked. "Why do you want to take so many?"

"The chances of getting a good photograph are better if I have more than one negative."

. "If that is true, why have you not done that with all the other photographs you have taken?"

"I don't have enough glass plates to take duplicates of all my landscape photographs. But since I haven't used this camera much, I have extra plates." She didn't dare look at him. Technically what she told him was true, but taking duplicate photographs was something only inexperienced photographers would do. She'd been taking photographs for so long that there was no need to use additional plates. Only rarely did she wash the chemicals off an exposed plate to reuse it because the photograph wasn't up to her usual high standards.

Ethan gave her a pensive look, then finally shrugged and moved to where she wanted him to stand.

They camped in the same spot for two more days. Mariah used the best hours of daylight to take a few additional photographs, then spent the remainder of each afternoon wandering through the mountains and exploring several other canyons with Ethan as her guide. He told her Cochise had kept the U.S. Army at bay for years by hiding his band in that mountain range—a statement she had no trouble believing, given the rugged terrain. Everywhere large boulders were piled precariously on top of one another, huge stone outcroppings above the tall bluffs with nearly inaccessible, barely visible footpaths. Only someone familiar with every rock and cranny, like Ethan, would know how to find and navigate the narrow, winding trails. The Army never stood a chance.

Although she enjoyed her days, Ethan made her nights even more memorable, far beyond anything she could have dreamed possible. The passion that blossomed so easily between them continued to gain strength each time he claimed her body. Though she knew she should call a halt to their lovemaking in order to save herself additional heartache, she couldn't bring herself to do so. Her days with Ethan would soon end, and she wanted to savor each one to the fullest.

Benita stopped outside the door of the Palace Hotel and turned toward Ned. "Are you sure this will not be too much for you?"

Ned smiled down at her. "It might've been if Doc Handy hadn't brought me this cane. Thank God I don't have to keep using those crutches." Seeing the worry in her eyes, he lifted a hand to stroke her cheek. "I'll be fine, darlin'." He offered her his arm. "While we're walking, tell me about this festival."

She looped her arm through his and smiled up at him. "*El día de San Juan*—the feast day of St. John the Baptist—is one of the most anticipated fiestas of the year."

Ned nodded, turning them to head north on Meyer Street. Though it was only late morning, the town was already abuzz. The streets were crowded, and cheering could be heard coming from the river. "So I see. Does everyone have the day off?"

"*Si,* for *Mexicanos* there is no work on San Juan's Day. In the morning, we go to Mass and pray for the summer rains we need to nourish our crops. Then the rest of the day is a celebration of our love for horses, an opportunity for the men to show off their riding skills. First is the *saco de gallo,* a contest where men on horseback run at a gallop and try to grab roosters buried up to their necks in the sand. Then there will be a promenade of young men on horseback, their sweethearts sitting in front of them. And of course there will also be many horse races and cockfights."

211

Ned's eyebrows shot up. "Cockfights! Surely, you don't enjoy such a bloodthirsty sport."

"No," she replied. "I do not approve of cockfights, but"—she shrugged—"they have been part of the *Mexicano* culture for generations. Only men attend cockfights. The women are content to watch the horse racing and wait for the nighttime festivities. The music and dancing."

"Yeah, I'm lookin' forward to those myself."

Her flush of excitement deepened. Tipping her head to one side, she batted her eyelashes at him. "Are you planning to ask me to dance, Señor Corbett?"

"Just try to stop me, Señora Solares," he replied, flashing her a cocky grin.

"Your cane will not prevent you from dancing?"

He stopped, then turned to face her. "Don't you go worryin' yer pretty head about this cane. I won't be needin' it while I'm holdin' you in my arms."

The hunger in her eyes made Ned want to haul her against him and kiss her senseless, but the middle of the street wasn't the appropriate place for such a demonstration. Clamping down the desire running hot through his veins, he said, "If you keep lookin' at me like that, darlin', I'm liable to turn us around and head back to the hotel." Dropping his voice, he added, "And if that happens, we might not come outta my room till mornin'."

Benita held his gaze, seeing her own need mirrored on his face. She swallowed, then said, "I love you, Ned."

"Ah, darlin' Benita, I love you, too," he replied, his voice gruff with emotion.

Her bright smile faded. "When is Señorita Corbett coming back?"

"I don't know. Not for at least a week, I reckon. Maybe longer."

She nodded but didn't respond, the happiness in her eyes changing to sadness.

"Benita, what is it?"

"When Señorita Corbett returns, the two of you will leave Tucson to go to the big Exposition you told me about."

"Mariah has worked long and hard to make a name for herself. Her bein' asked to display her photographs at the Centennial Exposition is a great honor and well deserved. I can't disappoint her by not bein' there to share such a fine occasion."

"*Sí*, I know," she replied, her bottom lip quivering. "But what about us?"

"I haven't thought that far ahead. You've got to remember, I've never been in love before, so I don't know exactly what I should be doin'. But I've waited a lifetime for you, and I don't want to lose you." He touched her cheek. "Don't worry, I'll figure out somethin'."

She nodded, blinking away her tears. "We must go," she said, giving him a watery smile. "I want to introduce you to my sister and her family. I told her we would meet them at the Courthouse Plaza."

After Mariah and Ethan loaded the mules, she followed him from the canyon where they'd camped for three days. He led them down the eastern slope of the mountains, back to the desert and another broad, flat valley.

213

"Tomorrow night, we will camp there," he said, pointing across the valley to the east. "In what my people call Land of the Standing-Up Rocks."

As Mariah looked at the mountain range that rose from the desert floor to dominate the eastern horizon, she repeated the name several times in her head. Turning her gaze on Ethan, she said, "With such an interesting name, I can't wait to see the mountains up close."

"They are called the Chiricahua Mountains by the White Eyes. But when you see the heart of the mountains, you will understand the reason for the name my people gave them."

She nodded absently, her gaze moving back to the distant and intriguing mountains.

Though Ethan said they would've been able to cross the valley in one day if it were just the two of them on horseback, the pack mules slowed them down. They spent the first night camped near a spring, resuming their journey at first light the next day.

By the time they arrived at the base of the mountains and Ethan led them to the mouth of a canyon, the sun had sunk low in the western sky. They followed a creek deeper into the canyon until they reached the place he'd selected for their camp.

The site wasn't far from the rocky banks of the creek, on a flat strip of ground surrounded by thickets of oak trees, several varieties of pine, and junipers with deeply grooved bark.

As Mariah helped unload the mules, she drew a deep breath of the pine-scented air. "I love the smell of a forest," she said. "So clean and fresh. Living in a place like this would be wonderful."

Nighthawk looked at her over the back of one of the mules. "I thought you liked traveling too much to live in one place."

"I do. But someday, when my photographs earn enough so I don't have to work all the time, I'd like to have a place where I could spend at least a few months each year."

Nighthawk thought about her response. The idea of traveling part of the year and having a home to go to for the remaining months caused a surprising pang of envy. Seeing the places he'd read about in Father Julian's books appealed to him, but as he'd told White-horse, he had no plans to leave the land of their ancestors. Not when he didn't know the Spirits' plans for his future. But maybe he should reconsider. He had the money he'd saved from the wages Father Julian paid him, and he remembered Mariah saying there were places where his Apache blood wouldn't matter. So maybe after she left Tucson, he would travel—with or without the Spirits' blessing. He'd have to do something to fill the emptiness in his life.

As Mariah and Ethan went through their routine of setting up camp, she thought he was unusually quiet. And later, his lovemaking was especially aggressive, taking her on an even wilder ride of sensual discovery and mind-boggling satisfaction. Though she wondered at the reason for his behavior, she kept silent. There were things she didn't want to tell him, so not prodding him for answers seemed a safer choice. No need to get into a discussion that might lead in a direction better avoided.

The following morning, Nighthawk accepted a cup of coffee from Mariah, then said, "Today, we will leave our supplies and mules here and ride higher into the mountains. Once you decide on the places you want to photograph, we will move our camp if possible. If not, we will use one or two of the mules to carry your equipment to each location for a day."

Mariah nodded. "Good idea." She stared into her coffee cup for a few moments, then lifted her gaze to meet his. "What does *shijei* mean?"

When he frowned at her, she said, "You said it again last night, so I was . . . uh . . . just wondering what it meant."

Nighthawk took a drink of coffee, then said, "It is Apache for *my heart*." He shrugged. "I must have said it when my mind was clouded with passion."

"Oh," she replied, staring at him for a long moment and wishing she hadn't asked. She shouldn't care that he claimed to have said the words only because of a moment of passion. Probably men, and even women, throughout the ages had said things they didn't mean while their minds were clouded with passion. Yet knowing he hadn't meant the endearment, hadn't begun to care for her, came as a crushing blow. Her mind told her she shouldn't let his casual brushing aside of the words bother her; after all, she didn't want a permanent relationship either. But her heart told her a different tale. Her heart wanted him to care for her, even return her love.

She jerked her gaze from him, silently chastising herself for allowing the secret hopes of her heart to creep into her thoughts. She had to finish her photographic field trip and head for Philadelphia. That had to be her one and only priority.

A few minutes later, they left their camp on

horseback, going deeper into the canyon before start-
ing up a narrow trail that wound around one of the
mountain peaks.

When they reached the summit, Nighthawk halted
his pinto on a rocky ledge and waited for Mariah. She
stopped her horse beside his, then followed his gaze
to the valley far below them. Her eyes went wide,
and she gave a soft gasp.

Nighthawk smiled and turned to look at her. He
didn't speak, taking great joy in watching her reaction. Her initial surprise quickly changed to disbelief,
then to astonished delight.

She glanced over at him, her cheeks flushed, eyes
sparkling. "This is . . . this is"—an infectious laugh
bubbled out—"unbelievable."

His smile widened. "Now you see why my people
call this the—"

"Land of the Standing-Up Rocks," she said in a
breathless voice. "The name is perfect. Absolutely
perfect." Her gaze drifted over the spectacular sight
stretching out below them. Hundreds of odd,
extraordinary rock formations—massive stone col-
umns, towering red-rock spires, and huge boulders
perched delicately on small carved pedestals—filled
the valley.

Mariah forced her gaze away from nature's
magnificent handiwork and turned to look at Ethan.
"I can't wait to take photographs of—" She looked
over her shoulder and frowned. "We'll be able to get
my photographic equipment up here, won't we?"

"Yes. The mules will have no trouble with the
trail."

"Tomorrow. Can we come back tomorrow?"

He chuckled. "If the weather is good. Yes, we will come back tomorrow."

She looked up at the perfectly clear, deep blue sky and frowned. "You think it's going to rain?"

"Summer storms are always possible. They strike quickly, filling a clear sky with dark clouds in a matter of minutes. Lightning can be very fierce, especially here. It was in these mountains that lightning almost struck me."

"When you had your first vision?"

"Yes. That day was as clear as today. Then suddenly a storm came over the mountains. We need to watch the sky for such a storm and take care not to get caught in the open."

"But you have lightning power," she said. "I thought that would protect you."

"That is true. But I do not know if my power will also protect you."

"Power can extend to someone besides the person who has it?"

He nodded. "Some power helps and protects only the one who received it. Other power might extend to the person's family or an entire band, as a medicine man uses his power to cure the sick.

"Because my people fear lightning, they will not ride a pinto during a storm, they hide everything that is red, and they will not eat until the storm ends. After I received lighting power, I no longer had to do those things. But I have never tested my power to see if I am the only one it protects."

"Well, if we get caught in a thunderstorm," she said, flashing him a smile, "I'm willing to find out."

Nighthawk couldn't help returning her smile. "Are

you saying you trust the power of Apache Spirits to protect you?"

"I guess I do, because I trust you to protect me," she replied, her smile fading.

"That troubles you?"

She shook her head. "That's not what—" She drew a deep breath, then released it slowly. "No, that doesn't trouble me."

Nighthawk stared at her for a moment, waiting to see if she would say anything else. When she didn't, he swung his pinto around. "There is more I want to show you."

Mariah sighed, then turned her horse to follow his. She'd almost slipped and told him she trusted him because she loved him. Her gaze moving over him and the way he rode his horse so effortlessly, she considered telling him her feelings. Then maybe he'd say he—Pressing her lips together, she gave herself a mental kick for allowing such a fantasy to enter her head.

Not long after they stopped at a creek to water the horses and let them rest, Mariah noticed a change in Ethan. The horses had rested only a few minutes when he abruptly announced it was time to leave. Though he hadn't been overly talkative, he became less so after they left the creek, and he seemed edgy, as if he were expecting something bad to happen.

Mariah made no comment until they reached their camp and dismounted. "Ethan, are you going to tell me what's wrong?"

"Why do you think something is wrong?" he replied, not turning to look at her but continuing to unsaddle his horse.

"I've been around you long enough to tell when something isn't right. Something happened when we stopped to water the horses. All of a sudden you said we had to get back here."

When he didn't respond, she said, "Did you hear something? Or see something?"

Nighthawk blew out his breath with a huff, then turned. "On the other side of the creek, I saw many horse tracks."

Mariah's brow furrowed. "Tracks? Someone else is in these mountains?"

"Perhaps. The tracks were several days old."

"You think whoever made those tracks will come back?"

"I do not know. It is possible."

"Could it have been an Army patrol?"

"No. Army horses have shoes. The tracks I saw did not."

She stared at him for a long moment, then said, "So what does this mean? Will I be able to take my photographs?"

"Yes, but we must be more careful. I do not want to leave you alone any longer than necessary, so I will stop hunting. And I want you to keep your gun near you at all times."

She swallowed but nodded.

They finished unsaddling their mounts in silence. Then, while Ethan led the horses to the creek and checked on the mules, Mariah fed Screech, her carbine within easy reach.

After several days of moving through the mountains—setting up camp in different canyons, then hauling

Mariah's photographic equipment to the locations she'd selected—without coming across more hoof-prints, Nighthawk began to relax. But he didn't re-scind his instructions to Mariah about keeping a weapon close by. And although he'd resumed hunting to add fresh meat to their diet, he stayed as close to their campsite as possible.

On their fifth day in the mountains, Mariah took the last of the photographs she wanted and began packing for their return trip to Tucson. By late after-noon she had her glass plates and chemicals all wrapped and carefully packed in their crates. As she made sure her cameras were properly secured in their strongboxes, Ethan told her he was heading to the creek to bathe. She nodded absently, her heart heavy with the knowledge that their time in mountains more beautiful than she could describe would end the fol-lowing morning.

She and Ethan would have the time it would take them to get to Tucson, then perhaps as much as a week more while she developed her latest group of negatives and arranged for her trip to Philadelphia. But then—She squeezed her eyes closed, the sharp pain in her chest making it difficult to breathe.

She opened her eyes, determined to finish her task and not let her thoughts dwell on anything but the moment. Once her cameras were packed to her sat-isfaction, she looked around camp, contemplating what she should do next. The sound of approaching horses interrupted her thoughts. In one movement, she grabbed her carbine, turned, and lifted the weapon to her shoulder.

When the riders came into view, her eyes widened, but she maintained her stance. As the Indian in the lead entered the clearing, he pulled his horse to a halt. The rest of the riders halted their horses abreast of his. There were six of them, including, to Mariah's surprise, a young woman. All had long straight black hair with strips of cloth in a variety of colors tied across their foreheads. The men were bare-chested; the woman wore a fringed buckskin shirt.

"Who are you," Mariah said, "and what do you want?"

None of them spoke, but after a moment, the leader touched his heels to his horse's sides to move the animal forward.

Mariah raised her voice and said, "Don't come any closer, or I'll shoot." She racked a shell into the carbine to emphasize her words.

She wasn't sure if the man understood, though his expression changed to what she thought could be labeled amusement, but he didn't stop. After his horse took a couple more steps toward her, she lowered the barrel of the carbine and pulled the trigger. The bullet hit the ground a few feet in front of the horse's hooves, sending up a spray of dust and dirt. The horse nearly reared, dancing sideways to avoid the sting of flying pebbles.

"I warned you," Mariah said, racking another shell into the carbine. "Now, what do you want?"

The rider didn't reply, easily controlling his horse with his knees, his anger-filled gaze locked on hers.

"Do you speak English?"

Again Mariah received no reply. She glanced briefly at each of the other riders. "Do any of you speak English?"

"Some of them do," a voice said from behind her.

Mariah nearly sagged with relief. Not lowering her carbine, she glanced over her shoulder to see Ethan step into the clearing and start toward her.

When he stopped beside her, she said, "Do you know them?"

"Yes," he replied, moving his gaze over the riders. He knew several of them and recognized the others. "The one who is trying your patience is Tseeltsui—Eagle Tail. He and the others refused to move to the reservation at San Carlos."

Eagle Tail dismounted and took a step toward Nighthawk. "We refused," he replied in the guttural Apache language, "because we will not live like cattle. You also did not go to San Carlos. You left our people to live among the White Eyes." He raked an insolent gaze over Mariah. "And now you are hiding behind the skirt of one of them."

Nighthawk clenched his jaw against the urge to make an angry retort. He knew Eagle Tail's words were meant to provoke him, but he refused to take the bait. Crossing his arms over his chest, he remained silent.

Mariah eased the hammer forward on her carbine, then lowered the weapon to waist level. Eagle Tail was shorter than Ethan and whipcord lean. He wore knee-high moccasins similar to Ethan's and an unusual garment the likes of which she had never seen. A long piece of fabric hung from his hips on some sort of belt, falling to his ankles in the back and to his knees in front. The open sides of the garment provided a glimpse of his bare thighs when he moved.

From what she could tell, the other men were dressed the same way.

Eagle Tail's sound of disgust jerked Mariah's gaze back to his face.

"I think you are no longer Apache," he said to Ethan, refusing to use English. "You speak the language of the White Eyes, live in one of their towns, dress like one of them." He indicated Mariah with his chin. "You even have your own White Eyes whore."

The muscles in Ethan's jaw worked. Determined not to let Eagle Tail goad him into doing something he'd regret, he drew a deep breath, then released it slowly. At last, he said, "You do not speak the truth. I am Apache. I will always be Apache. But the old ways of our people are gone."

"How can you say that?" Eagle Tail's eyes flashed with fury. "If all our people would fight, we could take back what is ours, could keep the old ways."

Nighthawk shook his head. "I wish that could be. But the Chokonen cannot defeat the White Eyes. Even with all other Apache bands fighting beside us, it would not be possible. The White Eyes have too many soldiers. They will keep sending more until they have killed all Apache."

When Eagle Tail's only response was a glare, Nighthawk said, "I speak the truth. If you refuse to believe my words, you will die fighting for what can never be."

Mariah had no idea what the two men said to each other, but there was no mistaking the tension hanging thick in the air.

A string of loud hoots suddenly broke the strained silence. Mariah bit back a groan. She'd completely forgotten about Screech. She sneaked a glance at Ethan, and relief washed over her. Other than a slight stiffening of his back, he hadn't reacted to Screech making his presence known. She shifted her gaze back to Eagle Tail. The color of the man's face had changed from copper to a sickly gray, his eyes wide with fear, his mouth hanging open—the same horrified expression Ethan had worn the first time he saw Screech.

Eagle Tail kept his gaze locked on Ethan and took a step backward, then another. When he bumped into his horse, he spun around and vaulted onto the animal's back in one lithe motion. Grabbing the reins, he looked at the others. In a choked voice, he said, "We must go. Nighthawk has powerful new medicine."

He whirled his horse around, then jabbed his heels into the animal's sides. In a flurry of movement, the others quickly turned their horses and raced down the trail behind him.

# Chapter Fourteen

Mariah waited until the sound of pounding hooves faded before speaking. "I'm sorry Screech scared off your friends."

Nighthawk turned to look at her. "I know Eagle Tail, but I do not consider him friend. As a boy, he always caused trouble, always wanted to be important." His gaze moved back to where the riders had disappeared from view. "Now he leads a group of renegades and thinks fighting will bring back the old ways of our people." He heaved a sigh. "He would not listen to me."

"He's fighting for what he believes in. I thought you would agree with that."

"Fighting for your beliefs is honorable. But continuing a fight that cannot be won is foolish. Apache training teaches the objective of war is to kill the enemy without losing even one of our warriors.

Retreating is not a disgrace." He sighed again. "Eagle Tail will never retreat. He and those who follow him will die for his foolishness."

"You tried to tell him. If he's killed, you can't blame yourself for his death."

Nighthawk frowned but didn't reply.

After a moment of silence, Mariah said, "Anyway, I'm sorry about Screech's poor timing."

The corners of his mouth lifted in a weak smile. "I thought his timing could not have been better. I was not sure I could convince Eagle Tail to leave. Insults were not enough for him. He wanted to fight. Screech stopped him."

"Insults! What did he say to you?"

"He said I was no longer Apache. That I have turned into a White Eyes, hiding behind the skirt of my—" He sucked in a deep breath and released it slowly. "What he said does not matter. He is full of hatred and lets his anger speak for him."

Mariah wasn't sure how to respond. Although Ethan tried to brush off Eagle Tail's rude behavior, she had the impression he hadn't accepted the excuse he gave her. Unsure what that meant, she decided to change the subject.

"Once Eagle Tail heard Screech," she said, "he didn't waste any time getting away from here. The look on his face was priceless. He looked just like—" She cleared her throat. "Uh . . . never mind. So what did he say before he rode off?"

"He told the others they had to leave because I have"—his brow furrowed—"powerful new medicine." He glanced at her, then added, "*Medicine* is another word for *power*."

Mariah's eyes widened. Flashing a smile, she said, "See? I told you. You have owl power. Do you believe me now?"

He didn't respond for a moment. Finally, he said, "I understand why you think that is true, and perhaps it is what the Spirits intend. But"—he turned to face her—"I have not been given owl power. Not yet."

Her smile faded. "So, you don't want one of Screech's feathers to put in your medicine bag?"

Nighthawk's gaze shifted to the owl's cage. He studied the small bird in silence for a moment, then shook his head. "It is too soon for that."

"I don't understand why you—" She blinked, remembering their discussion about obtaining power. "Ah, the Spirit of the owl hasn't spoken to you."

"No. I cannot acquire new power until that happens."

Mariah nodded. "It will. I have no doubts." As she turned to finish packing, she realized she hadn't said the words simply to placate Ethan. She actually believed them. Though she'd initially thought the entire notion of everything possessing power and people acquiring that power totally ridiculous, she now accepted the idea without so much as a qualm. Something else that had changed because of her love for Ethan.

She had neither planned nor expected to fall in love, and certainly not with a man whose way of life was so at odds with her own. Yet now she not only found herself deeply in love with Ethan Nighthawk, but her beliefs also had undergone a change, expanding to accept the ways of the Apache.

She gave her head a shake, hoping to clear her

mind of such thoughts. Somehow she had to stop her heart from taking control of her life. Photography was her life. It had to be.

"Mariah, are you all right?"

She started, Ethan's voice pulling her from her musings. Propping her rifle against one of the wooden packing crates, she glanced up at him and managed a smile. "I'm fine."

He crossed his arms over his chest; his dark eyes narrowed to stare into her face. "Would you have shot Eagle Tail if I had not returned to camp when I did?"

"Only as a last resort. I would've given him every opportunity to prevent that, but"—she drew a shuddering breath—"if he'd pushed me too far, I would have pulled the trigger."

"And what about the others? Would you have shot them?"

Her lips flattened. "Yes, to defend my life. Or yours. I told you, I'm an excellent shot. I wouldn't have missed."

Nighthawk nodded, biting the inside of his cheek to halt a smile. He didn't doubt her words in the least. "Whitehorse was right. He told me you would make a fine warrior," he said, surprised to hear himself say the words aloud.

"Who's Whitehorse?"

"A friend. I have known him since we were boys. He is the one who saw you fight with the woman in Tucson."

She gave him an embarrassed smile, then nodded for him to continue.

"Whitehorse also said that any man would be proud to have you fighting at his side. After watching you face a skilled Chokonen warrior like Eagle Tail, I agree."

"Thanks," she replied, trying not to let his words affect her but unable to completely squelch the surge of joy pumping through her veins. "That reminds me. There was a woman riding with Eagle Tail. Is that common among the Apache?"

"It is not forbidden for Apache women to ride with the warriors from their band, but it does not happen often. Apache girls spend their early years learning what they must know to become wives and mothers and taking care of younger brothers and sisters. They are not taught the skills of a warrior, but when they get older, a few choose to go with the men on raids or into battle. Some are widows. Others want to be with their husbands. And sometimes a woman chooses to ride with the warriors because she has special powers."

"What special powers?"

"Ones that can be used to help in raiding or fighting the enemy. I heard Little Star had such powers."

"Little Star? Is that the name of the woman riding with Eagle Tail?"

He nodded. "She was called Little Star as a child. She is sister to Black Wolf, a man I have known for many years. I have not seen Little Star since she was perhaps fourteen, so I do not know if she has been given a different name." He turned his head to look down the path the riders had taken. "I wonder if Black Wolf knows she rides with Eagle Tail."

"Would he object?"

"Little Star is many years younger than Black Wolf and had a wild side, not the calm nature of most

Apache women. He was very protective of her and the only one who could control her wildness." He turned back to look at Mariah and sighed. "I have not seen Black Wolf in many years. But if he is still the man I used to know, I do not think he would approve of his sister riding with a band led by Eagle Tail."

Mariah studied his face for several seconds. "What about you? Do you approve of her choice?"

"I do not know her reason for being part of Eagle Tail's band. Perhaps it is because of her special powers. Or perhaps it is because she shares his frustration and his hatred for what has been done to our people. If that is true, I understand. I, too, feel those things. And I understand why she and the others refused to go to San Carlos. But I do not approve of what they are doing. They cannot run forever. The White Eyes will not let them or any other Chokonen remain free. It is only a matter of time before Washington orders their soldiers to find those who would not go to San Carlos. The only chance our people have to survive is to live in peace with the White Eyes."

Mariah's heart ached at the pain and hopelessness she heard in Ethan's voice. Once again she longed to offer her aid, to try to ease his suffering. But knowing the futility of such a gesture, she kept her desire to help to herself.

She drew a deep breath and exhaled slowly. "I have a few more things to pack, then I'll fix supper." When her gaze fell on her rifle, she said, "It's okay to stop keeping my carbine near me, isn't it? Surely Eagle Tail won't come back now that he thinks you have owl power."

A smile teased the corners of his mouth. "I think

Eagle Tail's fear of owls is enough to keep him away. But if I am wrong, your skill with a rifle will be." His smile faded. "But to be safe, keep the weapon near you until after we leave these mountains."

"You think we'll run across another band of renegades?"

He dropped his arms to his sides. "I thought most Chokonen who would not go to San Carlos went far to the south, in the mountains of Mexico. Since Eagle Tail came back, it is possible others will, too."

Later that evening, Mariah lay in Ethan's arms, her body totally relaxed. His lovemaking had been particularly intense, guiding her to two closely spaced, incredibly powerful climaxes before he'd allowed himself to take his own pleasure. As her pulse slowly returned to normal, she ran a hand over his chest in lazy circles, loving the feel of the smooth, heated skin, the well-defined muscles beneath her fingertips.

"Ethan?"

"Yes," he replied in a drowsy voice.

"What do you call what Eagle Tail was wearing?"

"A breechcloth."

"Do all Apache men wear them?"

"It is the traditional clothing of Apache males. In winter they also wear a buckskin shirt and leggings."

"You wore a breechcloth like that?"

"Yes, when I lived with my people."

Mariah fell silent for a minute. Then, pushing herself up onto one elbow, she looked down into his face. "Do you still have a breechcloth?"

He opened his eyes a slit. "Why do you want to know?"

"I'd like to take a photograph of you wearing it."

He closed his eyes again, his lips twitching with a smile. "Are you sure that is the reason? Or could that be an excuse so you can see my legs?"

She leaned closer and pressed a quick kiss on his mouth. "Don't tell me you've forgotten?" she whispered, then gave his bottom lip a quick nip with her teeth. "I've already seen your legs"—she soothed her bite with a stroke of her tongue—"along with every other part of your body."

"It is true," he replied, laughter rumbling in his chest. Opening his eyes, he lifted a hand to thread his fingers through her hair. "I have a breechcloth in my room in Tucson," he said with a smile. "If it would please you, I will wear it so you can take a photograph of me."

She returned his smile, love squeezing her heart and pushing up to fill her throat. She swallowed hard, fighting the strong urge to say the words aloud. When she'd regained control, she kissed his smiling mouth, then managed a raspy thank-you before settling back beside him, her head tucked between his neck and shoulder.

The following morning, not long after dawn, Mariah followed Ethan from their camp and began their journey out of the Land of Standing-Up Rocks. Every few minutes, she looked over her shoulder, trying to commit everything she saw to memory. Images to add to the photographs she'd taken and the memories she'd accumulated from the days and nights spent with Ethan. Images she would recall in the years ahead. After she left Tucson, her nights would be much different, no longer spent in the arms of the man she loved. She'd have to be content with her memories.

An image flashed in her mind. Nighttime. She sat in a room. Alone. The glow of a lamp flickered on her gray hair, her gnarled hands, and the photographs lying in her lap. Photographs she'd taken of Arizona and Ethan. The cameras in the room told her she'd continued doing the work she loved, but the rest of the scene made her shudder. The sadness, the loneliness, the emptiness of her life as an old woman with only memories and fading photographs to fill the long hours of another night.

Mariah squeezed her eyes closed, trying to will the unsettling image from her mind. But her efforts didn't entirely erase the mental picture she'd painted of her pitiful future.

Nighthawk noticed Mariah's withdrawn mood, the way she'd slumped in her saddle. The sad, almost haunted look on her face tore at his own heavy heart. He clenched his teeth, determined not to think about anything except getting her safely to Tucson. Then, once she boarded a stage and left town, he'd have to deal with the emotions swirling inside him, find a purpose for his life. Lifting his face to the sky, he offered a brief prayer to the Great Spirit, asking for the strength he would need to endure the coming days.

Late in the afternoon, several days later, Nighthawk turned in the saddle to look at Mariah. "There is a spring not far ahead. We will camp there."

She nodded, then halted her horse and pulled her

hat from her head. After wiping the dampness from her forehead, she resettled the hat back in place. With a sigh, she nudged the gelding to follow Ethan's pinto over the valley's rolling terrain.

As she crested one hill, she heard voices. Her heart pounding with concern at what she might find, she pulled back on the reins, slipped her carbine from its scabbard, and dismounted. After tying the gelding to the branches of a mesquite tree, she racked a shell into her rifle before creeping toward Ethan. When she spotted him standing beside his horse, she eased out a relieved breath and shifted her gaze beyond him. Sitting cross-legged near a fire pit sat another man—a Chokonen, unless she was mistaken.

She lifted the barrel of her carbine and inched closer, stopping a few feet behind Ethan. Before she could say anything, he spoke.

"There is no need for your gun, Mariah. Bearclaw is a friend."

She uncocked the rifle and moved to stand beside Ethan. After he made the introductions, he said to Bearclaw, "I am surprised to see you. I heard you had taken a long journey."

Bearclaw nodded. "It is true. But I have been back a few days. I came here because I was told you needed my help."

"A dream sent you here?"

When Bearclaw nodded, Nighthawk turned his gaze on her. "Bearclaw and Whitehorse, another friend I told you about, were with me when I was nearly struck by lightning. We all had visions that day. Bearclaw was told his visions meant he would

235

acquire bear power and also become a dream shaman."

Mariah's eyebrows lifted. "What does that mean? Dream shaman?"

Nighthawk looked back at Bearclaw and saw his friend nod his permission. "Bearclaw lives his life based entirely on his dreams." When Mariah opened her mouth to speak, he held up a hand to silence her.

"Yes, I follow my visions, too. But Bearclaw's dreams are about more than his own life. He also uses his dreams to help others against sickness and danger. And sometimes others come to him to have their dreams explained. His great knowledge makes him a dream shaman."

Mariah studied Bearclaw in silence for a moment. He was a handsome man, his features similar to Ethan's. The same coppery skin, dark eyes, high cheekbones, and straight black hair, parted in the center and hanging past his shoulders. But his nose was straighter, his mouth a little fuller, with deep smile lines on both sides. She couldn't determine his height, but his chest was broad, his arms and legs muscular. At last, she said, "I understand. The Spirits told you to come here because they knew Ethan would be here."

Bearclaw grinned, deepening the grooves around his mouth, then said something in Apache to Nighthawk.

Nighthawk's chuckle brought Mariah's gaze back to him, her brow furrowed. "What's so funny?"

"Bearclaw said you are a rare find. Most White Eyes would not accept the words I just told you so easily."

"Well, I wouldn't have a few weeks ago," she said to Bearclaw. "Ethan has made me view life from a whole new perspective." She glanced at Ethan. "Things I thought were totally impossible I now know can actually happen."

Bearclaw looked at the two for a moment, then nodded. "*Nzhu.*"

Nighthawk jerked his gaze from Mariah to Bearclaw. Amusement sparkled in his friend's eyes.

Mariah watched a muscle jump in Ethan's jaw, his lips flatten. When he didn't speak, she said, "What did he say?"

"He said it is good."

"What's good?"

Ethan's eyes narrowed. In a soft voice, he said, "I do not know." Turning back to Bearclaw, he raised his voice to say, "We would like to share your camp, but Mariah has a pet owl. You may not want us to—"

"You are welcome here," Bearclaw replied, acting as if he hadn't heard Nighthawk's statement.

"You're not afraid of Screech?" Mariah said.

Bearclaw smiled again. "If Screech is an owl, yes, I am afraid. You have been told all Apache fear owls?" At her nod, he said, "You and the owl are welcome to share my camp." He met Nighthawk's gaze, then added, "With your new power, I am certain no harm will come to me."

Nighthawk heard Mariah's soft gasp of surprise and started to open his mouth to dispute Bearclaw's words. Changing his mind, he moved closer to his friend and said, "It is good to see you."

Mariah watched Bearclaw get to to his feet and the two men embrace. "I'll fetch my horse and the mules," she said, though she doubted either man heard her. As she walked away, the sound of their low voices drifting to her, she wondered where Bearclaw had learned to speak nearly flawless English. Untying her horse, she made a mental note to ask if he'd also been a student of Father Julian.

While the three of them sat around the fire eating their meal, Mariah kept Bearclaw busy answering her endless questions. Where had he learned English? What was it like being a dream shaman? And anything else she could think of to ask.

Then, after a momentary lull in the conversation, she said, "Why do you think Ethan needs your help? I mean, he isn't sick or injured, and Screech took care of Eagle Tail and his renegade band before trouble started."

"Eagle Tail?" Bearclaw looked at Nighthawk. "I heard he would not go to San Carlos."

"Yes, and many others as well." Nighthawk quickly told Bearclaw about Mariah's confrontation with Eagle Tail, concluding with how the warrior and his band had been scared off by Screech. When he finished, he said, "Now you see why Mariah asked why I needed your help. I wonder the same thing."

Bearclaw shifted his gaze back and forth between Nighthawk and Mariah, then shrugged. "The Spirits did not tell me why."

"Maybe the Spirits were wrong," Mariah said. "Is that possible?"

Bearclaw stared thoughtfully at her for a few seconds, then said, "That has never happened." Seeing the concern on her face, however, he decided to placate her. "Perhaps this time will be different." Her smile of relief told him he'd made the right choice.

Later than evening, after Mariah had turned in, Nighthawk banked the fire, then rose and joined Bearclaw on the opposite side of the campsite.

After a few minutes passed, Bearclaw said, "Mariah Corbett is a special woman. I can understand why you care for her."

Nighthawk hesitated briefly before deciding to answer honestly. "Yes, she is special, like no other woman I have ever known. I care for her more than I thought possible."

"And she cares deeply for you."

Nighthawk flicked a glance over his shoulder to where Mariah lay curled up in her blanket. "She has not said the words."

"Sometimes words are not necessary. There are other ways to know what is in another's heart."

Nighthawk frowned. "Maybe it is better not to know."

"Why would you not want to know?"

"There can be no future for a Chokonen Apache and a White Eyes woman. Knowing she cares for me would make watching her leave more painful."

Bearclaw mulled over Nighthawk's statement, then said, "Have the Spirits told you there is no future for you and this woman?"

"No, but Mariah did. She does not want a husband."

"Then you must change her mind."

"I did not say I wanted to be her husband," Nighthawk said in a fierce whisper.

"Not in words. But I see how you look at her. How

she looks at you. Your futures can be one. I believe this to be true."

Nighthawk stared off into the darkness for a long time, then shook his head. "I do not see how."

"When the time is right, the Spirits will show you."

Though Bearclaw's words offered a seed of hope, Nighthawk squelched the urge to grab the seed, plant it, then encourage it to take root and grow. To do so would be foolish. Regardless of what his friend believed, even if Mariah returned his love, he saw no way for them to have a future together.

The following morning, Nighthawk accepted Bearclaw's help to load the mules. As they worked, Nighthawk said, "Will you travel with us?"

Bearclaw shook his head. "I must take a different path."

"Another dream?"

"Yes, but like in your visions, the Spirits have not told me everything. Sometimes they send me dreams that I understand. Like the one that told me to come here to see you. Other dreams are not complete." He looked off across the valley. "This dream told me which way to travel but nothing more."

"It has been good seeing you," Nighthawk said. "I hope our paths cross again soon."

"I wish that, too."

The men worked in silence for a few minutes, then Nighthawk said, "The Spirits must have been wrong about my needing your help."

"I do not think they were wrong."

"What do you mean?"

"I gave you help. You just do not realize it. The Spirits did not mean for me to protect you from physical harm. They wanted me to help your mind and your heart."

Nighthawk frowned. "I do not understand."

"You will," Bearclaw said with a smile. "As I told you last night, when the time is right, the Spirits will speak to you, and you will understand everything."

Nighthawk stared at his friend for a long time. Releasing a heavy sigh, he loaded the last of the boxes onto one of the pack mules.

A short time later, Bearclaw bid Nighthawk and Mariah good-bye, then watched them ride away. After a few minutes, he mounted his horse and rode off in the opposite direction.

Two days later, Mariah and Ethan arrived back in Tucson. Though she knew the wise thing to do would be to cut all ties to him as quickly as possible, she couldn't bring herself to take her own advice. She selfishly wanted to spend as much time with him as she could—their separation would begin soon enough—so she asked him if he'd like to help her develop photographs from her latest group of glass negatives. When he agreed, relief washed over her.

Nighthawk helped Mariah take Screech and her personal belongings to the hotel. He waved hello to Ned from the doorway of the Corbett suite, then pulled her back into the hall for a lingering kiss.

"Do you want to come in?" she said in a breathless voice.

"Yes, but I am leaving," he replied, running the backs of his knuckles down her cheek. He brushed another kiss on her moist lips. "I have things I must do, but I will be back in the morning."

"Okay," she said, gathering the thick strands of his hair in her hands and pushing it over his shoulders. "I won't start developing the photographs until you get here."

After another scorching kiss, Nighthawk forced himself to pull away. He stared at Mariah for a few seconds, then turned and walked down the hall. At the head of the staircase he stopped, flashed her a quick smile, then started down the stairs.

Mariah returned his smile, hoping he couldn't see how her lips trembled. As soon as he disappeared from sight, she sagged against the wall, squeezing her eyes closed. *Dear God. I love him so much. How will I ever survive life without him?*

A full minute passed while she pulled herself together. Releasing her breath with a long sigh, she straightened. She couldn't let her uncle see her in such a miserable state. Ned would badger her until she confessed all, and she didn't want that to happen. Pasting what she hoped would pass for a happy expression on her face, she turned and entered the hotel suite.

As soon as she shut the door behind her, Ned called to her from his usual spot by the window. "Come over here, girlie." He waggled his fingers at her.

"Are you all right? Is your leg bothering you?"

"No, my leg's fine. Good as new. I got somethin' for ya."

In spite of the melancholy that had settled over her, the excitement in her uncle's voice piqued her curiosity. "What is it?"

He held out an envelope. "You got a letter. Looks real important."

"A letter? Who's it from? Didn't you open it?"

"It's addressed to you. But if you'd been gone any longer, I mighta opened it anyway."

Mariah took the envelope from her uncle. Her hands shook as she fumbled to get it open. Pulling out the sheet of paper, she unfolded it and quickly scanned the letter's contents. She let out a whoop of laughter, then looked at Ned. "It's from the editor of the *Philadelphia Photographer*. He wants to meet me at the Exposition to discuss terms of employment. As a special correspondent."

She reached down and pulled her uncle to his feet, then threw her arms around his neck. "Oh, Uncle Ned, this could be the opportunity we've worked so hard for!"

Ned grasped her waist and spun around, then held her away from him. "That it is, girlie, and well deserved. But yer the one who did most of the work. Just think about all the great places you'll get to visit. All the great photographs you'll take."

"*We'll* get to see." As the look on Ned's face registered, her smile faded. "You will be going with me, won't you?"

"Sit down, Mariah. There's something else I need to tell you."

The tone of his voice erasing the last of her excitement, she took a seat beside him on the settee.

Ned drew a deep breath, exhaled slowly, then said, "I asked Benita to marry me. We would've done it already, but since yer the only family I got, I wanted to wait till you got back. Now that yer here, I'll speak to Benita about making the final arrangements. We're figurin' on goin' with ya to Philadelphia. That'll be our honeymoon trip. And we'll stay until the Exposition closes, but then"—he swallowed hard—"Benita and me are comin' back here. Her brother-in-law offered me a partnership in his freight business, and I accepted."

Mariah stared at her uncle, her mouth agape. She knew Ned had fallen in love with Benita, so the news of their impending wedding shouldn't have been such a shock, yet his announcement stunned her. Closing her mouth, she gave him a genuine smile. "I'm so happy for you and Benita," she said, leaning over to give him a hug and kiss his cheek.

"Then yer not mad at me?"

"Mad at you? Why would I be mad that you found the woman you want to be with for the rest of your life?"

"But I won't be yer assistant anymore. Aren't ya mad about that?"

Mariah sighed. "No. I admit, finding another assistant as good as you will be difficult. But the Exposition runs through November, so I'll have plenty of time to find the right person."

Ned chuckled. "Well, that's certainly taken a load off my mind." He reached over to pat her hand. "Now tell me all about yer latest field trip."

Mariah did as Ned asked, carefully hiding her worry that, in spite of her words to the contrary, she would not be able to find a suitable replacement for him. The only person she could imagine working as her assistant wouldn't be interested in the job.

# Chapter Fifteen

Mariah spent a restless night, tossing and turning, her few snatches of sleep filled with disturbing dreams. Tormenting scenes of her exhibit being a miserable failure, her photographs the laughingstock of the entire Centennial Exposition. Then the scene shifted to one she'd imagined a few days earlier—an old woman sitting in a small room, alone and gravely unhappy. As the identity of the woman became apparent, Mariah cried out her shock and despair at seeing herself in her such pitiful circumstances. Her cry awakened her, ending the troubling dream but also her attempts to sleep.

As she unpacked the supplies she would need to make paper prints from her glass negatives, each troublesome dream replayed in her mind in vivid detail. Though they were all deeply disturbing, surprisingly it wasn't the dream where her work hadn't been well received that bothered her most. That distinction fell to the glimpse she'd had of herself as a desperately lonely old spinster.

What if her dream was an accurate prediction of what lay ahead for her? The possibility made her shudder. She closed her eyes and drew a deep breath. *Now I sound like Ethan. Thinking dreams and visions can really predict the future.* Blowing out her breath with a huff, she opened her eyes. Determined not to dwell on her depressing thoughts, she continued with her task.

A few minutes later, she took a step back and looked over the supplies she'd set out. She nodded with satisfaction. Yes, everything she needed was there. The only thing missing was Ethan.

As if responding to her mental cue, a knock sounded on the door.

Mariah crossed the room, tried to calm her racing heart, then opened the door. Seeing Ethan in the hallway, one shoulder leaning against the doorjamb, instantly lifted her sagging spirits. Smiling, she said, "Come in. I have everything ready."

Nighthawk returned her smile, then straightened and moved into the parlor. Looking around, he said, "Is your uncle here?"

"No, he went to see Señora Solares." Recalling the reason for Ned's sudden departure that morning and what his marriage meant to her career, Mariah's lightened mood slipped.

Ethan turned and arched an eyebrow at her. "Ah, so we are alone."

Mariah glanced up and caught the sparkle in his eyes, the flash of his teeth in a rakish grin. "Yes, but we have work to do," she replied, trying to sound businesslike.

He sobered. "Of course. Your work always comes first."

Mariah opened her mouth to make a comment, then decided she didn't need to defend her work to him or to anyone. Instead, she moved to the table and said, "If you'll join me, we can get started."

Nighthawk crossed the room to stand beside her. Looking at the supplies on the table, he noted the wooden trays, several bottles of chemicals, and a stack of paper. On a chair beside the table sat the crate containing her carefully wrapped glass plates.

"If you recall," she said, "I told you the paper used for photographs has been specially treated. So before we can transfer the negative image on this glass plate"—she pulled one of the plates from the crate— "to a positive image on paper, we must first sensitize the paper."

She set the plate aside, then picked up one of the bottles. "To do that, we need to dip the paper in two solutions. The first is chloride of sodium." She poured the solution into one of the large wooden trays on the table. "And the other contains nitrate of silver." She selected another bottle and poured the contents into the second wooden tray.

"Now, the paper is dipped in the first bath, then in the second, and finally placed on the glass plate."

Nighthawk watched Mariah, fascinated as always by her competence as well as the process she demonstrated.

A few minutes later, she lifted the paper from the glass plate. "Now we let it dry."

Nighthawk looked at the photograph in her hand, instantly recognizing the distinctive peaks of the mountains. A quick, sharp pain squeezed his heart and caused his breath to catch. His voice raspy, he said, "The mountains of my birth."

The obvious emotion in his response touched Mariah deeply. "Yes. You can keep it if you'd like. I can make another for my exhibit."

He looked up to meet her gaze. "Are you certain?"

She nodded. "That's why this photographic process is so much better than any of the older ways. Several hundred pictures, perhaps more, can be made from one glass plate, all as good as the first one."

His gaze drifted back to the photograph in her hand. "Then, yes, I would like to have this one."

"If there are others you'd like, just say so."

As they continued developing more of the photographs Mariah had taken on their last field trip, her eyes grew heavy, and she fought the urge to yawn.

"You did not sleep well?" Ethan said, studying her face.

"No," she replied, keeping her gaze averted from his. "Every time I fell asleep, I had awful dreams that woke me."

"Do you want to talk about them?" When she didn't respond, he said, "Sometimes when you speak the dream aloud, it will no longer be so bad."

She yawned, then shook her head. "They weren't that bad. I mean, they weren't nightmares, exactly. They were just . . . well . . . disturbing, I guess."

He stared at her for another moment, then turned his attention to watching her work. After several minutes, he surprised himself by saying, "I also did not sleep well last night."

"Did you have bad dreams, too? Is that why—" Her gaze snapped to his face. "You had another vision!" At his nod, she said, "Will you tell me about it?"

Though he wished he'd kept quiet about his visions, he realized he wanted to tell her, needed her input in trying to decipher the vision's meaning. He drew a deep breath, released it slowly, then began speaking in a soft voice. "The path I walked down did not divide this time. But, like in the other visions the Spirits sent me, the nighthawk appeared. He said again to look for the bridge. That I must look harder to find the bridge."

"And you still don't have any idea what bridge the nighthawk told you to find?"

When he shook his head, she said, "If it isn't a real bridge, then maybe the Spirits are speaking symbolically. They might mean something that acts like a bridge, something that connects two things."

"I have considered that. It is possible but does little to help me find such a bridge."

She gave him a sympathetic smile. "I guess that's something you'll have to figure out for yourself."

He nodded, knowing that the puzzle of finding a bridge was only the first of several issues he had to figure out.

They continued working together to develop more of the glass negatives, speaking only occasionally. As with the other phases of photography Mariah had explained to Ethan, he learned this step quickly. She glanced over at him, realizing again that his competence made him the perfect candidate to become her permanent assistant. And their personal relationship would be a wonderful bonus to such an arrangement.

As she selected another glass plate, she scowled. She had to stop thinking about a permanent anything with Ethan. She'd made her choices in life, had her goals, and she wasn't going to do anything to risk her career as a photographer. Then why did the plans she'd carefully laid out for herself no longer seem as appealing? Was it because Uncle Ned wouldn't be there to share each new experience with her? Or was it because her plans meant nothing without the man she loved?

Ah, there was the crux of the matter. She'd fallen in love. She closed her eyes for a moment, wishing she could go back in time. If she had a second chance, she would build an impenetrable wall around her heart, keeping her feelings for Ethan restricted to desire. But then she opened her eyes, traced his proud profile with her gaze, and knew the truth. She never could wish away her love for him. A love that strong would last until her dying breath. Having made that realization, one question remained. Was she going to do anything about it?

Over the next few days, Mariah developed the rest of her photographs, selected those she would include in her exhibit and wrote a caption for each, made her travel arrangements, and sent a telegram to the men at the Colorado Pavilion in Philadelphia to let them know when to expect her. The days passed quickly in spite of her efforts to make each one last as long as possible.

Then she awoke on the morning of her uncle's wedding—her last full day in Tucson. The following afternoon, she and the newlyweds would board a stage bound for San Diego. From there they would take a ship up the coast to San Francisco, and finally a train would take them cross-country to Philadelphia. Thinking about the long, hard journey filled her with both anticipation and dread. She couldn't wait to reach Philadelphia and get started on her exhibit, but she dreaded saying good-bye to Ethan. And she absolutely refused to think about never seeing him again.

Once again she hadn't slept well; the heat and her wildly fluctuating thoughts made for another fitful night. As she bathed and dressed for the wedding, she tried to shake her listlessness—a mood she knew had more to do with Ethan than lack of sleep.

She still hadn't told him about her uncle's decision to return to Tucson. When she'd asked Ned not to mention his plans to Ethan, he gave her a strange look but complied with her request. She wasn't sure if she hadn't told Ethan that she would be looking for a permanent assistant because she feared he'd offer to take the job, or because she was afraid he wouldn't.

Father Julian conducted Ned and Benita's wedding ceremony before a handful of guests: Benita's sister, her husband, and their children, several family acquaintances, Mariah, and Ethan.

The flickering of candlelight gave everything and everyone in the church a soft glow—an appropriate and beautiful setting, Mariah mused, for a couple pledging themselves to each other. By the time the service ended, tears filled Mariah's eyes—not because

251

her uncle's marriage meant the end of their working relationship but because of the unconditional love and joy she saw reflected on the faces of Ned and his new bride.

As she dabbed at her eyes, she cast a quick glance at Ethan from beneath her lowered lashes. What was he thinking? Had the reciting of vows, the joining of two people for life in the bonds of holy matrimony, affected him as strongly as it had her? As usual, she couldn't read his expression, his features carefully schooled not to reveal what went on behind those dark eyes.

She turned her attention back to the couple standing at the church altar, wondering at her reason for getting maudlin over a wedding. Her reaction had to be a combination of watching her only living relative get married, her lack of sleep, and her nervous anticipation of finally arriving at the Exposition. She decided that had to be the reason, since she certainly couldn't be crying because she envied her uncle. Given her firm position on marriage, that was too ridiculous to contemplate. Her breath caught in her throat. Or was it?

After those in attendance congratulated the newly proclaimed Mr. and Mrs. Ned Corbett, they all went to the home of Benita's sister, who had prepared a celebration meal. By midafternoon, the guests began leaving. Mariah and Ethan were the last to say their good-byes.

She kissed Benita's cheek and offered her congratulations again, then crossed the room to speak to her uncle.

The joy on his face was impossible to miss. Smiling at him, she said, "I love you, Uncle Ned, and I'm so happy for you."

His eyes turned misty. "Thanks, girly. I never thought my life could be any better than it was but"—he sniffed—"since I met Benita, I just can't tell ya how happy I am." He wrapped his arms around her and pulled her against his chest for a tight bear hug.

Mariah laughed, then whispered, "Since this is your wedding night, I think you should have the hotel suite all to yourself."

"What? That's not necessary," he replied, loosening his grip to hold her at arm's length. "Besides, where would you stay?"

"Don't worry about me." She glanced over to where Ethan stood talking to Benita. "I'll be fine."

Ned followed Mariah's gaze, then frowned. "I know ya ain't never said nothin', but I can tell you care about him. After the rocky start Nighthawk and me had, I wasn't sure we'd get along. But I gotta admit, he's a damn fine man." He stared at her for a moment. "I know ya didn't ask for it, but I'm gonna give you some advice anyway. A lotta folks go through an entire lifetime without findin' love. I damn near did. If ya love the man, don't throw it away."

Mariah's gaze snapped back to her uncle's face. "I'm not a child. I know what I'm doing."

"I hope so, girlie," he said, pulling her into his arms for another hug before releasing her. "I surely do hope so."

After Mariah and Ethan made their exit, they headed for the main section of town, walking beside each other in silence. After a few minutes, he said,

"This will be your last night in Tucson. Do you have plans?"

"Nothing except leaving Uncle Ned and Benita alone on their wedding night."

"Do you have another place to stay?"

"No, I haven't thought about it."

He reached for her arm, then stopped and turned her to face him. "You could spend the night with me."

She looked up at him, an enormous lump lodged in her throat. Swallowing hard, she managed a smile. "What would Father Julian say?"

His lips curved in a quick grin. "If he found out, you would not want to know. He is very good at giving lectures." His amusement fled. "But he will not find out. He does not live near my room."

Mariah needed only a second to make up her mind. "I have a couple of things I need to do this afternoon, but after that I'm all yours."

He stared at her for several moments, the strength of the possessiveness her words created catching him by surprise. *Mine. Yes, Mariah is mine.* A deep ache settled around his heart. *At least for one more night.* Refusing to allow himself to think about anything beyond the coming hours, he summoned the strength to smile. "Come to me as soon as you can. I will be waiting."

Mariah nodded, her love growing, expanding inside her until she thought there couldn't possibly be room left for her lungs to fill with air.

Mariah followed Ethan's directions to his room without any problem, arriving a little after six that evening. Never having been to where he lived, she took careful note of everything about the room and its sparse furnishings, wanting to remember even the smallest detail.

With silent indulgence, Nighthawk watched her look around. She ran her fingers over the small desk, picked up the books piled there to check their titles, then carefully put them back in the same order. When she finished her perusal, he said, "Have you eaten since we left your uncle and his wife?"

Mariah swung around to meet his gaze. For a moment she considered lying; then she shook her head. "Food probably would stick in my throat."

He nodded. "It is the same for me." Grabbing her hand, he said, "Come. It is cooler outside." He tossed a blanket over his shoulder, then led her to the door.

She followed him outside and across the rear yard to the shaded area beneath a lone tree, a secluded spot away from prying eyes and cooled by a light breeze. He spread the blanket on the ground and motioned for her to have a seat.

"Mmm, it's much better here," she said once she had settled beside him. She tipped her head to one side, listening to the whisper of the wind caressing the tree, enjoying the soft rustle of leaves above them.

"I come here when it is too hot to sleep inside."

"I can see why. You must miss the mountains on nights like this."

"Yes. Even in the summer, the nights are cool in the mountains of my people."

She nodded, remembering how soundly she'd slept in the mountains and wishing—She shoved the thought aside before it totally formed, refusing to think beyond the present.

They sat side by side, not speaking, content just to be in each other's company. Mariah saw a flash of lightning streak across the western sky, caught the faint rumble of distant thunder.

"A storm's coming," she said.

Ethan turned his head to look toward the west. "Perhaps. Sometimes storms lose their strength and do not reach here." Unable to bear not touching her a moment longer, he wrapped an arm around her and pulled her against him.

She sighed and let her head fall against his shoulder. "Ethan, I—"

"Shh, do not talk," he said in a whisper, shifting so he could lower his face closer to hers. "Let us enjoy this time."

Mariah drew a deep breath, his scent causing her head to swim. "Make love to me." She cupped the side of his jaw with one hand and pressed a gentle kiss to his lips. "Make me forget everything but the two of us here and now. Give me more memories to fill the long nights ahead."

Nighthawk thought his heart would break into a thousand pieces. Part of him wanted to completely eradicate Mariah from his brain so he wouldn't have to face the pain of her leaving. Yet, like her, another part also wanted more memories of their time together. Forcing himself to concentrate on only the present, he said, "We have all night to make memories." He ran his tongue over her bottom lip. "For both of us."

Though he throbbed with the need to tear off her clothes and take her quickly, he reined in the urgency pounding in his veins. Using every bit of self-restraint he could muster, he slowly and carefully pulled the pins from her hair, then loosened the silky mass so it tumbled over his hands and past her shoulders in a thick cascade of gold.

He pressed a soft kiss to her mouth, then eased her onto her back. After spreading her hair on the blanket in a sunburst pattern, he shifted so his upper body angled across hers. Then he spent a great deal of time just kissing her. Using every skill he'd learned and inventing more techniques of his own, he mixed gentle, barely touching kisses with more insistent, almost savage fusings of their lips.

As he guided her along in a dance of desire, her breathing became ragged, the fingers of one hand tightening in his hair, the other digging into his shoulder with increased force. He lifted his head, slowing the pace of the dance for a moment. She moaned, and her eyelids fluttered up. Blinking several times, her gaze finally focused on his face.

He smiled at her dazed expression. Running his fingertips down one flushed cheek, he said, "*Shijei,* you are even more beautiful when you are aroused. Your eyes become the color of the trees high in the mountains of my people. Your lips become red and plump like the berries Chokonen women gather in the summer."

Mariah flashed a smile. "Better be careful, or such silver-tongued flattery just might turn my head," she said, trying to keep her tone light. "With your exceptional skill at using flowery words, I bet every woman you've ever spoken to that way has fallen at your feet."

Nighthawk studied her in a silence for several seconds, his eyebrows drawn together in a frown. "I have never spoken words like that to any woman."

Her smiled widened. "Really?" She ran her fingers down his throat, noting that the wild pounding of his pulse matched hers. "Then I'm glad I was the first to inspire such charming behavior."

He nearly told her she was the first for far more than inspiring his newly acquired ability to recite pretty words, but he stopped himself in time. Admitting she was the first person he'd told so much about himself, the first woman to capture his heart, would serve no good purpose, not when their parting was only hours away.

He pressed his lips together, narrowing his eyes in a glare. "Apache warriors do not want to be called charming."

Her eyebrows lifted. "No, I suppose they don't." She wrapped her arms around his neck and pulled herself up so that their mouths were just an inch apart. "Don't worry," she murmured, tracing his upper lip with the tip of her tongue. "Your secret is safe with me."

He pressed his lips together with more force, but it didn't help. A chuckle worked its way up from his chest, shattering the mock fierceness he'd tried to maintain. Moving his hands to cup her face, he held her still while he brushed his lips over hers. Then, suddenly, a gentle touch wasn't enough. Grinding his mouth to hers, he swept them back into the dance of desire with the speed of lightning. He heard her gasp, felt her fingers slide from his shoulders and clutch his forearms. Keeping his mouth sealed to hers, he lowered her onto the blanket a second time.

The wildness of his kiss demanded her response, which she gave with a groan and the quick stab of her tongue into his mouth. White-hot need roared through his veins. A buzzing sound filled his head. Teetering on the brink of losing control, he fought to clear his senses. The battle raged for several minutes while he tried to counteract her assault on his rapidly declining defenses.

Somehow he recovered enough to make himself wrench his mouth from hers. Drawing a ragged breath, he closed his eyes for a moment, praying for strength and for the throbbing in his groin to ease.

When his senses finally righted themselves and the ache of raw need receded to a manageable level, he opened his eyes. His hands shaking slightly, he reached for the buttons on the bodice of Mariah's shirt.

As he removed each piece of her clothing, he mixed lingering kisses on her mouth with moist kisses on each newly exposed patch of skin. By the time he pulled the final garment from her body, she trembled with need, her breasts heaving with her labored breathing.

"Ethan. Please. I need—"

He pressed his fingers to her lips. "Shh. I know what you need, *shijei*. Be patient, and you will have it."

"I can't," she said with a moan, rolling her head from side to side. "I can't take anymore."

He bent toward the hardened peak of one breast. "Yes"—he laved his tongue over the rosy tip—"you can." He pulled the nipple into his mouth and suckled hard.

She gasped, pressed her heels into the blanket, and arched her back. "No, I can't." The last word ended in a high-pitched wail.

He lifted his head, kissed the tightly puckered nipple, then moved lower. He spent a moment exploring her navel before continuing his downward journey. Nuzzling the soft curls at the base of her stomach, he opened the moist folds with his fingers and touched her intimately with the tip of his tongue.

Mariah's breath hissed out from between her gritted teeth; her fingers curled into fists. Garnering all the strength she could, she said, "Ethan, stop toying with me." She winced to hear that her words sounded more like a pathetic whine than the assertive command she wanted.

He chuckled. "Toying," he said, nudging her legs apart. "An interesting way to put what I am doing." He nipped the inside of one thigh, then soothed the bite with a lingering kiss.

"Do I have to beg? Is that—" She drew a shuddering breath. "Is that what you want?"

"No, *shijei,* I do not want you to beg." He slipped a finger inside her, rubbing his thumb over her most sensitive place. Her hips bucked against his hand. "This is what I want," he whispered, continuing to move his thumb over the hardened bud in an unhurried rhythm. "To give you great pleasure."

"You're . . . certainly . . . doing . . . that," she said between gasping breaths. "So could you"—a moan vibrated in her throat—"do it a little faster?"

Nighthawk laughed, thoroughly delighted with the woman lying naked before him. "Still impatient." He clucked his tongue. "We will have to work harder on teaching you patience."

In spite of her pleading, he didn't relent. He took her close to her peak twice before he finally pushed her high enough to fly over the edge.

When Mariah's heart slowed enough to stop the thundering in her ears, she blinked away the fuzziness in her brain, then met Ethan's amused gaze.

She managed a halfhearted punch to his ribs. "I should be mad as hell at you."

His eyebrows lifted. "What did I do?"

She pushed herself up onto her elbows. "Don't play the innocent with me, Ethan Nighthawk. You darn well know what—" His mouth pressed to hers ended whatever she'd started to say.

When he broke the kiss, she said, "That's not fair." She scowled at him. "All you have to do is kiss me, and I melt like lard dropped in a hot frying pan."

He pulled his shirt over his head and tossed it aside. "I like that I make you melt. And quiver." He flashed a cocky grin. "And scream my name."

Before she could reply, he stretched out on his back and pulled her atop him. "I think I should make you scream again."

Though she tried to pretend outrage over his arrogance, she failed miserably. And as his lips found hers, she no longer cared. All she wanted was to experience more of the incredible skill of her Apache lover.

They alternately made love and dozed until well into the night. When the first splats of rain began, Ethan wrapped Mariah and their clothes in the blanket and carried her back to his room. There they made love again, the thunder drowning out Mariah's screams, before they fell into exhausted sleep.

Mariah awoke first, just as the blue-black velvet of the nighttime sky began to lighten with the pink blush of dawn. Not wanting to disturb Ethan, she lay quietly beside him, remembering the previous night, then re-evaluating her life, the goals she'd set for herself, her future. She turned to look at Ethan, his handsome face relaxed in sleep. Her heart nearly bursting with love and longing to awaken beside him every morning, she made a decision.

She gave his arm a gentle shake. "Ethan."

He awakened instantly, blinked his eyes, then turned his head toward her. "What is it?" he said in a sleep-roughened voice. After searching her face and finding no sign of panic, he curved his mouth into a lazy smile. "Again?" He touched her swollen lips. "I cannot believe how greedy you—"

"That's not why I woke you," Mariah replied, her cheeks growing hot at the reminder of her insatiable hunger for him during the night. Pulling herself together, she said, "We need to talk."

# Chapter Sixteen

Nighthawk's light mood dissolved instantly. "Maybe we should get dressed first."

She nodded, then rose and started pulling on her clothes. When she finished, she turned to find Ethan staring at her. She licked her dry lips and said, "Uncle Ned isn't going to be my assistant any longer. Now that he's married, he doesn't want to travel all the time. He and Benita are going to Philadelphia with me, but after the Exposition closes, they'll be coming back here. Therefore, I . . . um . . . I need someone to be my assistant on a permanent basis."

She studied Ethan's face, but other than slightly arched eyebrows, his expression revealed nothing. After a moment, she dropped her gaze to a spot on the floor. "Anyway, I'd like you to be that someone." She swallowed the lump of apprehension in her throat. "I need you to be my assistant, but, more important, I need you to be my husband."

When he didn't respond, she forced herself to look at him. "I love you, Ethan, and I want us to get married."

Long seconds passed before he spoke. "I thought you were not interested in marriage. That you would not risk your career as a photographer."

"That's true. I did feel that way. But I've done a lot of thinking about my attitude about marriage, and I realize I was wrong. I still don't want to give up being a photographer. But if you were to ask me to, then I . . . I guess I would, because I love you, and I want us to be together. It's too late to arrange a wedding here, but as soon as we reach San Diego, I'm sure we could find someone to marry us before we board a ship to San Francisco."

Nighthawk moved to stare out the window. Of all the things Mariah could have said to him, an offer of marriage was definitely not on the list. For a moment, he let himself consider what accepting her proposal would mean. He would have a chance to travel and to learn more about photography, perhaps even become a photographer himself. He would get to spend every day with Mariah, sleep beside her every night. He drew a deep breath, then exhaled slowly, knowing his daydreams were just that. Finally, he said, "I would never ask you to give up doing what you love, but I cannot marry you."

Mariah's heart sank. "I understand. You don't love me, so why would—"

"No," he said with a growl, spinning around to face her. "That is not the reason. I do love you."

Her heart soared at the words, then plummeted. "Then what is the reason?" When he seemed reluctant to answer, she said, "Is it your visions? The Spirits haven't told you it's okay to marry me, so you'll just let your love wither and die?"

"Yes. No." He rubbed a hand over his face. "I do not know what I mean."

"Talk to me, Ethan. Help me understand."

He moved to the bed and sat down beside her. "I do not know what my future holds. The Spirits have not revealed that to me. I do know that I would not like to let my love for you die, but I see no other choice. I am Chokonen Apache. You are a White Eyes. The life-ways of our people have many differences, too many differences for us to live as husband and wife."

"Yes, we're from different cultures, but that should only enhance our relationship. Learning from each other, taking what each of us brings to the marriage, blending those differences to form a new, richer life for ourselves. I've already learned a lot from you. I told Bearclaw you taught me to view life from a whole new perspective, remember? And I hope you'll teach me more. A desire to learn is one of the things we have in common. And we both enjoy and appreciate being out in the open, exploring what nature has created. I sense you've already begun to appreciate photography, and I'd enjoy teaching you more if you'd like. I'm sure you'd love traveling as much as I do, visiting places you've read about, plus lots of other wonderful sites."

She paused to draw a deep breath. "And you can't deny that we're compatible in a physical sense." Ignoring the blush heating her face, she continued. "With all of those things as a base, plus the most important one, our love for each other, we can make it work."

He stared at her thoughtfully for a moment, then gave his head a shake. "Some of what you say is true. But I have done things you may never be able to forgive. I have raided and killed. Things you hate."

"Yes, I hate the thought of raiding and killing. And when you first told me you did those things, I admit I was disturbed. But that was before you explained why raiding became a necessary part of the Apache way of life. I'm not saying I approve. Even if the raids are for food, it's still stealing to me. But I do understand why your people believed they had no other choice. And I promise you, I'll never hold your past against you." When he didn't look convinced, she said, "Do you plan to do more raiding and killing?"

"No. The time for the old ways has passed."

"Right, and now it's time to concentrate on the present and the future—our future."

He didn't respond, his jaw clenched, his eyes turning cold.

The sinking sensation in Mariah's chest changed to an icy prickle of apprehension. Ignoring her uneasiness, she said, "We would have a great life. Traveling. Taking photographs. There are so many places I want to show you. So many new places we can see and explore together. Doesn't that sound wonderful?"

He continued looking at her with the same detached expression, making no attempt to answer, giving no indication he'd even heard what she said.

Her frustration over his continued refusal to respond caused her temper to flare. She lifted her chin and glared at him. "I knew you were afraid of owls, but I didn't think you were also afraid of love."

Other than the slight tightening of his mouth, he didn't react, and he didn't speak.

As quickly as her temper had flared, it cooled. Her apprehension returned, intensifying into full-blown fear. The pain in her chest made breathing nearly impossible, made the backs of her eyes burn. She blinked away the tears, then cleared her throat. "Well, I . . . uh . . . guess I'd better leave."

When he said nothing to stop her, she got to her feet and crossed the room to the door. Keeping her back to him, she swallowed her pride and said, "Think about what I told you, Ethan. Please." She drew a deep breath, then added, "I'll be taking the afternoon stage, and I'd like you to go with me."

She opened the door, then turned to look at him for what she hoped wouldn't be the last time. In a choked whisper, she said, "I love you, Ethan Nighthawk." After gazing at him a moment longer, she stepped outside and softly closed the door behind her.

After Mariah left, Nighthawk continued to stare at the door, unable to move. Apache warriors were taught to withstand great physical pain without making a sound, but nothing in his training had prepared him for the devastating emotional pain ripping at his heart. How would he endure the days, the weeks, the months ahead?

He needed to clear his mind, to find some peace, to ease the ache of letting the woman he loved walk out of his life. A long time passed before he made a

decision and rose from the bed. He quickly gathered
what he needed and stuffed everything into a rawhide
bag. At the door he looked back to see if he'd missed
anything, carefully keeping his gaze away from the
photograph Mariah had given him. Seeing nothing
else he wanted to take with him, he left to find Father
Julian.

Later that afternoon, Mariah stood in front of the
stage station, watching her luggage and photographic
equipment being loaded onto the stage that would
take her away from Tucson. Away from Ethan. Her
usual attentiveness to the handling of her equipment
was broken by her periodic glances up the street. Each
time she looked away from the stagecoach, a flicker
of hope blossomed in her chest. Hope that Ethan had
taken her last words to heart and thought about their
future. Hope she would see him walking toward her.
By the time the last of the luggage had been secured
and the driver called for the passengers to board the
stage, Ethan hadn't appeared. The last of her hope
shriveled and blew down the street with the desert
wind.

Nighthawk rode his pinto out of Tucson, heading for
the mountains he and Mariah had visited several
weeks earlier. In the Land of the Standing-Up Rocks,
he would go to the holy home of his lightning
power—the place his power was first revealed to
him—to seek answers. Because the path his life had
taken left him unable to deal with the confusing emotions roiling inside him, he feared his power had deserted him. So he would go to the source of his power,
where he would pray and sing to the Spirits, then wait

for a sign assuring him he had not been abandoned.

From first light until well past sunset, he pushed his pinto at a relentless pace, stopping only when necessary to water and rest the horse. He ate little, and after finding sleep elusive the first night, he gave up trying.

Weak and exhausted, he rode into the valley where he'd received his first vision. But as soon as he dismounted and took a deep breath of the fresh mountain air, his exhaustion began to fade, and the crushing ache in his chest began to ease. He exhaled, certain his decision to make the journey had been the right one.

After seeing to his horse, he gathered wood, small pieces of bark, and dried grass. He dug a shallow hole, placed the bark and grass in the bottom, then reached for his rawhide bag and removed his *kuugish*—fire-making stick. Lighting the fire took much longer using the fire-stick, but he needed to show the Spirits he hadn't forgotten the ways of his people.

He placed a flat piece of a sotol stalk next to the grass and bark, inserted the tapered, blunt end of the fire-stick into a small hole carved in the sotol, then began twirling the stick between his hands. When sparks ignited the grass, he removed the fire-stick and piece of sotol and carefully added more bark. As the flames consumed the grass and bark, he slowly arranged larger pieces of wood atop the blaze.

When the wood caught fire, he sat back on his haunches, pleased by his efforts. He hoped the rest of his stay in the mountains would be as satisfying.

But the first days of his quest for answers proved to be the opposite. He still had trouble sleeping, and the Spirits remained silent. A week later, he spent an entire day praying and singing to the Spirits. When darkness fell, he was more exhausted than he'd ever been. He stretched out on his blanket and almost immediately fell into a deep sleep.

*Nighthawk stood in the middle of the road. Ahead of him, the road divided. Unable to see anything down either path, he didn't know which to take. So he waited. He knew he'd soon hear the call of the nighthawk. Then the bird would appear and tell him which path to follow.*

*When long minutes passed and the nighthawk's call did not reach him, he grew anxious. Glancing all around, he finally noticed a dark spot in the sky off in the distance. He concentrated on that spot, watching it come closer until he could see the movement of wings, yet he heard nothing. He frowned. The nighthawk always made sounds—its distinctive call and the flapping of wings. But the bird flying toward him did so in complete silence.*

*As Nighthawk watched in amazement, the bird gently landed on the road in front of him, folded its wings, then blinked its huge yellow eyes. The bird was not a nighthawk. It was an owl.*

*He wanted to ask what had happened to the nighthawk, but he knew he must wait for the owl to speak first.*

*"You are not afraid of me," the owl said. "That is good."*

*"Your presence startled me, but I am not afraid."* When the owl didn't respond, Nighthawk said, *"Why are you here?"*

"To find out if you have a desire strong enough to learn the songs and prayers of the ceremony for a new power."

Nighthawk nodded, knowing he would be put to a test to determine if he was worthy of receiving owl power.

The owl blinked several times, then said. "You have been told to look for the bridge."

"Yes."

"Yet you have not done this."

"No. I have tried, but I do not know what to look for."

"You have seen the bridge with your eyes. Now you must look harder to see it with your mind and your heart. You must find the bridge, because it leads to your happiness."

Nighthawk frowned. "I do not understand."

"Look deep inside, and you will." Without making a sound, the owl spread its wings and took flight.

"Wait." Nighthawk called after the owl. "Which path do I take?" He turned back to look at the divided road. He blinked with surprise. Down one path he saw the distinctive wickiups of an Apache village. Down the other path he saw the buildings of a White Eyes town, a town much too big to be Tucson.

As he moved his gaze back and forth between the two paths, the voice of the owl drifted to him. "When you find the bridge, you will know which path to follow."

Nighthawk awoke with a start, then looked around him. He saw no forked road, no owl, just the darkness of night cloaking the valley where he'd made camp.

271

He sat up and wiped the last of the sleep from his eyes. He thought about the vision the Spirits had sent him, going over it again and again, hoping to make sense of what he'd been told.

His vision had confirmed one thing—Mariah's claim, and his own suspicions, about being given owl power. He had been selected to receive the power, but first there was the matter of the test the owl had given him. He had to find a bridge. A bridge that led to his happiness.

He closed his eyes, clenching his hands into fists. Where was this bridge? How could he have seen it with his eyes yet not know what it was? How could he look for the bridge with his mind and heart? *Mind and heart.* Those were the words Bearclaw had used— he said the Spirits had sent him to help Nighthawk's mind and heart. But he still didn't know what all of that meant.

The questions continued to swirl in his brain, but no answers came. Knowing there was no point in trying to return to the first decent night's sleep he'd had in more than a week, he stirred the fire to life, then added more wood. He had a lot of thinking to do.

Several more days passed before all the pieces of the puzzle fell into place. Once Nighthawk realized he'd found the answer, he was amazed he hadn't thought of the solution sooner. Both the owl and Bearclaw had been correct. Once he'd followed the owl's instructions and looked deep inside, his friend's words had helped him open his mind and heart. As soon as those doors opened, finding the bridge had been simple.

Though he'd solved the mystery of the bridge, his last question to the owl remained unanswered. Remembering his first vision, when the shaman Spotted Wolf told him he would have to make a great decision one day, he knew that day had arrived. He must decide which path his future would take.

Again Nighthawk prayed and sang to the Spirits, asking for the strength and wisdom to make the decision. Near dawn, he rested. As he lay in a half-doze, thinking about his last vision and solving the mystery of finding a bridge, he heard again the owl's final words to him. He considered the words for a moment; then, for the first time in many days, he smiled. The owl had spoken the truth. Now that he'd found the bridge, he knew which path to follow.

Mariah smiled at another of her admirers, her face aching from smiling so much. As the man walked away, she shook her head. Though she'd been in Philadelphia for nearly two months, she still hadn't recovered from the shock of her exhibit's instant success or the number of people who came to see her photographs. No matter the time of day, a steady stream of people filed past her Photographic Documentation of the American Southwest. And once her identity had become known, every time she put in an appearance at the Colorado Pavilion she was besieged with congratulations, inquiries about buying her work, and more offers of employment. She'd already accepted positions with two publications, yet, to her amazement, she continued to receive job offers.

She still found it hard to believe that her future was assured, that all her years of hard work had paid off.

But one look around her exhibit and she knew it was true. So why didn't the thought cheer her?

The weeks since she'd left Arizona had been difficult. The trip east had been long and more tiring than she'd expected. And after arriving in Philadelphia, she'd worked almost continually for two days and nights to get her exhibit ready. She had yet to catch up on her sleep, her appetite had fled, and she suffered sudden bouts of tears—a consequence she attributed to everything that had happened in the past several months.

Though she considered her participation in the Exposition an honor, a once-in-a-lifetime experience she would never forget, she couldn't wait for it to close. She wanted her life to get back to normal— though after what she'd been through the past few months, she didn't know what normal was anymore.

She looked at the crowd moving through the pavilion, trying to stifle a yawn. It would be another long day. As she scanned the sea of faces, someone raised a hand to wave. Recognizing Ned and Benita, she waved in reply. When they had worked their way through the press of people and reached her side, Ned flashed a quick grin.

"I never thought I'd ever see the likes of this," he said. "Other than the Machinery Hall, your exhibit is the most popular attraction of the entire Exposition."

Mariah smiled. "That's what I've heard. The past couple of months have been amazing. I just wish—" Her smile wobbled. "Did you check the hotel for messages?"

"I checked," Ned replied, his heart aching at not

being able to give her better news. "No telegrams. No letters. Sorry, girlie."

"Don't be," she said, lifting her chin and squaring her shoulders. "I shouldn't have sent a letter to Ethan telling him where we were staying. It was foolish of me to think he would change his mind and want to contact me. I'll just have to accept the fact that he's made his decision. I was—" She blinked several times to stop another spurt of tears. "I was stupid to keep my hope alive this long."

"It is never stupid to hope," Benita said.

Mariah shrugged. "Maybe not. But sometimes, no matter how much we hope for something, it just isn't meant to be."

Benita gave her a hug. "I wish I could take the pain from your eyes."

"I'll be fine," she said. "Eventually." She drew a steadying breath, then managed to work up a smile for her uncle. "So, did you two have a nice morning?"

Ned smiled at his wife. "Yes. I showed Benita more of the city, didn't I, darlin'?"

"*Sí*, there are many interesting things to see in Philadelphia, but"—she lowered her voice—"the city is so big, and there are so many people. I feel very— how do you say?—closed in."

Mariah chuckled. "Yes, I imagine you do feel closed in. It's certainly nothing like the open spaces of Arizona Territory." She turned to her uncle. "You two don't have to stay in town until the Exposition closes. I'm sure you're anxious to get back to Tucson, so why don't you go ahead and leave?"

"We don't want to leave you here by yerself."

Mariah glanced around the crowded exhibit hall. "I'd hardly call this being by myself."

"That ain't what I meant," Ned replied, "and you know it. I don't like the idea of leaving you alone while yer goin' through such a rough patch."

Mariah looped her arm through his. "I know that, Uncle Ned, and I appreciate your worrying about me. But I assure you, I'll be fine. I want you and Benita to make arrangements to go to Tucson."

"Well . . . you will come visit us, won't ya?"

"As soon as the Exposition closes, I'm going to be real busy taking photographs for my two employers. So I won't have much free time." Seeing the disappointment on her uncle's face, she added, "But I promise I'll try to come for a visit the first chance I get."

Ned heaved a sigh. "Okay, girlie, we'll go. But I plan to hold ya to yer promise."

The following morning, Mariah rose and prepared for another day at the Exposition. Though it wasn't necessary for her to attend every day, she preferred being where she could keep her mind occupied. If she remained in the hotel, her thoughts invariably wandered into areas she wanted to avoid.

She finished pinning up her hair, then looked at her reflection in the mirror above the dressing table. *Oh, my God, what happened? I look terrible!* As she touched a pale cheek, traced one of the dark circles under her eyes, she realized she was going to have to start taking better care of herself. Because for the first time, she faced what she'd been avoiding for several weeks—the reason for the tears that came so easily and the queasiness of her stomach that made eating difficult or impossible. On her last night with Ethan, she'd asked him to give her enough memories to last a lifetime, but he'd given her something else as well. His child.

When the possibility of pregnancy had first occurred to her, she pushed the idea aside, refusing to believe it could be true. She conveniently blamed the symptoms, which she chose to ignore, on the strain of the long trip from Tucson, the stress of getting her exhibit set up, the pain of a broken heart. But she could no longer make excuses; she accepted the truth. Harder to accept was how she'd let it happen.

Because she'd eliminated a wedding from her future, she'd also never considered having a child, foolishly viewing marriage and motherhood as going hand in hand. She wasn't naive. She knew how babies were conceived. Yet not once had she considered the possible consequences of her relationship with Ethan. Such irresponsible behavior made her cringe, especially since it went against what her uncle had tried to teach her—always consider the consequences of your actions *before* leaping into a situation. But, in her defense, she'd never been in love before, so perhaps her behavior wasn't completely unforgivable. She wasn't looking for excuses, but she also wasn't sorry for what she'd done.

She drew a deep breath and released it slowly. Scolding herself or trying to justify what she'd allowed to happen wouldn't change anything. She had a future to think of, one that included bringing a child into the world. Which meant she had some serious thinking to do, some decisions to make.

First on the list was telling her uncle about her

condition. He might not be happy with her for allowing herself to end up pregnant and unmarried, but she knew he would never pass judgment. She was more concerned about her timing, especially since he and Benita planned to leave for Arizona Territory the following week.

Mariah knew if she waited to break the news until after he returned to Tucson, he would be furious with her for not telling him sooner. But if she told him before he left Philadelphia, she knew in all probability he would refuse to go, insisting his place was with her. As much as she would like having him nearby, she couldn't allow him to change his plans. His future was with Benita, and their life was in Tucson.

After considering her options, she decided she would wait until a few days before Ned and Benita were to board a westbound train. Hopefully by then she would have come up with satisfactory arguments to all the objections she anticipated he would voice.

When that day dawned, she wasn't sure she had sufficiently prepared herself to face whatever her uncle might throw at her, but she was determined to try. After she summoned Ned and Benita to her hotel room and made her announcement, his first reaction had been what she expected. Anger directed at Ethan.

She let him rant for a few minutes, then interrupted his tirade by saying, "Don't blame Ethan, Uncle Ned. He didn't force me to do anything I didn't want to do."

He'd grumbled something indecipherable but remained silent while she outlined her plans. When she finished, he said, "I don't have a problem with you wantin' to work for as long as ya can. Not as long as ya promise me ya won't take any unnecessary chances while yer carrying this child. But I'm more concerned about when yer time comes and after the child's born. What will ya do then?"

"When it gets close to the baby's birth, I'll take some time off. Then, afterward, I'll hire someone to help me with the baby so I can resume working."

"You'd let some stranger take care o' yer child?"

"Yes," she replied, mustering a smile. "Lots of women hire a nurse to care for their children. If it will ease your mind, I promise to take my time looking for qualified help."

"Well, I still don't like the idea," he replied.

"Ned," Benita said, "Mariah is a grown woman. You should respect her decision."

"Yeah, I know, darlin'." He rubbed a hand over his jaw. "It's just that I'll worry about her."

"I know you will," Mariah replied, reaching over to squeeze his arm.

Ned stared at his niece for a moment, then said, "You ain't said nothin' about Nighthawk. Are you gonna tell him?"

Mariah dropped her gaze. "I haven't decided."

"A man deserves to know he's fathered a child."

"I know," she said in a low voice. "But since he doesn't want me, he might not want to know about his child. I'm not sure I could stand that."

Ned wished he knew the words that would ease her pain. Rubbing a hand over his jaw again, he said, "Are ya sure you don't want Benita and me to stick around for a while longer?"

"No. I think it would be best if I get used to being alone right away."

Ned looked at his wife, then back at Mariah. He released a heavy sigh. "Okay, girlie, we'll leave on Thursday like we planned."

The next morning, Mariah arrived at the Exposition just as the gates opened. She enjoyed arriving early, when the crowds were light and the grounds nearly deserted, so she could wander through the other pavilions, view the other exhibits without being jostled by elbow-to-elbow people.

An hour later, she entered the Colorado Pavilion. The man stationed at the entrance smiled at her. "Oh, Miss Corbett, I'm so glad you're here. A man asked for you a while ago. He seemed real anxious to speak to you."

Mariah nodded. "Probably another reporter."

"Or maybe he's come to offer you a job," the man said with a wink. Apparently word of her being swamped with job offers had become common knowledge.

"I never thought I'd say this," she replied in a low voice, "but I hope not. I already have plenty of work lined up." She looked around. "So where is this man?"

"I believe he's waiting by your exhibit."

"Okay, thanks."

The man bobbed his head. "My pleasure."

Mariah took a deep breath, then started through the pavilion. As she approached her exhibit, she saw a man in a dark suit standing in front of one of her photographs, his arms crossed over his chest. A leather satchel sat on the floor beside his feet. His face was angled away from her, but she could see he wore his dark hair long, pulled back, and tied at his nape.

Her breath caught in her throat. Could it—She gave her head a shake. No, that wasn't possible. Trying to collect herself, she moved closer to the exhibit. Just as she opened her mouth to announce her presence, the man turned toward her and smiled.

She sucked in a sharp breath, then stumbled to a halt. A hand pressed over her racing heart, she stared into a face she'd thought she would never see again.

# *Chapter Seventeen*

"What . . . what are—" For a moment, Mariah thought she might she might faint. When her head stopped spinning, she said, "What are you doing here?"

Ethan's smile disappeared. "I did not mean to startle you," he said, moving closer. He raked his gaze over her face, his eyebrows pulled together in a frown. "What is wrong? You are very pale."

She didn't respond. She couldn't. The tightness in her throat prevented any words from getting through. She could only stare at him.

"Mariah? Talk to me."

She swallowed, then ran her tongue over her dry lips. "I'm fine. Just surprised to see you."

He stroked her cheek, the harshness of his expression softening. "I should have let you know I was coming."

His statement snapped her out of her trance. "How did you get to Philadelphia? Where did you get the clothes? How did you find me? And why—" She took a gulping breath. "Why are you here?"

"I got to Philadelphia the same way as you. The stagecoach was very uncomfortable. But the ship and the train . . ." He smiled again, his eyes sparkling. "I cannot describe what riding in them was like."

"Yes, traveling by ship and train definitely beats a dusty ride in a bouncing stagecoach."

He nodded, then said, "When I told Father Julian I planned to come here, he said I should buy White Eyes clothes when I got to San Francisco. He had been there and told me the name of a store." Seeing her frown, he added, "Is something wrong with this suit? The man in the store told me this is the current fashion."

"No, the suit's fine. It's just that I'm stunned to see you in Philadelphia, especially dressed like this." She pursed her lips, running her gaze from his face down to the toes of his shiny boots. Meeting his gaze again, she said, "But you do look wonderful. As handsome as ever."

He cleared his throat, both embarrassed and pleased by her words. Running his fingers along the inside of his collar, he said, "I do not know how White Eyes men can wear something this tight around their neck all the time."

"I've often wondered the same thing," she replied. "So, are you going to tell me why you're here?"

"When you were not at your hotel, I knew you must be here. Several people heard me ask for directions to the Exposition and offered to let me share their carriage." He shrugged. "It was not difficult."

"I didn't mean why are you here at the Exposition, I meant why did you come to Philadelphia?"

"I came for two reasons." He glanced at the display of photographs. "I wanted to see your exhibit. While I was in San Francisco, I read what a reporter said about it."

He retrieved his satchel and pulled out a newspaper. "I brought it with me. Let me read part of it to you."

He opened the paper and began reading. " 'Miss Mariah Corbett, one of the pioneer photographers of the Wild West, deserves great credit for her exhibit presently on display in the Colorado Pavilion at the Centennial Exposition in Philadelphia. Her Photographic Documentation of the American Southwest is beyond compare. A most impressive addition to the Exposition, her work reveals the tremendous skill and energy required to produce such magnificent views of lofty mountains and wondrous rock formations most of us will never see in person. The quality of her work is all the more extraordinary due to the fact that her photographic equipment had to be carried to remote locations on muleback. We all owe Miss Corbett our most profound gratitude for sharing her photographic masterpieces with America and the world.' "

He refolded the newspaper, then shifted his gaze to her face. "I am so proud of you, *shijei*," he said with a smile.

The use of the endearment sent her pulse racing again. "Was that the other reason you came here? To read me a review?"

"No," he said with a chuckle. He immediately sobered, his throat working with a swallow. "The other reason was to ask if you have hired a new assistant."

She shook her head. "I haven't had time to look for one."

"And the other position?" He ran the backs of his knuckles down the side of her face, glad to see a rosy flush replace the former paleness of her cheeks. "Have you found someone willing to become your husband?"

She shook her head a second time. "I haven't been looking."

Nighthawk took a deep breath, relieved the tight knot of apprehension inside his chest had begun to loosen. "Then I would like to recommend someone. Someone I believe is perfect for both positions."

Her eyebrows arched. "Really? Do I know this someone?"

He lowered his head until his lips brushed her ear. "Yes," he whispered. "You know him intimately."

Mariah bit the inside of her cheek to keep herself from smiling. Now that he'd revealed his reason for making the trip from Tucson, she relaxed. Pretending to mull over his statement, she said, "Someone I know intimately, hmm? Well, that narrows the field considerably. To only a handful."

His head snapped up. "What?" His voice was a low growl, the previous warmth in his eyes intensifying to a blistering heat. "Have there been other men since me?"

She dropped her gaze, desperately trying to hold in her amusement. But another peek at his scowling expression and she lost the battle. A laugh bubbled up from her chest and burst out.

Nighthawk narrowed his gaze. "You did that on purpose. You let me think there have been other men so I would be jealous."

"Yes," she managed to say before another hoot of laughter escaped. "You should have seen the look on your face. It was—" Realizing he wasn't laughing, she immediately curtailed her merriment. She cleared her throat and said, "Never mind. Now, what was it you were saying?"

He stared at her for a moment, his brief stab of jealousy quickly dissolving. The woman standing before him totally befuddled him, continually keeping him off balance. But, if he were honest with himself, that was one of the reasons he loved her. "I was recommending someone to be both your assistant and your husband. Me."

She searched his face, looking for any sign of insincerity. She found none. "What changed your mind?"

"After you left Tucson, I went to the mountains, to the holy home of the Lightning Spirit to search for answers. I stayed there many days. I did not leave until I understood what the Spirits had been trying to tell me."

"The bridge?"

He nodded. "I had a vision while I was in the mountains. It was much like the others, the Spirits telling me I must find the bridge. The bridge would lead to my happiness. But in that vision, I was told I had already seen the bridge with my eyes and must look for it with my mind and my heart."

Her brow furrowed. "Did that make sense to you?"

"No, not at first. I spent a lot of time thinking about

the meaning of the words. When the answer came to me, I could not believe I had not thought of it sooner." He cupped one side of her face with his palm. "The bridge I was told I must find is you, Mariah."

She blinked. "Me?"

"I did as the Spirits told me. I looked deeper inside myself, looked with my mind and my heart. And I saw only you."

"I still don't understand. How does that make me the bridge?"

"Do you remember I told you I do not belong with my people or with the White Eyes?" At her nod, he said, "When you asked me to be your husband, you told me that blending the differences in our cultures would make a richer life for us. I did not believe your words because I could see no way for them to be true. Do you also remember Bearclaw saying the Spirits sent him to find me because they told him he needed to help me?"

"I remember. Did you ever figure out why the Spirits told him you needed his help?"

"Not before he left. I told him I thought the Spirits must have been wrong. He did not agree. He said he had been sent to help my mind and heart. I did not know what he meant, but he said when the time was right, the Spirits would speak to me, and I would understand.

"After I realized you were the bridge the Spirits told me to find, everything became clear. What Bearclaw told me was the truth. And part of what Eagle Tail told me was also true. I do not live the old ways of my people, but I am still Apache. I live among the

White Eyes, but I have not completely become a White Eyes. I do not want to be one or the other. That is the reason the Spirits brought us together. To capture each other's heart so you would become the bridge that connects the two parts of me."

He touched a finger to her trembling lips. "I want our futures to be one."

Mariah's breath caught on a sob. "Oh, Ethan," she managed to say, her eyes flooding with tears and spilling over to run down her cheeks.

His brow knitted with a frown. "Tears?" he said, catching a glistening drop with a fingertip. "What happened to the Mariah Corbett I met in Tucson? Where is the brave, confident woman who walked into the jail and offered a job to a wild Apache? The hot-tempered woman who fought on the street to defend me? The fierce woman warrior who faced down a band of renegade Apaches?" He caught another tear. "I did not think that woman would cry so easily."

"I'm still that woman," she said with a sniffle, wiping the last of her tears from her cheeks. "It's just that my emotions are really close to the surface because of the ba—um, well, because of all the stress I've been under." She glanced up at him, relieved to see that his expression revealed nothing to indicate he'd caught the near slip of her tongue. She wanted to save that announcement for a more private moment. First they needed to settle an important piece of business.

"What was it we were discussing before we got sidetracked?" she said, tapping a finger on her chin. "Oh, yes, the candidate you're recommending to be my assistant and my husband. You."

She placed a hand on his chest and looked him

straight in the eyes. "Since I also think you're perfect for both positions, and because I love you, I accept your proposal." Her gaze narrowed. "You were proposing, weren't you?"

He managed a rasping, "Yes."

She smiled, sliding her hand up his chest and around his neck. "Ethan, now would be a good time to kiss me."

He grinned, then pulled her into his arms and gave her what she asked for and more.

When he finally ended his devouring kiss and lifted his head, she took a step back. Her breathing ragged, she straightened the bodice of her dress. When she could trust herself to speak, she said, "Don't you think we should go someplace private to ... um ... celebrate?" She lowered her voice to add, "Like my hotel room?" Grabbing his arm, she tried to turn him toward the entrance.

"Wait," he said, shaking off her hand. "I thought you would want to show me the rest of your exhibit."

She stared up at him for a moment, her bottom lip caught between her teeth. Finally she said, "I do, but can't it wait until later? Maybe even a whole lot later?"

He chuckled. "Ah, there is the hot-blooded, greedy woman I love," he said, bending to pick up his satchel. "Yes, I will see your exhibit later." As he offered her his arm, his mouth curved in a wicked grin. "Much later, after we 'celebrate.'"

As they walked toward the pavilion door, he said, "Do you still have Screech?"

"Of course, why?"

"I need one of his feathers."

"One of his—" Her hand tightened on his arm. "Does that mean you had a vision where an owl spoke to you?"

He smiled and nodded. "In the vision I told you about. The bird that spoke to me was not the nighthawk. It was an owl."

"Oh, Ethan, you have owl power!" A couple walking the opposite way gave them a strange look, prompting Mariah to drop her voice to a whisper. "You do, don't you?"

"Yes," he replied, choking back a laugh. "But only after the owl tested me to make sure I was worthy. I had to find the bridge. Once I did, I received the power."

"I hate to say it," she said, trying but failing to maintain a stern expression, "but, I told you so."

"Yes, you did tell me," he replied, unable to hold in his laughter. "But I do not believe you hate saying so."

Her temper flickered, but she quickly doused the tiny flame, refusing to allow anything to ruin the moment. Her heart nearly bursting with love, she let her laughter join his.

Hours later, Nighthawk held Mariah pressed against his side, one arm wrapped around her waist, her head resting on his shoulder. While his breathing and heart rate returned to normal, he played with her hair, lifting the pale golden strands, then letting them sift through his fingers to fall onto his chest.

"The first time I touched you," he said in a raspy whisper, "when we shook hands in the jail, I could not believe my reaction. I had never felt desire that

290

strong." He picked up another strand of her hair. "Later, I had erotic fantasies about your hair."

She smiled against his neck, then shifted one leg and draped it over his thighs. "I remember the first time I saw you. It was from my hotel window. The morning the marshal took you to jail. Looking at you left me breathless, my fingers itching to touch you." She moved her hand to caress the smooth skin of his muscular chest. "You still affect me that way."

Nighthawk looked down at her hand resting on his chest, her leg thrown over his thighs. Her pale skin looked even whiter against the copper of his. "We are so different," he said, tucking her hair behind her ear. "I wonder what our children will look like."

She lifted her head and met his gaze. She flashed a smile, and before she lost her nerve, she said, "In about seven months we'll find out."

His smile faltered. "Seven months?" He swallowed the sudden lump in his throat. "Are you saying we will have a child? In seven months?"

She nodded. "In the spring." When he didn't respond but continued to stare at her with a stunned expression on his face, she said, "Ethan, are you all right?"

He inhaled a deep breath, released it slowly, then nodded. "What about your work?" On the way to the hotel, Mariah had told him about all the job offers, and he knew how important continuing her work was to her. "Will you have to change your plans?"

"The only change will be having you with me while I work. I'll take some time off when it gets closer to the birth of our child. Then, afterward, I'll hire someone to help with the baby so I can resume work—"

"Hire someone?" he said, sitting up and holding her at arm's length. "You will not hire someone to care for our child."

"But I'll be taking photographs. I won't be able to look after a baby every minute."

"You will not hire someone," he said again, a muscle ticking in his jaw. "I will do it."

"You're going to be working as my assistant, remember?"

"I have not forgotten. I will carry the boxes of glass plates and chemicals. I will help set up your tent and your cameras. *And* I will care for our child while you are taking photographs or developing negatives."

She stared at him for a moment, then gave her head a shake. "I don't know a lot about the ways of your people, but I doubt taking care of babies falls under the duties of a husband."

"That is true. Apache women and their oldest daughters care for the youngest children. But we will be not living in an Apache village. So I will do it."

When Mariah still didn't look convinced, he said, "You told me we can be very adaptable when we set our minds to it. Do you remember saying those words?"

"Yes."

"Then you should understand why I want to take care of our child." He dipped his head and pressed a soft kiss on her mouth. "I am setting my mind to being adaptable."

Mariah shook her head again, but this time she was

smiling. "When we get back to Tucson, I really do need to thank Carmen."

He didn't reply but merely raised his eyebrows in anticipation of her explanation.

"If not for Carmen, you wouldn't have spent the night in the bordello or tried to help one of the other women. You wouldn't have been arrested, and I wouldn't have seen you walking down the street bare-chested and—" Her eyes widened. "That reminds me, there's something else we need to discuss."

"What?" he replied, his attention snared by one breast playing peekaboo through her hair. He touched the tightened tip with his fingers, then gently squeezed.

"I never—" She sucked in a sharp breath. "I never—Ethan, I can't think while you're doing that."

He gave her a crooked smile, then reluctantly withdrew his hand. "You never what?"

"I never got to take a photograph of you in your breechcloth." She glanced at where he'd dropped his leather satchel. "Did you happen to . . . um . . . bring it with you?"

He chuckled, lying back on the bed and pulling her with him. "Yes, but before you insist on taking my photograph, we have more 'celebrating' to do." He nuzzled the side of her neck, then settled his lips atop hers in a gentle, fleeting kiss. His mouth still touching hers, he said, "A lot more."

"That's blackmail," she whispered.

"That is true. But I do not hear you complaining."

"No," she replied, sliding her body fully atop his. "And you won't."

# *Epilogue*

Mariah stood beside the editor of the *Philadelphia Photographer* in the parlor of his home, where she would be a guest for the next few days. He and his wife were hosting a party to celebrate Mariah's fifth anniversary as the publication's premier special correspondent. Many of the firm's employees were present, along with a select group of city dignitaries and a number of photography enthusiasts.

Mariah usually preferred not to attend such events. She'd been back to Philadelphia only twice in the years since the Centennial Exposition, but when she learned the party would help the journal's prestige, she knew she couldn't refuse.

From the moment she'd agreed to work for the editor of the *Philadelphia Photographer,* she'd been given carte blanche regarding her photographs, allowing her to choose whatever subject matter she wanted.

Just as important to her, he'd agreed to publish any essays she sent with her photographs. Then, when she sent him a telegram telling him Ethan would be taking over the writing of the essays, he never flinched. He simply responded by saying he looked forward to receiving their work.

Though Mariah was still thrilled to see her photographs appear in the *Philadelphia Photographer*, her greatest pleasure came from seeing Ethan's essays published alongside her work. For agreeing to publish Ethan's essays before he'd even seen the first one and for rarely changing even a single word, her editor would have her eternal gratitude.

The day she discovered Ethan's writing talent remained a vivid memory. They'd been married less than a month and had traveled to Yellowstone National Park to do a series of photographs. After a week of hauling her cameras around the park, she'd sat down with her notes to try to write an essay about one of the photographs she'd taken.

When Ethan heard her grumbling about her efforts, he offered to help. Though he spoke English as well as anyone she knew, she'd never considered the depth of his ability with the written language. But the chance to be relieved of the burdensome chore, even for a little while, was too much of a temptation, so she happily turned over her notes.

What she discovered, after reading the essay he wrote, stunned her. He not only had a wonderful command of English, he also had a natural flair for writing, a rare talent that allowed him to paint beautiful pictures with words. He possessed an ability she would never attain, no matter how long she tried.

When she suggested he take over writing the essays to accompany her photographs, he refused, thinking he would be intruding on her territory. She quickly assured him that it would not be an intrusion: in fact, she welcomed the opportunity to pass the responsibility to him.

She would never forget the look on his face the first time he saw his work in print, his name prominently displayed in the credits. Her heart had nearly burst with pride.

Realizing she'd let her mind wander from the party, she cast another glance toward the doorway, then turned her attention back to her editor.

"Have you seen Mariah's latest photographs?" he was saying to the guests who'd formed a small group around him and Mariah. "They're absolutely stunning. Her best work yet."

Mariah smiled. "It's always nice to hear that my work is appreciated."

"How long will you be in town, Mrs. Nighthawk?" one of the other guests said.

"I'm not sure," she replied. "Probably only a few days."

"Can't wait to get back to the Wild West and photograph more of that spectacular scenery, eh?"

She wanted to say that wasn't the entire reason, but instead she smiled again and said, "You could say that."

Someone else started to make a comment but was cut off by a collective gasp directly behind Mariah. When she turned, she saw three women all fluttering their fans in front of their faces.

In a loud whisper, one of them said, "My stars, isn't

he the man in that photograph of hers? You know the one I mean."

"I know exactly which photograph," a second woman said. "The one where the man's practically naked."

"Yes, that's definitely him," the third woman said, her voice breathless. She fluttered her fan even faster and released a long sigh. "My, he is a handsome devil, isn't he?"

Mariah bit her lip to halt a smile. She also knew which photograph the three were discussing. It was one of her personal favorites. Entitled *Chokonen Warrior,* the photograph was of Ethan, arms crossed over his chest, wearing only his breechcloth, moccasins, and what she called his Apache face—stoic, fierce, proud. Tamping down her amusement over the stir the photograph had caused among the three women— and probably all the other females who had seen it— she excused herself and headed toward the door.

When she reached the women, she paused long enough to say, "You're absolutely right, ladies. He is the man in the photograph you found so interesting, and, yes, he is handsome. He's also my husband."

Mariah continued toward the door, vaguely aware of the soft tittering of embarrassed laughter behind her. All her senses were focused on the man standing just inside the parlor and the child in his arms.

"*Shima,*" the child said when she spotted Mariah, using the Apache word for *mother.*

Mariah smiled at Ethan, then turned her attention to their four-year-old daughter. "Sophie, you're supposed to be asleep by now. Remember the talk we had about what time little girls and boys should go to bed?"

Sophie tilted her chin in precisely the same stubborn angle Mariah's often took. "I'm a big girl, not a baby like Lucas. 'Sides, Daddy said I could come tell you g'night."

"I said I would think about it," Ethan said.

"No, Daddy. You said I could."

Mariah shook her head, wondering again if she'd been such a handful at her daughter's age. She met Ethan's gaze; the love she saw shining there sometimes still caught her by surprise. She was so unbelievably lucky. Her career was everything she'd ever hoped for, but she considered her personal life, as a wife and mother, her biggest success.

"Lucas is sleeping?" she said, referring to their one-year-old son.

Ethan nodded. "He went to sleep without any trouble. Not like this little lady," he said, ruffling Sophie's hair, as black and shiny as his.

Sophie wrinkled her nose, her green eyes flashing. "Not little, Daddy. I'm big. 'Member, that's what you said when I ate my supper all gone."

He leaned closer to Mariah and whispered, "I have to pay better attention to what I say to her. She remembers everything."

Mariah nodded, then turned her attention to Sophie. "Yes, you're getting to be a big girl. So, give me a kiss good night, then let Daddy take you upstairs and put you to bed so he can come back down and be with me for a while. Will you do that, sweetheart?"

Sophie bobbed her head in agreement. "Maybe I'll

have a vision tonight." She puckered her rosy lips and leaned forward.

Mariah kissed her daughter, then said, "Maybe. But your Daddy was much older than you before he had his first vision."

Sophie shrugged. "I know, but maybe Daddy's 'pache Spirits will send me a vision anyway." She tucked her head beneath her father's chin and closed her eyes.

Ethan shook his head. "I should have waited a few years before I told her about Apache Spirits and visions."

"No, telling her when you did was fine," Mariah replied, walking with him out into the hallway. "She's just a very bright child. Look how easily she learned the Apache and Spanish you taught her."

At the foot of the staircase, he turned to Mariah and brushed his mouth over hers. "I will be down as soon as she falls asleep."

She nodded, reaching up to touch his face. "I hope this party doesn't drag on too long," she said in a low voice.

He flashed a grin. "Ah, you want to be alone with me. Maybe we will create another baby."

"I'd love to have more of your children," she said, returning his smile, "but not right away. Besides, a third child wouldn't be fair to you. You already take care of Sophie and Lucas while I'm working. And you still work as my assistant and write essays to go with my photographs. Taking care of another child would be too much to ask."

"You do not have to ask me to take care of our

children, *shijei.* I do it because of love. My love for you and for them."

Mariah swallowed the sudden lump in her throat. "I want to go home," she said in a raw voice, speaking of the house in a mountain canyon not far from Tucson, their private hideaway for whatever free time Mariah's schedule permitted.

"I have already purchased the tickets," he replied, just as eager as his wife to return to their home.

Five years earlier, Ethan Nighthawk had had no place where he felt he belonged. Then he'd had a vision predicting he would meet a yellow-haired White Eyes woman. From the moment they met, Mariah turned his world upside down. But now not a day went by that he didn't offer his thanks to the Spirits for bringing her into his life.

With Mariah he'd found the peace he craved, a reason for an English-speaking Apache to live among the White Eyes, a future filled with more love and happiness then he'd thought possible. With Mariah, he'd found where he belonged.

# Lair of the Wolf

## Chapter Eleven

Madeline George

*Lair of the Wolf* also appears in these *Leisure* books:

On January 1, 1997, *Romance Communications*, the Romance Magazine for the 21st century made its Internet debut. One year later, it was named a Lycos Top 5% site on the Web in terms of both content and graphics!

One of *Romance Communications*' most popular features is The Romantic Relay, an original romance novel divided into twelve monthly installments, with each chapter written by a different author. Our first offering was *Lair of the Wolf*, a tale of medieval Wales, created by, in alphabetical order, celebrated authors Emily Carmichael, Debra Dier, Madeline George, Martha Hix, Deana James, Elizabeth Mayne, Constance O'Banyon, Evelyn Rogers, Sharon Schulze, June Lund Shiplett, and Bobbi Smith.

We put no restrictions on the authors, letting each pick up the tale where the previous author had left off and going forward as she wished. The authors tell us they had a lot of fun, each trying to write her successor into a corner!

Now, preserving the fun and suspense of our month-by-month installments, Leisure Books presents, in print, one chapter a month of *Lair of the Wolf*. In addition to the entire online story, the authors have added some brand-new material to their existing chapters. So if you think you've read *Lair of the Wolf* already, you may find a few surprises. Please enjoy this unique offering, watch for each new monthly installment in the back of your Leisure Books, and make sure you visit our website, where another romantic relay is already in progress.

*Romance Communications*

http://www.romcom.com

Pamela Monck, Editor-in-Chief

Mary D. Pinto, Senior Editor

S. Lee Meyer, Web Mistress

# Chapter Eleven

*By Madeline George*

Dame Allison crumbled the leaves carefully between her dry palms, then sprinkled them into the mead, stirring well to conceal their presence. It had taken most of an hour to learn who held the key to Sir Olyver's irons. Captain Hanes would be the one to savor her concoction this day.

A twinge of guilt slowed her pace as she carried the mead to where Hanes sat dozing by the fire. Treason was the only name for what she was about to do. And treason would be Sir Garon's accusation if ever he learned of her deception. If all went as planned, though, Longshanks' Wolf would not live to know the truth.

Some evil potion or spell must have mesmerized Lady Meredyth. There could be no other explanation for her acquiescence—or for her apparent fondness for the conqueror. The day he'd arrived, her lady's feelings were clear at the announcement that he meant to take her as bride.

*I shall never submit to his demands, nor will I pledge him my fidelity.*

The thought of her lady in that man's bed caused a ripple of revulsion to shiver down Dame Allison's crooked spine.

Lady Meredyth must be rescued. As sure as Sir Olyver sat imprisoned in the dank, rotting bowels of Glendire, her lady had been imprisoned by the black magic worked on her by Longshanks' Wolf. That evil man must die. And Sir Olyver Martain was the only man who could accomplish such a deed.

Dame Allison's lip curled at the thought of having to free the man who'd cruelly beaten Mott, the kennel boy. Only a few were privy to the knowledge that Mott was her grandson. When she'd tended the welts on the poor dear's tender back, she'd vowed to see Sir Olyver dead before the next full moon.

The minute Olyver had slain the Wolf, she would be there with a celebratory cup of mead mixed especially for him. The leaves crumbled in that cup would assure that he would sleep forever.

Dame Allison quickened her pace. Even now, Mott waited until the appointed hour, when he would summon Lady Meredyth to tend an imaginary ailment suffered by her loyal lady-in-waiting. Dame Allison's dry lips slid back over her teeth, twisting into a malevolent grin. By nightfall, both Englishmen, scum that they were, would be dead, and Lady Meredyth would be free from the spell holding her captive.

Hanes roused when Allison drew near.

"Halt, woman. You have no duties here. Why have you come?"

"You commanded a cup of mead, and I have obeyed."

"I gave no such command."

"Very well, then, I'll drink it myself." She turned to go, lifting the heavy cup to her lips.

"Hold. My throat would cheer to a bit of refreshment." He took the cup from her hands and drained half of it before dragging one sleeve over his mouth.

"At least my efforts were not wasted. If you'll finish the brew, I'll take the cup with me to the kitchen."

Hanes complied with a wide grin, then handed the cup over.

Dame Allison retreated to a dark corner, where he could not detect her presence. Within a quarter of an hour, he slumped in his chair and snored contentedly.

She wasted no time finding the key to the cell and irons, then headed for the dungeon.

Meredyth paused before opening the door. "Who's there?"

A quavering voice answered, " 'Tis Mott, my lady. You must come quick!"

Meredyth opened the door wide, gasping at the sight of a festering stripe on the lad's cheek. "What happened to your face?"

"Sir Olyver, my lady. I spoke too freely about the English bastards, and he lashed me."

She remembered now. Owain had spoken of the incident that day when she'd been on her way to the chapel to pray.

"Quick, boy. Why have you come?"

"Dame Allison be in a bad way, my lady. Her guts are churning like she's been poisoned. She bade me fetch you. Please come!"

Garon shifted in his bed, groaning at the pain it caused in his wound. "See to her, Merrie. Then come straight back." His scowl proved his lack of affection for Dame Allison. "If she requires nursing, find another for it. I, too, require your tender care."

"Yes, I know." She burned with the thought of the *care* he would require this night. "Take me to her, Mott." She followed him down the dark hallway.

"This way, my lady."

"The torches have burned out, Mott. See to them the minute I'm with your grandmother."

"Yes, my lady." His eyes darted back and forth as they proceeded toward Allison's room, but not once did he look directly at her.

Meredyth felt the chill of fear as shadows engulfed them. Too clearly, she was reminded of the captivity that had ensued when Sir Olyver led her along just such a darkened passageway.

Mott didn't stop at Dame Allison's room but kept going toward the kitchen.

"Mott, where is Dame Allison?"

"This way. Not far now." He quickened his pace.

Warnings echoed in Meredyth's brain. This wasn't right. She could feel the wrongness of it as they hastened on. "Mott, wait!"

He broke into a run, shouting over his shoulder. "She made me do it, my lady! I had no choice! Please don't have me lashed again!" He disappeared into the gloom, the sound of his crying fading as he left her in almost complete darkness.

Meredyth remained where she was as she pondered Mott's actions. Dame Allison's illness was obviously a ruse, but who had concocted the tale, and why? Had someone thought to lure her away from Garon to kidnap her again? No, Mott would never do anything to endanger her. He was as loyal as his grandmother, and he hated the English conquerors, as his wounded face bore witness.

"She made me do it," he had cried. No one but Dame Allison could have forced Mott to lie to Meredyth. But for what purpose? She had been lured away from Garon, but she was not the target! "Dear God, no. Garon!"

She turned and ran, praying she wouldn't be too late.

Sir Olyver rubbed his raw wrists, now freed from the cruel irons. "I assume you brought my sword?"

Dame Allison grimaced at her oversight. "I did not think to bring it. I'll fetch—"

"I'll do it myself. Give me the keys." She handed them over. He shoved her aside and strode out of the cell, heading for the guard station, opening cell doors as he went, releasing his men.

Captain Hanes showed no signs of waking. Sir Olyver snatched the sword from the soldier's sheath, then glanced back at Dame Allison with a grin that shivered through her like an icy winter's blast.

"Why, woman? I would've thought you'd rather see me rot. Yet you've freed us all."

After a moment's hesitation, she blurted, "I want Sir Garon dead! The Wolf has bewitched my lady with some potion. She would never submit to him

311

otherwise. I want her freed from his control." She quivered with the intensity of her hatred.

Olyver nodded. "She will be free of Saunders, and mine before the sun sets, as will all of Glendire."

Dame Allison watched him go, then nodded, mocking him. The mead she had prepared for him would mean true freedom for Lady Meredyth.

Meredyth stumbled through the dark passageway, blinded with fear and anger. How could her own lady-in-waiting betray her so grievously?

Climbing the last stairs, Meredyth heard, then saw, the throng of men between her and the bedroom where Garon waited. Olyver's men! Traitors all, somehow freed from the dungeon. Unarmed, but blocking any escape from the room.

She glared at them, demanding with her presence that passage between them be permitted. As she walked, chin high, praying her trembling would not betray her fear, the traitors yielded and granted the lady room to advance.

Inside the room, she found Sir Olyver standing over Garon, who was lying on the floor, his wound broken open and bleeding. The point of Olyver's sword had already pierced the skin of Garon's throat.

"Harm him at your peril," Meredyth warned him.

"At my peril?" Sir Olyver broke into gruff laughter, raising his sword to point toward her. "And who will cause me peril, my lady? You, who arranged to have me and my men set free?"

With a snarl, Garon sprang to his feet, but he was stopped from advancing as Sir Olyver's sword swung in his direction once more.

312

"You lie!" Meredyth cried. "I gave no order to release you."

"Oh, but you did. Your lady-in-waiting brought the key herself. We are here by your desire. And I promise you, I shall accomplish the task you've assigned me."

"Task? I assigned you no task." She looked at Garon pleadingly, willing the doubt she saw in his eyes to fade.

Sir Olyver grinned knowingly. "Did you think you could betray him and leave him ignorant of the betrayal? I think not, Lady Meredyth. Your treachery makes his death all the sweeter."

Meredyth saw Garon's scowl. "Surely you don't believe—" she began in her defense.

"I thought you cared for me. Supported me. It's been nothing but a lie," her husband accused.

Dame Allison pushed her way into the room. "Kill him, you miserable swine! Do what you've come to do, then drink to your future at Glendire." She shoved the cup of mead toward Sir Olyver, sloshing a bit onto the floor.

Meredyth glared at her. "What have you done?"

"Only what you wanted, my lady. You said you'd rather die than submit—"

The words came back to her, bitter and unpalatable. How could she convince Garon that her heart had changed toward him since she'd uttered that oath?

Before she could form the words to beg Garon to believe her, a soldier barged into the room, calling out excitedly.

"Forgive the intrusion, Sir Garon, but the outlaw band is less than an hour's march from here." The seasoned warrior looked confused when he saw his lord at sword point. In an instant, he had unleashed his own blade and aimed it at Sir Olyver's back.

"Give to, Sir Olyver," he growled, "lest ye meet your own end."

"Fool," Sir Olyver spat, his own sword unwavering. "You'll never make it out of this room alive. One word from me, and my men will come swarming through yon door."

The man stood unyielding.

Garon shoved Sir Olyver's sword aside, wincing as pain from his newly opened wound seared his body. "Enough," he commanded. "It appears, Olyver, that you are once again my prisoner."

Sir Olyver grudgingly yielded his sword to Garon, then shrugged. "Luck has always favored you, Garon, but this game has not yet been played to its conclusion. At the moment, you need me, and you need my men. It will take all of us to defeat these Welsh bandits."

Garon nodded reluctantly, recognizing the truth of Sir Olyver's words, and he indicated for his man to put away his sword.

"No, don't trust him, Garon!" Meredyth cried.

Garon looked at her for a long moment. "Fear not," he said without expression. "Never again will I put my trust in anyone but myself. But 'tis true that Sir Olyver and I need each other if any of us are to come out of this battle alive."

Meredyth gave a cry of anguish, but Garon turned away from her.

"What say you, Olyver? Will you fight with me for the sake of Glendire? Our differences can be sorted and solved after the marauders are dispatched. Right now, let's get ready for battle."

Olyver took back the sword that Garon offered him. "Gladly. Let's put this behind us quickly, so the celebration of victory can begin."

He strode from the room, shouting orders to his men and sending them scurrying to their positions.

In less than a minute the room had emptied, save for Lady Meredyth and Garon. Meredyth pleaded with her eyes for Garon to hear the truth in her words.

"I love you. I would die for you. Please, my lord . . ." she said as she grasped his arm.

"I've known from the beginning that it was a mistake to love you. I only wish your treachery had been revealed before I lost my heart so foolishly." He trailed a fingertip down her silken cheek.

Meredyth's tears ran freely now. "Garon, I never—"

He hardened his heart and turned away from her. "Your plan failed, Lady Meredyth. Olyver and I are united once more. And we shall fight, side by side, to defend Glendire. Not because it is your home, but because it now belongs to me." He took a deep breath. "And, if God is kind, I shall never have to look upon your traitorous face again."

*Watch for the stirring conclusion of* Lair of the Wolf— *Chapter Twelve, by Constance O'Banyon—appearing in November 2000 in* White Dreams *by Susan Edwards.*

# Lair of the Wolf

Constance O'Banyon, Bobbi Smith, Evelyn
Rogers, Emily Carmichael, Martha Hix,
Deana James, Sharon Schulze, June Lund
Shiplett, Elizabeth Mayne, Debra Dier,
and Madeline George

Be sure not to miss a single installment of Leisure Books's star-studded new serialized romance, *Lair of the Wolf*! Preserving the fun and suspense of the month-by-month installments, Leisure presents one chapter a month of the entire on-line story, including some brand new material the authors have added to their existing chapters. Watch for a new installment of *Lair of the Wolf* every month in the back of select Leisure books!

Previous Chapters of *Lair of the Wolf* can be found in: